THIS OLD BILL

By Loren D. Estleman

THIS OLD BILL

LOREN D. ESTLEMAN

DOUBLEDAY & COMPANY, INC.

GARDEN CITY, NEW YORK

1984

Library of Congress Cataloging in Publication Data

Estleman, Loren D.
This old Bill.

1. Bill, Buffalo, 1846–1917—Fiction. I. Title.
PS3555.S84T45   1984   813'.54
ISBN: 0-385-19165-0
Library of Congress Catalog Card Number 83–20766
Copyright © 1984 by Loren D. Estleman
All Rights Reserved
Printed in the United States of America
First Edition

To Ray, who knows damn well why.

"I am sorry to have to lie so outrageously in this yarn. My hero has killed more Indians on one war trail than I have killed in all my life. But I understand this is what is expected of border tales. If you think the revolver and Bowie knife are used too freely, you may cut out a fatal shot or stab wherever you think wise."

—William F. Cody to his editors, 1875

THIS OLD BILL

PORTSMOUTH, VIRGINIA
NOVEMBER 11, 1916

The old man is dying.

There is death in his eyes, and under the glare of the electric bulb behind the curtains there is bare skull beneath his mottled skin. In his blue flannel shirt and yellow kerchief and buckskin pants and high black boots he looks like a wax figure wearing the wrong head. The famous mane and moustache and spray of whiskers are as dry and white as feathers on a hen's carcass. His glove gauntlets flap on his emaciated wrists. A broad belt with a square buckle cinches his loose belly and there is about him the stench of corruption, certain and sweet.

Johnny Baker, his own long locks graying now, too old to be called Johnny, escorts the old man to his horse McKinley, not touching him but close at his elbow, although he has never collapsed on the way in. The tent smells of chewed earth and mildew and the thick warm stink of fresh manure. On the other side of the curtains applause swells and recedes under the buzz of brass, the tubas farting and making the ground tingle. McKinley flicks his tail at a late moth and looks bored. More applause, and then the band hurls itself into "The Girl I Left Behind Me."

"We're late, Colonel," says Johnny.

The old man nods and places his Stetson on his white head, looking a little less fragile after he has adjusted it in the old rakish tilt. "I'm afraid."

He retains the milk-smooth baritone of his youth, but it is sour around the edges and too loud for normal conversation. It has rung across too many tents, reverberated from the back rows of too many theaters and auditoriums. Long whistling pauses between words.

"Not you, Colonel. You're not afraid of anything."

"It's not doing it that scares me, understand. It's doing it out there in front of all those people in the arena. The Indians believe that when a man's time comes he must be alone or his soul will wander forever between heaven and earth."

"The trail hasn't been beaten that can lose you."

The old man looks at him with the death in his eyes and closes them, lifting one foot.

With Johnny's help he hooks the boot in the stirrup and is boosted grunting into the saddle. Once there he sinks his chin onto his chest and shuts his eyes a second time against the flaming pain in his crotch. His breathing is audible across the enclosure, where a pair of roustabouts prepare to work the curtains. In shadow he waits.

"Ready, Colonel!"

The music swells and the curtains glide open, spilling in blinding light from the spot mounted over the grandstand. Raising his chin he rides out into the lighted arena and sweeps his big hat from his head while the cheers wash over him.

A pinwheel of color and light and noise and movement, Johnny throwing the blue glass balls into the air, the old man's special smooth-bore Winchester cracking and spraying sand at the flashing targets, the reports thudding dully against his thickened eardrums. The balls pop obligingly, and soon the earth is coated with fine twinkling powder. Pewter-colored fog fills the arena.

The last ball. Johnny hesitates with his arm poised, his eyes on the Colonel. The old man hoists the rifle and drops his head a fraction of an inch. The ball is launched. It climbs toward the lights, slows, hangs at the top of its arc before the descent. The old man cups the globe lovingly like a woman's breast in the Winchester's iron notch, draws a deep breath and releases half of it. The light strikes the ball and he squeezes the trigger. The glass bursts. Fragments of iridescence shower down.

Cheering, new music, the grand parade of performers around the arena— bronc riders, bulldoggers, and clowns—the old man in the lead, and then the wait alone under the sterile spot while the band subsides and the white horse dips its great head and shakes its mane and the cheering crests and breaks and retreats into coughs and silence.

"This farewell visit will be my last hail and farewell to you all. . . ."

The round tones curl in the tent corners like the last traces of blue smoke. The tightness in his throat and his harsh breathing die at ground level. Flecks of sweat glitter like diamond dust at his hairline, but his thick brow shadows the death in his eyes.

". . . Thirty years ago you gave me my first welcome. I am grateful for your loyal devotion to me. During that time many of my friends among you and many of those with me have been long since gathered to the great, unknown arena of another life. There are only a few of us left. When I went away from here each year before, I merely said good night; this time it will mean good-bye. To my little friends in the gallery, and the grownups who used to sit there, I thank you once again. God bless you all. Good-bye."

Silence while he turns the horse. The jingle of the raiments is a dry rattle in the center of the emptiness. Then, as at the flip of a switch, cheering.

The beast voice is a strong wind at his back as he approaches the curtains. After a lifetime the heat of the spotlight swings away from him and cold darkness overtakes horse and rider. His inner spring unwinding in a rush, the old man slides off the saddle into Johnny Baker's waiting arms.

"I didn't do it, Johnny."

"I knew you wouldn't, Colonel."

On the way out of the tent the old man's long frame leans on his friend's smaller one. In the arena the band whirls and crashes as the spectators shuffle toward the exits. The two roustabouts watch the pair's retreating backs.

"How many times you figure the old fart's made that speech now?" murmurs one.

His companion splatters the ground with brown tobacco juice. "I was in the audience first time he give it in 1910."

BOOK ONE
1854–1872

THE PRAIRIE BLOSSOM

". . . a dissolute and reckless life."
—William F. Cody, 1879

CHAPTER ONE

Big Isaac Cody, whiskered like a border raider, with the build of a canal-boat puller and the eyes of a boy on his first visit to a Leavenworth whore-house, rested a horned hand on his eight-year-old son's shoulder and watched Kansas bleed.

"If I had my way I'd hang every goddamned abolitionist!" Editor String-fellow shook a bony fist at God and the rafters of the Salt Creek Trading Post. His graying hair and beard were parted in the center and his eyes were white all around the irises. "And everyone born north of the Mason-Dixon line is a goddamned abolitionist!"

The smelly crowd of homesteaders buzzed approval. An animal shriek rose from among the standees near the door, raising the down on the backs of unprepared necks. It was one of the first rebel yells that had been heard in the territory.

Scents of ground coffee and unwashed humanity mingled in the room's closeness, odors a boy could carry with him to the end of his life.

"I was born north of the line," Cody muttered.

"Who said that?" Stringfellow's mad eyes raked the faces gathered below him.

"This'n here!" shouted a voice behind the elder Cody. Hands shoved him. Young Will clung to his father's coat.

The editor glared. "Do you hold me a liar?"

"I call no man liar in the presence of strangers." Cody thrust out his jaw.

"What views have you on the subject of slavery in Kansas?"

"If you'll climb down off that box I'll tell you."

"Let's hear how he stands!" someone cried.

Stringfellow stepped down and Cody took his place on the speaker's box. He was taller than his predecessor and carried considerably more meat, two facts that commanded silence while his dark eyes brooded over the assem-blage. His speech started low and climbed slowly to the assured volume Will had heard so many times at table.

"I was one of the pioneers of the state of Iowa," he said. "I aided its settlement and helped organize it as a state. I voted it should be a white state, that Negroes, free or slave, should never be allowed to locate within its limits."

Angry murmurs. Will moved closer to the box and his father, who ignored them.

"I say to you now, and I say it boldly, that I propose to exert whatever power I possess to make Kansas the same kind of state."

"You black abolitionist!"

"And I shall always oppose the further extension of slavery—"

"Get off that box or I'll put you off!"

"Let me finish—"

Grunts and movement, a man (Will later learned his name was Dunne) scrambling onto the box with something in his hand, young Will fighting to reach him and getting trampled, his father swaying to keep his balance, not paying attention to the man, the quick, bright flash of the bowie knife, the gasp and the blood, red as boiled jam. His father toppling into the cursing, roiling crowd. Hot tears on Will's face, he kicking and flailing his small fists. A familiar face and voice, a neighbor's arm around his sagging father, the struggle toward the door and out into the sweet air. Tumbling into a waiting wagon, no time for doctoring or even gentle handling. A snap of the reins and the jouncing, teeth-rattling ride across country to the neighbor's cabin and hasty dressing for the deep tear in Isaac Cody's side, then the ferry trip across the Missouri under cover of darkness to Will's uncle's house.

"You all right, Pa?" the boy asked as they were helping the wounded man inside.

"Oh, Will, I've gone and killed us all."

The peaceful days tore like flesh and muscle before a blade, but only sour green pus poured out. Salt Creek, Leavenworth, Kickapoo, and Atchison voted proslavery; Lawrence, against. Border roughs towing Negro slaves rode in from Missouri to trade votes against the Free Staters for gold. Sharps rifles rode ferries in long crates stenciled "BOOKS," and a new term, "Beecher's Bibles," was born. Every other man carried one. Musket flares spiked the night and the dawn came up through blue clouds. Blazing memories for a boy, extending over three years but compacted by time and distance into a single long night: the proslavery election of 1854 and the righteous fervor on the victors' faces; the terror-filled eyes of an abolitionist preacher staring from a coat of tar and feathers over the tail end of a switched mule; the pitched battle at Hickory Point, slavers versus Free Staters, spent powder stinking like rotten eggs, bodies floating downriver; the chest-pounding terror of riding to warn his father of a fresh plot, shouts of recognition behind him, lead cracking past his ears; houses torched;

stables burning, the porklike smell of cooked horseflesh. Once Isaac donned a bonnet and shawl to escape the armed mob encircling their home. Will watched his father shuffling along like an old woman and decided that he had lost respect for him, though he made no outward show of it because of his father's temper and the handiness of his belt. But of course a boy's attitude toward a man he had seen wearing a bonnet could never be the same, even if he did have to remind himself of that fact now and again. And the last memory, of sunlight lying flat and amber on the floor of Isaac's bedroom that last time, Will's father succumbing at last to exhaustion and a three-year-old knife attack.

"You're the man now, Will. You'll grow to hate me for that soon enough."

The boy, eleven now, opened his mouth but could make no protest. His throat felt as if he'd swallowed a fist. He didn't know why, having seen his father in woman's clothes, he should feel this way. Isaac's bloodless hand lay gray and unmoving on the white counterpane. He clearly wanted Will to hold it, but the boy kept his own hands at his sides. The man's eyes were sunken in his face. They glistened and grew soft as the death came into them.

"Your mother is convinced you'll be President someday. I hold lower goals for you. Not that you're unworthy, but a boy growing up in times like these will have to devote most of his energy to the business of survival. You're not to tell her that."

Will moved his head from side to side carefully, as if it might topple off if he shook it.

"I'm going to tell you something I think you'll understand because you watched your older brother die when Betsy rolled over him in Iowa and because you've seen what happens to people when they get caught up in what they believe."

Will waited. It hurt his father to talk and at times his voice receded and the boy had to lean forward to hear the whispered words.

"You must suspend finer things like honor in times like these, Will. Know when to tell an untruth and then stick to it like fresh sap. I didn't and see where it got me. If it means your life or the lives of the ones you hold dear, lie like a nigger. It's all right as long as you know what the truth is. If you forget everything else I'm saying, remember that. God never made a worse fool than a man who's a liar to himself. Do you understand that?"

He swallowed past the fist. The saliva burned in his throat. "Yes, sir."

His father watched him, and it was in his eyes now. "No, you don't. You're a boy still. But you will. Just remember the words. Ask your mother to come in now."

He gave his mother the message. She mopped nervous hands off on her apron and went in, her skirt slurring the clay floor. Will ignored the weeping of his sisters and small brother. He hadn't cried since the stabbing. Isaac lived another day, but they spoke no more and for the boy he was already dead.

The new Leavenworth offices of Russell, Majors & Waddell, freighters, smelled cleanly of sawdust and fresh lumber. Alexander Majors, a tall man with hard eyes and a square black beard shot with gray, took the measure of the boy who stood before his desk with his mother behind him. For months his family's provider, Will was striking for his deep tan and mop of hair bleached yellow by the sun—carefully dampened and combed for this interview—but he was small for his age and skinny. He had large brown eyes with a direct cast.

"Freighting is hard enough work for a man grown, Mary Ann," Majors told the woman. "I'm not certain that young Will could stand to it. The wagon master will be busy enough with a thousand head of beef and two and a half tons of freight without having to pick him up every time he falls."

"I won't fall," said Will. "And if I do, I'll pick myself up."

Mrs. Cody pinched the nape of his neck hard enough to hurt. "Don't be disrespectful." To Majors: "He can ride as well as most men and he's a fine shot. He's managed to keep us in game all this time. And he knows something of herding cattle." She paused. "If nothing else you can make him a messenger. You need messengers." Her voice was firm, but her eyes pleaded.

Majors hooked his thumbs in his vest pockets and frowned. "Uncle Aleck" to Will and his sisters and younger brother, he was well aware of the family's plight since Isaac's death.

"It's dangerous work," he told the boy. "The ground turns to axle grease when it rains. You could slide under one of the wagons and lose a leg. Or a bullwhacker could take your eye out with the end of his whip if you make a wrong step. Then there are Indians. And Mormons. It's them the soldiers at Fort Kearney will be fighting, with the supplies we're bringing them."

"I'm not afraid."

"Boys never are." He looked at the woman. "Forty a month and found. I'll hold his wages and pay them to you at the close of the drive."

"Thank you, Alexander."

She squeezed the boy's shoulder and went out, her back straight. Majors watched her. If he hadn't a wife and three daughters already. . . . He scowled down at Will. "Can you write your name?"

"Not yet, sir. But I can cipher."

"That won't help with this." He drew a copy of the pledge from a pigeonhole above his desk and read it aloud.

" 'While I am in the employ of A. Majors, I agree not to use profane language, not to get drunk, not to gamble, not to treat animals cruelly, and not to do anything else that is incompatible with the conduct of a gentleman. And I agree, if I violate any of the above conditions, to accept my discharge without any pay for my services.' " He slapped it down in front of Will. "Questions?"

"I don't understand the big word, sir."

" 'Incompatible'?" Will nodded. "It merely means that you promise to be a good Christian while you're working for me. Do you find that unsatisfactory?"

"Not at all, sir."

"Make your mark then." Majors dipped a pen in his inkwell, shook off the excess, and handed it with a flourish to the boy, who scratched a lopsided *X* at the bottom of the sheet. The manager then opened a desk drawer and held out a new leather-bound Bible. "Every man receives one over and above his wages. See that you learn to read it. Sundays the crew pauses to rest the stock and make its peace with God. Work hard the rest of the week, follow those provisions, and if it's a regular job you're after, you'll look no further."

He took along his father's Mississippi Jaeger muzzle-loader, veteran of a hundred hunts, short and heavy and carrying a slug and two buckshot to a charge. They called him an "extra," which he soon learned meant an extra pair of hands and legs whenever they were needed. They were needed every minute. From first light to last he rode or walked beside the teams of oxen, drove cattle, carried messages between wagons, handed tools to the bullwhackers when a vehicle broke down, inspected the water barrels for leaks, helped extricate bawling heifers sunk to their haunches in river mud, and when the crew made camp he gathered, chopped, and split firewood and fetched water for the animals. He wondered that Majors had thought his pledge necessary, as there was hardly an idle moment to violate its conditions. By the time he crawled into his bedroll the first night, he ached in a thousand places. Five minutes later, it seemed, someone prodded him awake with a toe to help the cook with breakfast. The sky was still dark when he rolled out.

The wagon boss was Frank McCarthy, a former bullwhacker who called Will "Billy" and took all his meals in the saddle. He kept the wagons within sight of one another and sent drivers after stray cattle and settled disputes with a terse word and a rolled whip in one hand. Sundays he read from the Bible to all who cared to listen while the stock grazed and the men rested and wrote letters home. Will slept Sundays while his body grew and his limbs hardened.

The prairie breathed under empty blue sky, shrugging its coat of waist-high grass in the ceaseless wind—living land, taking no notice of the back-ward-leaning Conestogas and their shapeless bovine escort moving sedately across its back. Great black fists of buffalo pushed northward, and a lost eagle sailed among fat clouds in search of a mountain. Quail exploded from underfoot, making a boy's heart stop until they were almost out of range. Then the thump and crash of the Jaeger and bursting feathers and the long straight drop to earth. Additional stew meat for evening camp. Meanwhile eighteen yoke of oxen watched the ground and tramped out their fourteen miles a day. The earth revolved.

Purple twilight on the mealy banks of the Platte. Thirty-five miles of wading through brackish water alive with wigglers and silt to the knees to avoid hostile Indians. Exhaustion spreading through him cozily, Will dragged behind the train, shifting hands on the heavy rifle from time to time to ease the deadness in one arm. His face, neck, and wrists were smeared with mud to protect them from the dense cloud of mosquitoes surrounding him; close up, the cracked yellow surface resembled the skin of a very old man. Still, he was content, cloaked in the warmth of his own solitude and fatigue. Ahead of him the moon rose swollen and orange. While he was admiring it, the head and feathers of a savage came to its face and paused, looking like the engraving on a coin.

Hunting reflex took over. The rifle raised itself, pulsed against Will's shoulder. Feathers burst and the nightmare figure toppled, rolling down the bank, picking up speed as it rustled through the reeds until it landed with a splash at the bottom, one arm in the water, while the echo of the report growled in the distance and died hissing.

Will kept his position, swaying a little under the weight of the lifted rifle. Metallic smoke drifted up and shredded in the wind blowing across the banks. McCarthy came splashing back through the water astride his big wall-eyed roan and drew rein. He looked from the boy to the dead Indian and back to the boy.

"How old are you, Billy?"

He was borne behind McCarthy's saddle to the train, where upon hear-ing the news the delighted bullwhackers and drivers pummeled his back and shoulders and rubbed his head for luck and called him the youngest Indian slayer on the plains. When McCarthy left to supervise camping arrange-ments, a long-haired bullwhacker in his late teens named Jim passed Will a canteen with a broad wink. Dry-mouthed, the boy thanked him and tipped it up and choked on his first swallow of pure grain alcohol. When he finally stopped coughing, he responded to the others' laughter with a sheepish smile and helped himself to a more judicious sip before handing back the vessel. They pummeled him some more and someone gave him berries to chew to sweeten his breath, and when he got back to his bedroll the others were busy rewriting an old ballad to immortalize his feat of arms.

The next evening, killing some rare slack time before supper, Will turned around at the click of an iron shoe on a pebble to see Alexander Majors looking down at him from the back of a large dun. The boy hid his charred stick behind his back and stepped in front of the evidence, but the firm's manager had already read the scrawled legend "William Frederick Cody" on the wagon sheet.

"You learn quickly," he observed. The top half of his face was shadowed by his black hat and the lower half was all beard. "Have you been reading your Bible as I directed?"

"Yes, sir."

"Who slew Abel?"

"It wasn't me, sir."

Majors put a hand in front of his whiskers. "Well, read on. You've seen no Mormons?"

"I don't know what one looks like, sir."

"If you see one, you'll know him. They wear the devil on their faces. Keep your eyes open and report anything unusual to Mr. McCarthy."

Will replied that he would. Majors looked him over closely.

"I've visited three trains tonight and they're all buzzing about the boy who killed an Indian. How does it feel to take a man's life, Will?"

"Sir, there's a commandment that says 'Thou shalt not kill.'"

"I'm well aware of it."

"Sir, I don't believe Moses ever met a Cheyenne."

"Don't blaspheme, boy." He started his horse walking. "See me when you return to Leavenworth. We need Indian fighters."

Watering the animals at a creek the following noon, Will felt a hand on his shoulder and glanced up at Frank McCarthy, whose gaze was directed at the top of the hill. At first, Will thought it was Majors standing there holding a rifle, but then he saw that the man's beard was too long and the crown of his black hat too high. His companions were similarly shaggy and attired in somber black suits to match their hats. They were all armed.

"Throw up your hands, brothers," said the man in the center calmly.

"Who are you?" someone demanded.

"We're Danites. And you're surrounded."

The men in the river looked back toward the bank, where the wagons were ringed in by more bearded men in black hats and rifles. McCarthy's men raised their hands.

"Danites?" muttered Will to the boss.

"Destroying angels. Mormons."

They were ordered out of the water and promptly relieved of their weapons. Two of the intruders trained their muzzles on Jim, the young bullwhacker who had handed Will the canteen full of whiskey, while a third took away his six-guns. His face was drawn tight and pale as a clenched fist.

"We're God-fearing men, brother," the Mormon leader told McCarthy. "We will let you have one wagon with oxen to get you back to where you came from."

"That's almost a thousand miles!" protested the wagon master.

"Some of the others would rather you never left this spot."

"Can we at least have our guns?"

"No, nothing but food and blankets."

"If you faced us like white men instead of sneaking around like thieving Indians," Jim snarled, "things might of went different."

"And if you didn't make war on a peaceful people we'd have no need to meet at all." The leader gestured with his rifle. "Choose a wagon and load it with what you require."

When the wagon was filled, a bullwhacker climbed into the driver's seat and the rest of the party fell into step behind it, the Mormons' eyes burning holes in their backs. When they were over the first hill someone exclaimed and they looked back and saw the smoke from the flaming wagons.

"Devil's sons," complained a driver.

"It's enough to make a man use profane language, ain't it, Cap'n?" said Jim, managing a feeble grin.

McCarthy told him to shut the hell up and walk.

Stand back and give a young colt three years to kick up fresh earth and taste the short sweet spring grass. Teach him to write more than just his name and find out who slew Abel, hand him a whip and sit him behind the oxen on an uneventful trip to Fort Laramie to feel their sure and steady pull on the traces, introduce him at the end of the trail to small, clerkly Kit Carson with his Quaker haircut and gentle speech and loud, profane, hickory-limbed Jim Bridger. Fill him with information on distinguishing a Sioux sign from a gopher mound and the way a fresh wolf track in wet sand has sharp edges until the wind comes along to blur them. Lengthen his limbs, deepen his voice, and sharpen his aim so that game that takes flight is table fare in the twitch of an eyelid. Make a man.

"I'm fourteen, sir."

Shooting up now, growing thick through the chest and shoulders, Will stood in the middle of the Holladay Overland Mail & Express Company headquarters grounds at Horseshoe Station, dressed in the lightweight attire favored by his fellow Pony Express couriers. Coppery down glittered on his upper lip.

"Captain Jack" Slade grunted. Although no taller than the boy, the superintendent of the Sweetwater stage route from Julesburg, Colorado, to Rocky Ridge, Wyoming, outweighed him by sixty pounds, most of it around the belly. His face was as brutal as his reputation and there was lint in his chin stubble that looked as if it had been there long enough to get mail.

"That's high green even for an express rider," he said. "I wouldn't of took you on at all except for that letter from Majors' partner. But you've worked out fair. Savvy the situation, do you?"

"Indians, sir."

"Thievin' Cheyennes been hitting every other stage I send through and running off with the teams. I'll nail their brown hides to the station wall!"

Will resisted an urge to move his shoulders. His employer had earned his nickname of "the terrible Slade" when, while still recovering from an encounter in which a horse-stealing stationmaster had emptied a revolver into his body, he came back with a party of company agents, tied his former assailant to a corral post, and used him for target practice, finally riding off with the man's ears in his saddlebags after shooting him twenty-two times. The boy could see those hides now, drying bloody in the sun.

"I fought Indians before, Captain."

"So I hear. How are you at tracking?"

"I learned from Kit Carson and Jim Bridger at Fort Laramie."

The superintendent sucked at a bad tooth. "We'll find out on the trail what them references is worth."

He called over a very tall man from a knot of drivers in front of the station building. In his early twenties, the newcomer had very broad shoulders tapering to no hips at all and wore his tawny hair in ringlets below his collar. His drooping moustache couldn't quite conceal a protruding upper lip that together with his short chin gave him a definite facial resemblance to a duck. He was smoking a long black cheroot and wore the company uniform of wide-brimmed sombrero, high-heeled boots, and corduroy jacket and trousers trimmed with velvet. On him it looked natural.

"Jim Hickok, meet Will Cody. The boy's coming with us." To Will: "Jim was constable at Monticello, and you'll not find a better hand with a pistol in these parts."

Will grinned recognition. "How are you?"

"Hoss." Hickok nodded, but the puzzlement in his eyes made it plain that he hadn't placed the youth.

"You two know each other?"

"If you don't know a man after you've hiked with him a thousand miles, I don't guess you ever will." The courier told of the Mormon raid on the wagon train, his first Indian, and his first drink of whiskey courtesy of the young bullwhacker whose last name he had only just learned. The narrative had assumed distinct shape after several repetitions to others. Will had discovered a talent for storytelling. Hickok, who knew him now, wore a faint, painful smile throughout.

Slade said, "You let them take your guns?"

He dropped the cheroot and ground it under the heel of an exceptionally small boot. "Reckon you had to of been there, Cap'n, and seen how it was."

"Reckon it's too bad I wasn't. You that obliging with redskins?"

The driver went white to the hairline, and Slade set his feet. Both men were armed, the superintendent with an old Paterson revolver in a soft holster on his hip, Hickok with two Navy Colts riding in a sash around his waist with the butts twisted forward. Will shrank back out of the line of fire. Then Hickok showed tobacco-dull teeth behind his moustache.

"I like you, Cap'n Jack," he said. "I surely must."

Tension slid away through cracks in the earth. Slade nodded shortly.

"Folks generally do. Draw some grub, the two of you, and put on trail clothes. Let the company pay for its own advertising."

Hickok watched the little stage officer stumping back toward the station building, his round-crowned hat tipped down to his eyes. "There is a fellow who ain't bound to die the natural way," observed the driver.

"A body might say the same thing about you," the boy reminded him.

Night tarred the prairie and spat stars like carpenter's tacks across the sky. Amid stitching crickets the yellow flutter of fire at the base of the long slope looked impossibly remote, yet breathtakingly close, like a bright moth trapped in the small end of a field glass. Then an owl hoot wrinkled the peace and dimmed the illusion. Slade waited, then raised his hands to his mouth and answered with a whippoorwill whistle. Crickets again, and then the soft thudding of bound hoofs on grass.

"There's forty or fifty of them in camp," reported Will when the thudding stopped. His face was a smoky uncertainty two feet from Slade's. "Corral's west about a hundred yards."

"Shit." Slade wasn't a Majors man. "I wasn't counting on them odds. I fold my hand at four to one."

Others in the party murmured agreement.

Hickok said, "I never have. Let's split up, half to the corral and the rest to camp. Hot things up a mite while the others get the horses."

When the superintendent hesitated, Will spoke up. "Indians aren't natural organizers, Captain. Once you surprise them, they stay surprised. But we got to move fast."

"Well, seeing as how we come this far."

Slade, Hickok, and Will rode with the group that was to attack the camp. They walked their horses in downwind of the dogs that were to be found wherever there were Indians, untied the rag bundles from their hoofs for maximum speed and noise, mounted, and at a low whistle from the corral they thundered between tipis, whooping and shrieking and snapping caps at the targets that flashed in the firelight. Blue and orange flame spiked the darkness. Hickok's gray whinnied and lunged, its eyes rolling over white, while its master hammered away first on this side, then that, with a Navy Colt in each hand and his reins clamped between his teeth. Most of the party, Will included, was shooting just to make noise, but the former constable seldom missed. A brave would make a dash for the horses in the corral and before he got five steps, a hole the size of a ten-dollar gold piece would open in his forehead and he'd flop on his face. One unarmed Cheyenne plucked a flat rock from the ground and hurled it desperately at Hickok. The first bullet sent the projectile spinning into the night. The second tore through the brave's throat. Will wounded an Indian in the leg with a ball from his Dragoon Colt and plunged through a cloud of stinging smoke into the clear, and then they were swinging east to join the men who had stolen back the horses. Dogs were yapping in camp. The whole raid had taken less than thirty seconds.

"Who's hit?" Slade demanded breathlessly when after two miles they stopped to blow the horses.

There was a general patting of limbs and torsos. No one spoke up.

"Damned heathens never could hit the obvious side of a buffalo in broad daylight. Slow now. We don't want to bust any of these bastards' legs after we went to so much trouble to get 'em back."

They resumed at a walk.

"That horse of yours is pretty fast," Hickok told Will.

"Old Mountain?" He patted the big stallion's steaming neck. "He can beat anything on four legs."

"I believe you're right. You ever been to St. Louis? They race for money there, but I bet they ain't seen nothing like your mountain runner."

"I'd like to see St. Louis," Will said.

St. Louis swam in summer heat, the air like raw silk. A man and a youth walked along the levee, eyes on the ground, ignoring the pumpkin-shell highwheelers paddling down the Missouri trailing dirty cotton smoke, two hundred miles downriver from the spot where a child and his wounded father had crossed into hiding seven years before.

"You got any money at all, Jim?"

Hickok turned his head and spat into the water. The white spittle bobbed on the steamers' wake. "They cleaned me out too. Goddamn skinny mare from Peoria. I always did hate that town."

"Flat country hereabouts. Old Mountain favored the high ground. We shouldn't of bet him too."

" 'Shouldn't of' don't change what's past."

"Where to now, Jim?"

He shrugged. "There's war back East. I'm thinking I might join up, see the elephant."

"Which side?"

"How many sides can an elephant have?"

"You know what I mean."

"I'm Yankee to the bone. What about you?"

"Me too. My father was an abolitionist. I might just join up myself."

"If your ma lets you."

Will stopped walking. "What's that mean?"

"Means I was fifteen once too."

"Not for long, I bet." The boy sprinted to catch up.

"Don't say 'bet.' "

Will's laugh was as deep and hearty as a man's.

CHAPTER TWO

"Louisa Frederici, William F. Cody."

She spread her skirts, taffeta and lace rustling loud enough to spook a band of Sioux or stop a Confederate charge, and offered up a plump hand, over which he bowed neatly, touching her palm with sandpapery fingers. Her rather coarse features were dominated by thick, arched brows and she wore her dark hair piled carelessly on top of her head and lanced in place with pins. Her speech was throaty and frenchified.

"Are you just back from the fighting, Mr. Cody?"

The tall young man in blue dress uniform said something about hospital duty in St. Louis, while Louisa's cousin, having performed his gentlemanly duty, drifted away unnoticed. Voices droned in the large room as the first truly fine social gathering of the postwar period gathered fine social dust. Private Cody was saying something now about General Sterling Price and the rebel rout at Westport, but as usual when the conversation turned to the war, she wasn't listening. He had the features her mother liked to call classic and brown hair with a thread of auburn gleaming through it, although it was a little long for St. Louis, and as he talked, very white teeth flashed behind his well-kept moustache. She liked to hear his mellow baritone even if she wasn't paying attention to the words. Local tone ran toward phlegmy French and nasal American.

". . . killed my first hostile Indian. Have you ever been West, Miss Frederici?"

"West?" She hesitated, wondering how he had got to Indians from Westport. "Heavens, no. Is that where your people are from?" Her heart dropped a little as she searched his face for savage characteristics.

"I was born in Iowa. But my father and mother took my younger brother and five sisters and me to Kansas when I was seven."

"Do they live there yet?"

"My brother and four sisters do. My father died eight years ago and my mother followed him last November. My sister Martha also preceded her."

"I am so sorry. But six children! Do you support your brother and sisters as well as yourself?"

"There were eight originally. My older brother Samuel was killed when a horse fell on him in Iowa. I try to send money home, but that hasn't always been possible on a soldier's salary. I have a chance to become an Army scout when my enlistment is up. The pay is much better."

"But isn't that terribly dangerous?"

And then he was telling another story, about stolen horses and Cheyennes and a person named Hickok. It was all very boring after four years of war news, but she kept her eyes on him, widening them instinctively at just the right moments even as the details slid through her grasp, taking her cues from the expression on his face. He had doe-brown eyes with little gold flecks in them.

"Surely you will adopt some steady vocation eventually?" she put in when he paused for breath.

"Well, yes"—thoughtfully—"I suppose I'll have to, when I get too old for the other."

They were married the following March, after he had carried dispatches through Cheyenne country for General Sherman and driven stagecoach in Kansas. When he returned, she almost didn't recognize him in his frontier trappings, hair to his shoulders now and the beginnings of a goatee showing red on his chin. But his manner remained courtly and she forgave him the affectation. For the ceremony at her parents' home the twenty-year-old bridegroom donned bleached doeskins trimmed with ermine and fringe and soft winter moccasins decorated with porcupine quills dyed red and white, the whole topped incongruously by a conventional collar and tie. Louisa felt pride and a twinge of jealousy at the other than familial glances her tall plainsman drew from some of her female cousins at the reception, but he was preoccupied with her and appeared not to notice. Although she found his sisters cordial (his young brother Charles had died within a year of his mother), she was disappointed to see them looking at her with her husband's eyes and speaking with his mannerisms, as if something that she'd thought was hers alone had turned out to be just another in a line of ready-made items available to all. She dismissed the feeling as part of the inevitable letdown at the end of a long period of anticipation, and didn't come back to it for years.

Will was a surprisingly good dancer, graceful on his feet even if some of the steps he knew were foreign to St. Louis (he blamed them on his sister Martha's nonconformist teaching), and the applause that greeted the couple upon the completion of their first turn around the floor brought the blood to her cheeks. The hasty embraces and frantic farewells when they left were just delirious features of the same fevered dream.

It was on board the river steamer *Morning Star* for their honeymoon trip up the Missouri to Leavenworth that she first heard Will explaining to an interested party from New Hampshire that they had met when her bridle rein parted during a morning ride and he caught the runaway horse. When they were alone, she asked him why he had lied.

"Easterners expect it," was the only answer he would give.

In Salt Creek, scene of his father's stabbing and the abrupt end of his own childhood, Will put an arm around his bride's waist, familiar territory now, and watched the boy he had hired tapping nails into the new sign over the door of his mother's old boarding house: The Golden Rule Hotel, lettered in bright gilt with curling serifs.

"Well, Lulu, you married a businessman."

"I couldn't be prouder if you owned your own railroad."

"Maybe someday I will. Wear a stovepipe hat and travel in a private car."

"You don't regret your promise to me?"

"Regret!" He spun her around, laid his other hand on her waist, and lifted her off her feet. "I gave up the word when I gave up scouting!"

"Put me down, please, William."

"What you doing, Will, guessing her weight?" This from a gray-bearded trapper in otter skins standing on the boardwalk.

"Light as a feather!" he bellowed, and whirled her around, sending her skirt and petticoats flying.

"William!"

Roaring with laughter, he set her down gently on the boardwalk. She adjusted her clothes with a hurried glance around at the small crowd they had attracted. Her face was flushed and angry.

"No luck, Rufe?" Will asked.

The trapper paused with one moccasined foot on the hotel threshold and shook his head. He was carrying a bale of pelts slung over one shoulder. "Getting a fair market price out of Gunderson's like prying a Texas leech out of your behind. Beg pardon, Miz Cody. Sure am obliged to you for waiting on the rent, Will."

"Take all the time you need."

Louisa looked sharply at her husband, but he was admiring the new sign.

The Golden Rule had a new name but the same old black dirt in the damp corners where sow bugs dwelt, fluffy brown cobwebs hammocking from the ceilings, and yellow rivulets of calcified grease striping the black iron stove. Louisa hired a fifteen-year-old colored girl whose husband had been killed fighting in the 10th Cavalry, and together they scrubbed the windows and scoured the walls and polished the floors until the building glistened from attic to basement. They hung curtains and spread rugs over the dented floorboards, and when Will timidly ventured back inside after being chased out for the twelfth time by furious womanhood and a dust mop, he wandered from room to room with a handkerchief wrapped around his hand to avoid smearing the gleaming china doorknobs.

Bookkeeping was her next big project, although she had had no training in it and thus was forced to develop her own system based on information obtained from local merchants who were only too glad to help out the caretaker of what they deemed Salt Creek's future in the face of peace and westward expansion. When after four weeks in business she learned that Will had yet to write down a single transaction, she tramped down to the mercantile and bought two large ledgers bound in brown buckram with brass corners and a bottle apiece of red and black ink and came back and cleared the rolltop desk in Will's study of black powder and cartridge-loading paraphernalia and set to work to reconstruct the finances of the past month. She was lighting the lamp after two hours at this labor when Will came in carrying an armload of wood and dumped it into the coal scuttle next to the fireplace. Dust rolled out, settling unheeded over the figures neatly inked into the ruled columns.

"Good news, Lulu! Dingle says he saw a team of surveyors working east of town this morning. You know what that means."

"More guests to stay here free of charge, no doubt." She redipped her pen.

"Means the railroad's coming just like we heard. When it gets here, we'll be turning guests away."

"That's because by then you'll have given away all the rooms."

"Now, Lulu."

She slapped down the pen, spraying scarlet tadpoles across the creamy page. Dull fire glowed in her eyes. "Understand me, William," she said. "I think it admirable that you've invited your sisters to live here at no charge. Your Christian good fellowship in allowing every prairie rat for a hundred miles to come in and partake of the famous Cody hospitality without concern to his pocketbook is above criticism. I am certain they sing your praises around the campfire. But it's no way to run a business. In the past four weeks we've paid out more for food and room maintenance than your mother laid down for the entire building, and we've not taken in a Confederate dollar. Will, we're running out of money."

"When the railroad comes—"

"It will just bring more freeloaders faster. Soon we'll be applying for charity to carry on our good works. We certainly are not operating a hotel."

"These people are my family and friends. What am I supposed to do, just up and turn them out?"

"If your friends don't pay, yes. Your sisters can stay."

"A man survives upon the goodwill of his friends. There's no telling when it might mean the difference between a close call and your fingers swinging from a thong around some buck's neck."

She lowered her voice. "I've asked you not to speak of such things."

"Sorry, Lulu. I forgot."

"Anyway, those days are over. You promised me a conventional life."

"I have no intention of going back on my word."

"It would carry more conviction if you made an effort to look like a hotel keeper. That hair, and those clothes. Even the lowliest trapper puts on a dusty suit when he's in civilization."

He glanced down at his buckskins. "I was dressed this way the day you married me. I didn't hear you complain then."

"We weren't alone then. But if I'd thought it was permanent, I would have. Your hair is longer than mine."

"If I cut it off now, everyone will think I'm afraid of having my scalp lifted."

"Stop that! Stop talking like that!" Angry tears burned her cheeks. "I am tired of hearing about scalps and savages and horses and killing! Every time you come together with your horrible friends, that's all you talk about! Isn't it enough that I left my family and my friends in St. Louis and came out here to live with animals? Must I put up with your interminable horror stories as well?"

Her speech broke into bitter sobs. They were standing very close now, and Will's arms went around her automatically and drew her face into his chest. "There, there, Louisa," his voice rumbled. It was as if he were soothing a skittish mare. Deep inside she felt a trickle of doubt, like the first rusty water entering a rain barrel from a gutter on the roof.

On the surface they prospered. Advance men for the railroad came to compare sites and stayed at the hotel asking Will hundreds of questions about the terrain to the west and the Indian situation, then moved on, followed by surveyors and graders, their pockets full of eastern money. Behind them came men in suits and derbies to scout the high ground above the river for stores and restaurants. Will would register them and give the proceeds to Louisa, who would put it in the cash box and record the transaction in her ledgers. But when she went to take money out later for shopping or improvements, she would find less there than before she had put it in. Confronted, Will would shrug and say that he had used it to entertain his guests, that he had been meaning to tell her but hadn't got around to it. She would scold him and he would drop his eyes and promise not to repeat the offense and the cycle would start all over. At the end of six months they owed every merchant in town and the bank was threatening to foreclose on a mortgage she hadn't known existed unless the couple either sold out or gave permission to appoint a business manager. Neither Will nor Louisa had ever heard the word "receivership" before, but its sibilant sound repelled them both.

Coming up dawn in Leavenworth. Orange light slid between rows of new buildings, pushing ahead September shadows that chilled like ice water when they touched bare skin. Helen Cody, almost twenty, with Isaac's sturdy frame and her mother's erect bearing, saw Will to her door and paused on the threshold. He was nearly a foot taller than his sister now, broad across the chest and lean of hip, a long, hard board of a man who moved like clear water spilling over a bed of rocks. The sun at his back accentuated his massiveness. He was too big to keep indoors.

"What I got for the hotel ought to stand her keep till I can send more," he said. "I'm obliged to you for putting her up, Nellie."

"You never left any of us dry yet when you weren't dry yourself."

He slid the brim of his slouch hat through his hands. "Reckon you think I'm not much of a husband, dumping her off on you this way."

"I don't know what much of a husband is, Will. Pa was always off someplace in hiding or fighting secessionists."

"I'll make it up to her when I get back."

"How long will you be away this time?"

"Long enough to shake six months of civilized living out of my hair. Melt off the tallow. I hear the railroad's hiring at Salina."

"Good luck, Will. Write when you can."

He nodded and started to turn, stopped, glanced up at the windows on the second floor. "Tell her how it is with me, can you? Maybe coming from a woman she'll see."

"She sees right enough."

The door closed. He stood on the porch a moment, then stepped off and returned to the buckboard, putting on his hat.

Junction City, Kansas. Cowhands and railroad rowdies and cavalrymen and buffalo runners trailing clouds of flies. Fresh lumber and beer and manure, growth smells. The drunk at the back table in one of the busier saloons slumped in dusty buckskins, fighting the weight of his eyelids, his cards leaning in his clumsy left hand and almost exposing their faces.

"Come on, come on, you sot!" demanded the player across from him, a thin, red-eyed man in a travel-stained black suit and string tie. "That's five to you. In or out?"

The drunk belched and reached down to scratch himself. "Got t'see somethin' firs'."

"You can't even see your cards, rummy."

A Navy Colt appeared quick as thought in the other's right hand, the hammer rolling back with a noise like knuckles cracking. "Let's start with the ones up your left sleeve."

His speech was unslurred now and he was sitting up straight.

The red-eyed man hesitated, jerked his own gun hand, stopped, jerked it again, then lowered it to the table. He considered death's single empty eye.

The other two players at the table watched in brittle silence. The man with the gun caught the eye of the gambler to his right, who grasped the red-eyed man's left arm and shook the ace of hearts and the ace of clubs out of the sleeve.

"Leave everything on the table and skedaddle," said the bogus drunk.

Red-eye rose awkwardly. "I got to have a stake to get out of town on."

"Don't lean on your luck."

"Who the hell are you?"

"James Butler Hickok." He spaced out the names.

The blood slid out of the cheater's face. "You're Wild Bill Hickok?"

"I been called that. I been called worse, but not by anybody you'll meet."

The other stood unmoving for a long time. Then he turned and stumbled toward the batwing doors, colliding with a big man in sweat-stiffened clothes who was just coming in. Gasping, he glanced up at the newcomer's face and slid around him with a muttered comment about the town being full of long-haired killers.

The big man gazed around the humming saloon and spotted the man playing poker with his back to the wall and a revolver in his hand. "Jim," he roared, "can't I turn my back on you for a few years that you don't cut the bear loose?"

The expression on Hickok's carved-idol face went slowly from wariness to recognition. The ends of his moustache turned up suddenly. "Will, you little rascal, you went and growed up!" He took the Navy off cock with a flourish and thrust it into his belt in the old butt-forward position. To his table companions: "Split the tinhorn's checks three ways and go try the faro wheel."

When the hand crushing and backslapping were done, Hickok called for a fresh bottle, and he and Will sat down. The gunman counted his checks into stacks according to color with his left hand, leaving his right free as always. "You heard Slade's dead."

"Can't say I'm surprised." Will drank. "Who pulled the trigger?"

"No one. After Holladay fired him he went up to Virginia City and got hisself lynched for disorderly conduct."

"Hell, I'd known they could string you up for that, I'd of gone into church work years ago."

But Hickok wasn't laughing. "Goddamn civilization's ruining everything, Will. Everyplace I go there's people there ahead of me making rules. They been pouring out here like piss out of a boot ever since the war got over. It's how come I left Illinois, and I got to go farther and farther West to get clear of it."

"You left Illinois on account of that mule skinner you near drowned in the Illinois and Michigan Canal. This is me you're talking to, Wild Bill."

"It's Jim, damn it. That's another thing about these carpetbaggers—they can't even get a man's name right."

The younger man grinned. "Anyway, you don't appear to be suffering."

"It's how come I took up scouting for the Army. This way I get to see what a place is like before the women and Bible-tooters get a chance to hang curtains on it."

They worked on the bottle for a while, inflating the details of past experiences shared. Drinkers came in and went out, pausing to look at the two long-haired frontiersmen making guns out of their forefingers and hammering the table for punctuation.

"What they got you doing these days?" Hickok asked finally, uncorking a second vessel.

"Grading track for the Kansas Pacific."

"How is it?"

"I've ate grass and it beats that. How's scouting?"

"Sometimes you eat lots worse than grass. But it pays better than the railroad and you're your own boss nine days out of ten."

"They hiring?"

"They got more jobs at Fort Hays than men to fill them." The gunman paused. "I got to say though, it ain't work for a married man. I heard you got roped."

"That make any difference with who gets picked?"

"Not where I was around to see."

"All right then," said Will.

Hickok grinned slowly, his only gradual act, and refilled their glasses.

First light bled cold and steel-blue into the deep black over Fort Hays, limning a man on a gray mule, their breath curling in the glacial air. On the porch of the commanding officer's quarters stood a tall, bony man in a Confederate officer's hat and a buckskin shirt over cavalry trousers with a stripe, copper-colored hair curling to the nape of his neck, and a great tragic moustache of a somewhat lighter hue the size and shape of an inverted horseshoe covering most of the lower half of his face. His blue-gray eyes were set deep under bushy brows that tilted downward sadly from a large, slightly hooking nose. His gaze slid icily over the mounted man and came to rest on the uniformed officer who shared the porch.

"Captain, I left orders to have a guide ready on the best mount to be had at this post. My regiment is waiting for me at Fort Larned and I haven't time to dilly-dally along the road with a mule. Get him a horse, and a good one."

His voice was pitched high, the words bitten off with an audible snap and almost stuttered.

"This is the best horse at the post, sir," the mounted man insisted. "I assure you he—"

"That isn't a horse at all."

The captain said, "General, the horses are all run out from chasing hostiles. Mules are all we have. Cody swears by this one and I trust his judgment in matters of this nature."

"Backwoods Aristotles and plodding mules. The material they expect me to win wars with. Very well, if that's the best you have, let's get started." He clomped down the wooden steps, jerking on his gauntleted gloves.

Will touched two fingers to his hat brim. "General Custer," he greeted, referring to the lieutenant colonel's wartime rank, as was the polite custom.

A small group of officers and enlisted men and their guide strung out against a bright steel sky. Tents of sand stretched to the horizon, the grains sliding and sucking under the mounts' bicycling hoofs. The horses' sides heaved, slick with lather. Will's mule flared its nostrils and breathed normally. Custer, riding a little in front, turned his head as if to note the sun's position, but Will suspected that he was watching the mule and rider out of the corner of his eye. When the commander faced front, his guide put spurs to the mule. It snorted and lunged ahead.

"Whoa, there! Easy, old fellow. We got us a ways to go."

A bright steel sky and a small group of officers and enlisted men and their guide strung out against it. More sand. The horses' eyes rolled over white and their breath came in chugs. The mule was in front now, moving along at a swift walk. Spurs when Custer wasn't looking, the surge forward, more soothing words. The commander raked his own mount's flanks and drew abreast.

"That's more horse than mule."

"He's no good till he finds his second wind," Will remarked.

They rode tandem for several hundred yards without saying anything.

"What sort of tactician is this Chief Black Kettle?" Custer asked finally.

Will said, "It's his stomping ground."

"I've known many a field commander to lose simply because he considered that the only advantage he needed. The victories that decided the war all took place below the Mason-Dixon line."

"Beg pardon, General, but Black Kettle is no regular officer and the Cheyennes aren't proper soldiers. They've lived and fought here for centuries and their rules aren't the same. When the chief makes a decision, for instance, the braves have to get together and vote on it before it can be carried out, and if the vote goes against it, they do something else. They don't follow orders blindly like men in uniform."

"That's a very poor system in an exercise where moments count."

"Maybe so, but that way you can't count on one man's mistake acting in your favor."

A few miles farther on they stopped to let Custer's escort catch up. The General's thoroughbred bellied and blew. Will patted the gray mule's neck and leaned the bit tight as if to keep the animal from bolting.

"I am told that the Cheyennes are excellent horsemen and that the time to attack them is in spring, when there is no snow to impede maneuvers and before the weather gets too hot," Custer announced. "Do you agree with that?"

"No, sir, I'd choose winter."

"Why winter?"

"They're used to fighting in warm weather. In winter they rest. If you want to surprise them, pick a time when there's a lot of snow on the ground. They hold it their best protection."

"My sentiments exactly. But the scouts I spoke with in St. Louis advised me against it."

"St. Louis scouts don't like cold weather."

"And you do."

"Given my druthers I'd take warm. But I work when I'm paid to."

"Cody, you're a breath of fresh air, even if you do ride a mouse-colored mule."

The others dragged in astride their foaming mounts.

"Move out," rapped Custer, kneeing his forward.

The party approached a shadowy line in the sand hills that was the Pawnee Fork Creek, the mule pacing itself, Custer half trotting to keep up. They drew rein to wait again for the officers and orderlies.

"Larned's about fifteen miles downstream," Will explained, pointing. "All you have to do is follow the creek, General. I'll carry any dispatches you might have on ahead and wait for you there."

"You're having sport with me for what I said about your mule earlier." The commander turned to an officer who had just joined them, straddling a wheezing and fistulous chestnut. "Captain, you will bring the escort in. I'm going on ahead with Cody."

First light at Fort Larned and a man on a gray mule throwing a long shadow with a sharp edge. Custer glowered at him from the porch of the commanding officer's quarters in uniform, thumbs hooked inside his belt.

"I'm not in good humor this morning," he announced. "My horse died during the night."

"I'm sorry he got into fast company, General."

Custer said nothing.

"If you have any messages for Fort Hays, me and my mouse-colored mule will just be plodding back now."

The commander grunted. "Well, hereafter I will have nothing to say against a mule."

Coming dusk on the Great Plains. Thick black smoke from the burning wagons stained the violet sky. Drumming hoofs and the rattle of repeaters against the more stately thud and crack of Army Springfields and the hissing of arrows. Mounted warriors in red and black paint flashed past Will's position swinging bows and lances, a few carrying Winchesters, some in feathers and breastplates made from the bones of small animals but most nearly naked. The sharp ululant cries with which they had launched the attack had abated to preoccupied yelps. Will withdrew farther under the ambulance to reload the converted Springfield .50-caliber breechloader he called Lucretia Borgia while Sergeant Monroe of the 10th Cavalry, a Negro regiment, occupied the savages with bullets from his own rifle and side arm. Spent powder had darkened the sergeant's cinnamon features. When he spoke, his teeth cut a white gash in his face.

"Wish to hell Gen'ral Custer would show up," he said. "We's running out of niggers."

"Quit wishing and keep shooting."

A Sioux bullet pierced the canvas sheet of the grub wagon next to the ambulance and clanged against a skillet.

"Bet you wishes you was back home, Mistuh Cody."

Will crawled forward on his elbows and took aim at the glistening brown back of a brave leaning a mustang around the circled wagons. "I am home, Sergeant." He shot the Indian.

CHAPTER THREE

Ellsworth, Kansas.

Gloved and hatted against the drifting cinders, holding little Arta tightly to her bosom, she stepped directly from the train onto bare earth—there was no platform—and looked for her husband among the bearded faces sprinkled between the unpainted and weatherworn buildings that stood at arm's length from one another on two sides of a rutted street as broad as a pasture. At first she saw only strangers and gaps of empty sky that made her sick at heart. Then he was there, striding out from a cluster of train watchers, bigger than she remembered, six feet of buckskin and leather and dust and sweat, the shock of his presence like a sudden gust of hot wind. He started to throw his long arms around her, but she shrank back, clutching the blanket-wrapped baby. Hurt flickered in his eyes; then they dropped to the reason and grew warm and soft and shining with wonder. His lips parted, a little boy's lips after all.

"Is that—?"

"Why don't you hold your daughter, William?"

He accepted the bundle as if it contained fine crystal. While Louisa watched anxiously, it stirred and a little red face stared into Will's mahogany one with its beard gone fair in the sun, and a black hole opened and it bawled like a sheep.

"I'd holler too, I woke up to a face like that," one of the watchers called out. The crowd broke into guffaws and the baby cried louder.

Will returned the bundle awkwardly. "She's wet."

"She's a beauty, Will!" someone said.

"Yeah, she don't look like you a-tall," commented another. More laughter. Will joined in. Still laughing, he swept his little family into a carriage, behind which waited three wagons piled high with furniture and a band of armed men on horseback with hard, sunburned faces, and climbed in beside his wife.

"So many guns." As they lurched into motion, Louisa adjusted the baby's blanket to keep the sun out of her eyes.

"The hunting is good hereabouts," replied Will, shifting the reins.

After they had traveled almost a mile, Will said, "I'm a millionaire, Lulu, or almost."

"You said in your letter you had a quarter of a million dollars."

"Well, not yet, exactly. But I'm worth that much on paper. This fellow Rose that I'm partners with has a grading contract with the Kansas Pacific. We're laying out a city on the west bank of Big Creek and reserving corner lots for ourselves. I figure if we sell them for two fifty each, we'll be sitting on two hundred and fifty thousand easy." He grinned. "You'll not fall out of love with me when I'm a rich man, Mama?"

"I'm the mother of your daughter, William. That won't change if you've a quarter million or just a quarter."

His heart soared.

At night the heavens sat on the prairie. The crickets' stoic serenade paused at the sound of footsteps, so that as he walked, Will towed silence like a shadow. He approached his sentries noisily, crunching his heels on last year's brittle grass and whistling to keep the jumpier ones from blowing out his brains in panic when he addressed them. The exchange was always the same; repetition had scaled it down to the essentials.

"Anything?"

"Nothing, Cap'n."

"Well, keep your eyes and ears open. You know how fast these bastards hit."

The same words would be spoken all down the ragged line of deputized settlers that defined the camp's perimeters. On his way between guard posts Will paused often to listen to the occasional cries of night birds, cocking his ears for an echo. The voices of birds carried none. There were no echoes, and after completing his rounds he rejoined his wife in the bed they shared in one of the wagons of furniture. Little Arta slept quietly in the cradle her father had made.

"That's the third time you've got up tonight," said Louisa when he had drawn the covers over both of them, having removed only his boots and shirt. "Is anything wrong?"

"Just restless, Mama. I can't wait to show you our town."

"Will, are we in danger from Indians?"

"Of course not. The cavalry has them under control. Sleep now. We'll be traveling all day tomorrow and most of the next."

She wanted to continue the conversation, but her husband's even breathing told her he was already asleep. She stared up at the darkness inside the wagon sheet and listened to the rise and fall of her daughter's tiny lungs and heard the crunching footsteps of the guard patrols outside.

The infant town of Rome occupied a level spot high above Big Creek a mile from Fort Hays. Clapboard stores and a hotel rose clean and white from a sea of tents and bare lots drawn with stakes, between which men drove wagons and pushed wheelbarrows stacked with planks along the grassy streets. Hammers clattered and saws wheezed. A haze of sawdust blurred the sun. Indoors, the prostitutes slept, their establishments having closed for the day along with the saloons and gambling houses in honor of the cofounder and his wife and child.

Louisa stared dubiously at the hotel as their things were being carried inside a small house across the street. Will laughed.

"That's someone else's worry, Mama. We're in real estate."

The settlers, many of whom were waiting for their own wives and families, tipped their hats and pitched in to help empty the wagons. The deference they showed one of Rome's first respectable women charmed Louisa, who took it as proof of her husband's high local standing. The couple dined on simple fare at the hotel and returned by nightfall to find the house in order, Arta's cradle awaiting the baby beside the bed where her mother could reach out and rock it without getting up. As they were preparing to retire, a chorus of shots rattled outside the bedroom window.

A brief pause, and then another ragged volley. The prairie warped the reports and hurled them back with a growl.

"What is *that?*" Louisa scooped Arta up out of a sound sleep. The baby cried.

Will was peeling off his suspenders. "Just a serenade. It means they approve of you."

"Are they firing blank cartridges?"

He chuckled. "Certainly not. Nobody carries blank cartridges in his pistol. The whole town is armed."

"Why, in heaven's name?"

"To keep law and order."

"Don't you have policemen like in St. Louis?"

"A St. Louis policeman wouldn't last long in a town like Rome."

The baby was quiet now. She returned her to the cradle, tucked the blanket around her, then stepped out of her skirt and spent a few minutes folding it carefully before fitting it into its hanger. "I don't think I'm going to like your city, William."

He swept an arm behind her while she was hanging up the skirt and pulled her to him. Skirt and hanger dropped in a heap to the floor of the wardrobe. Smiling down at her: "But you like me."

"I love you."

"You'll learn to love Rome as well."

While they were kissing, his hand slid down from the small of her back to her rump. She squirmed and placed a hand against his chest.

"No, William. I'm exhausted from the trip."

"I have just the thing to relax you."

The baby started crying again.

Rose was a slender extrovert six inches shorter than Will, with lively eyes and hands and silver whiskers that after three days glinted like metal shavings on his sunburned cheeks, although he was only a few years older than his partner. He collected Will in the morning and together the pair walked all over Rome, building factories and opera houses and a mayor's mansion on the only lot in town where the sun shone the same length of time on the backyard in the afternoon as on the front in the morning, lined the main street with shops whose red-and-white-striped awnings turned the boardwalk into a shady grove, and laid pipe from the creek so that no one would be bothered with pumps and wells. Thirsty from so much head work, they stopped off at a saloon before parting company at the hotel, in which Rose owned a half interest with his foreman. Will then returned home, where Louisa informed him he had a visitor.

He didn't recognize the man who strode across his parlor and seized his hand in both of his.

"Mr. Cody? My name is Webb. Seeing you in person, I'm beginning to understand the stories I've been hearing about you since I left Chicago."

A good-looking Easterner, Webb had straight teeth behind a sandy moustache and wore his sturdy frontier clothes as if they had been made to order. Will was cautious. "What can I do for you, Mr. Webb?"

"They said you were direct. I itch to kill buffaloes and I'm told none is more expert upon the subject than you. I thought perhaps—"

Will let out his breath. "Say no more, Mr. Webb. How soon can you be mounted?"

The bull he selected was old and half blind, one eye clouded, its gray beard worn almost to the chin from decades spent dragging the ground. From an enormous chest and shoulders under a close clustering mass of dusty curls, its frame tapered back to a narrow, muscular rump, above which a short tail like a twist of rope raised its shaggy pompon, signaling rage. The beast still rolled in its own urine, although cows had stopped responding to the strong male stench long ago and it drew only flies whose bites left bleeding sores where its hair had fallen away in patches. Its clumsy lope was deceptive. Puffs of yellow dust erupted from under its drumming hoofs and hot air burst from its nostrils. If the thick scars crisscrossing its walnut hide were any indication, it had killed many times.

Mounted on his best buffalo horse Brigham, Will stayed abreast of the lone bull, out of range of the sharp rear hoofs and veering farther away whenever it brought its great head and curving horns hooking sideways at the thing coming up on its blind side. The horse made these maneuvers even as they occurred to the man. For two hundred yards the pursuit continued in this fashion, until they were well clear of the rest of the small herd of old-timers. Then Will brought up Lucretia Borgia from her perch across the throat of his saddle, took aim while steering with his knees, and fired.

Dust exploded from the beast's side. It wheeled suddenly in the direction of the shot, forcing the horse left quickly to avoid collision, ran twenty more yards, and then its legs folded and it went down head first, plowing a furrow with its great shovel-shaped snout for ten feet before shuddering to a stop. Its lungs filled slowly and emptied with a mighty grunt. Then they were still.

Clouds of dust drifted past and settled with an audible sifting noise.

"Splendid!" Webb put spurs to his dun and joined the marksman. His eyes were as bright and his face was as flushed as if he'd been the one who had chased and killed the bull. "You make it look easy."

"Anything's easy after you've done it a thousand times for the railroad, Mr. Webb. And the horse does most of the work."

"You're much too modest. Would you do me the honor of accepting my dinner invitation in town?"

"I can't do that."

Webb's politician's smile faded.

"In Rome," said the frontiersman, "I buy."

The hotel restaurant was clean and quiet. Finishing his meal, Webb placed his utensils on the empty plate with a slight clatter. "Excellent. I never knew buffalo meat was so good."

"A lot of folks prefer it," Will replied over his wine. "It's always tender coming off the hump and the fat won't make you sick like with beef. Also, it's practically the only meat they serve here outside of sage hen, so they know how to fix it."

"When my colleagues learned I was coming West, they warned me I'd lose my scalp. So far the only Indian I've seen rented me the horse I'm using at the livery."

"They generally behave themselves this close to the fort."

The Easterner refilled his companion's glass and his own from the carafe on the table. "I'm quite impressed with what I've seen of Rome. It's an excellent site."

"We like it."

"I'm told you had a great deal to do with selecting the location and supervised construction."

"My parents were pioneers. I reckon some of it rubbed off."

Webb swirled the red liquid, watching it cloud and clear. "I'll give you one eighth of this townsite," he said.

Will paused with his glass halfway to his lips, then raised it the rest of the way and sipped. Smiling, he set it down. "I haven't time to discuss such matters, Mr. Webb. Dessert? They make a fine dried apple pie here."

The other shook his head, watching his host curiously. Later Will told Louisa laughingly about the man who had offered him one eighth of his own town.

At dawn he left to fulfill some more of his contract to furnish buffalo meat for the Kansas Pacific track gangs and was gone three days. Returning, sweaty, sunburned, smelling of innards, he walked Brigham to the top of the ridge above Rome and reined in, blinking against the late afternoon sunlight. More than half the town was gone.

Pieces of discarded lumber lying in empty lots were all that remained of some buildings. Others were being dismantled by the same men who had erected them, the boards piled into wagons and wheelbarrows pointed east. The blank spaces looked like missing teeth.

Will's house stood alone on what had been a crowded street when he left. He found Rose, his eyes less lively now, whittling with his back against a porch post. The earth at his feet was covered with coiled shavings. Louisa came out just as Will was stepping down into the yard. He took one look at the furious expression on her face and turned to Rose.

"What happened?"

"You wrote me you were worth two hundred and fifty thousand dollars," Louisa said.

"Later, Mama."

His partner peeled off an eight-inch curl. "That fellow Webb you had dinner with is in charge of building the division site for the Kansas Pacific," he explained without looking up. "Soon as you left to go hunting, he invited everyone over to see Hays City."

"There's no such place."

"There is now."

"Oh."

"He started selling lots on the spot and loaned government wagons to the folks that bought them to cart everything over in. That's some of them there." He pointed with his knife at the vehicles into which Will's former neighbors were stacking beams and doors.

"Can he do that?"

"Appears he did."

"William, what about that two hundred and fifty thousand dollars?"

He looked around. Almost everything was gone now. Only his house and a few stone foundations were left. "You're standing in it," he said, "or what's left of it." He drew a deep breath and grinned at Rose. "How does it feel to drop from a millionaire to a pauper in just three days?"

"It's quite a fall. I haven't got over it yet. I'd get drunk, but they took the saloons too."

"You should have accepted Mr. Webb's offer," Louisa told Will.

"I agree. But you don't put spurs to a horse after the race is lost. Anyway, I'm only twenty-one. I believe I have time to make it."

Rose flipped what was left of his stick into the debris at his feet and folded the knife. "Well, I still have a grading contract with the KP. You want a job?"

"I'm getting five hundred a month from the Goddard brothers in Ellsworth to feed the railroad workers. Being a tycoon, I was thinking of quitting. But the job's starting to smell better."

"If you need a place to put your family, I hear the folks in Hays City are friendly." His grin came and went quickly.

"I reckon it's as good as any till I can get them on the train back to St. Louis."

They shook hands. And laughed.

Louisa said, "You should have accepted Mr. Webb's offer."

"Will Cody?"

The man addressing him was a few years older than Will, lean, with a mane of dark hair cut square across the back of his neck like an Apache's, a drooping moustache, and pale blue eyes that contrasted sharply with his sunburned skin. He wore a buckskin shirt over denims faded to the same buff color, and the hand with which he grasped Will's was powerful and callused between thumb and forefinger like his own where the reins rubbed. He was riding a buckskin mare and carried a Henry rifle in a saddle scabbard.

"You have the advantage," Will said.

"Billy Comstock. Folks call me Buffalo Bill."

"I've been called that a time or two myself. You're chief of scouts over at Fort Wallace."

"I'm also the finest buffalo runner west of the Platte."

"Perhaps so. When I'm east of it."

They grinned at each other tightly, like two young bulls pawing the ground. Will was astride Brigham. Nearby, his skinners were at work hooking wagons to the hides of the buffaloes he had shot that morning, preparing to drag the hides off the pink and gray carcasses. The prairie air was thick with buzzing flies. Will felt the crew watching out of the corners of their eyes.

"They tell me you been making a fair job of it shooting meat for the KP," Comstock remarked.

"Coming up on two thousand so far this season. I hear you're not one to grow grass under your feet either."

"I done my share. You use that needle gun all the time?"

Will patted Lucretia, resting across his thighs. "Wouldn't change for gold."

"You'd do better with a repeater."

"Not for caliber. Anyway, I'm not interested in doing better. I'm the best there is now."

"I got officers backing me with five hundred dollars says you're not."

"That straight?"

"It'd take a bigger whopper than that to bring me out here."

"Well then," said Will.

The arrangements were made through Fort Hays. It called for a special train from St. Louis, which on a bright steel day in late spring disgorged a cargo of gentlemen and their ladies into an empty stretch of plain twenty miles from Sheridan, the women raising their skirts clear of the dust and chips. Parasols blossomed pink and white as they made their way to the horses and wagons waiting to take them to the hunting grounds. Will rode out from a group of officers and dismounted to embrace Louisa, who had come out from Hays City with Arta. This time he made care not to crush the tiny bundle.

"I don't know why you invited me, William," Louisa said. "You know I don't approve of slaughtering dumb brutes for sport."

"The meat won't go to waste, Mama. Those wagons are set to deliver it to the gandies and steel-wallopers as soon as the contest is finished. And five hundred dollars is five hundred dollars. I'd be a month earning it the regular way."

"You aren't doing this for money and you know it."

He ground-hitched Brigham and helped her into the seat of a buckboard with a fresh-faced lieutenant in the driver's seat who touched his hat to his passenger before reaching down to untie the team's reins. Two couples Louisa had ridden out with from St. Louis were already seated in back.

As the excursion was about to get under way, a little man in a stovepipe hat and cutaway climbed onto the back of a wagon and addressed the spectators in an astonishingly sonorous voice. The contestants were just swinging into leather. When his name was called, Will stood in his stirrups and swept off his hat to an ovation from the visitors and a raucous cheer from the Fort Hays delegation. Louisa uncovered Arta's face and held her up so that she could tell her when she was old enough to understand that she saw her father on that day, ignoring the admiring comments she overheard from women charmed by her husband's physique and the chestnut lock that fell over one eye when he removed his hat. Comstock, seated on his buckskin with one leg resting on the pommel of his saddle, merely waved when introduced. The officers and enlisted men from Fort Wallace shouted encouragement. A lone catcall rose from among Will's supporters.

"Messrs. Cody and Comstock will hunt for eight hours, at the end of which the man who has shot the largest number of buffaloes will be declared the winner," announced the little man in his big voice. "A referee will follow each man on horseback to count the carcasses. Once we have reached the hunting ground, spectators will please remain where directed until the shooting has begun, after which they may move up for a closer look."

The announcer abandoned the wagon box for a seat next to the driver, and the vehicles started rolling, accompanied by a cavalry escort from the two interested forts.

Scouts who had been tracking the migratory herds for days awaited the party at its destination, rolling terrain from where dark clumps of the curly-haired beasts were just visible grazing several hundred yards to the west. When the wagons stopped, the little man caught the attention of the two principals and produced a watch from a vest pocket. He kept his voice down to avoid spooking the buffaloes.

"It is now eight o'clock. You have until four. Good luck, gentlemen."

The hunters took off at a gallop. Their hoofbeats started the prey moving, lumbering at first, then picking up speed in that ragged lope that shook the ground, heads sunk between their shoulders, humps moving up and down like living hills. At the horsemen's approach the herd separated. Comstock took the bunch that went left. Will let his reins go slack, giving the little roan its head, and without hesitation Brigham peeled right, aiming for the leaders. By this time Comstock's Henry was cracking and stragglers were dropping at the rear of the bunch he was after. Will waited until he was almost abreast of the cow in front of his half before raising his heavy Springfield. Cows took the lead in times of stress. The butt pushed his shoulder an instant ahead of the roar. The bullet knocked dust off the beast's side just behind the left shoulder. It grunted loudly and heeled over.

The animal galloping behind stumbled on the fallen cow with a startled bellow, then caught its balance and crowded left, starting a chain reaction among the leaders. Will reloaded, aimed, dropped another. The rest turned hard left. Brigham stayed parallel with the herd while his master poked new cartridges into the breech and fired three more times, nudging the beasts ever left. He had them moving in a tight circle now.

The more rapid reports of his opponent's repeater grew faint as his herd drew him farther away in a straight line littered with carcasses.

At the end of the first round, which lasted as long as there were buffaloes to be shot, Will had killed thirty-eight, the shaggy hulks describing a circle four hundred feet in diameter. As the skinners and butchers set to work, he trotted back toward the wagons and found glasses and a number of tall green bottles waiting for him in the bed of a buckboard. He stepped down to allow a soldier to water Brigham from a bucket and picked up one of the bottles, examining the label. It was in French.

"Wine?"

"Champagne, Mr. Cody," explained a young trooper with freckles. "Compliments of the St. Louis excursionists."

Will peeled off the gold foil, whooped when the cork shot out of the bottle on a jet of white foam, filled a glass with sparkling liquid, raised it in the direction of his well-dressed benefactors, and emptied it in a draft. Smacking his lips: "Well, it sure beats water for killing a man's thirst." He topped off the glass a second time. "What's Comstock's score?" he asked the youngster.

"Not in yet, sir. He's still shooting."

"You mean he's still chasing them."

The chief of scouts at Fort Wallace reappeared ten minutes later, walking his weary buckskin along a trail paved with meat for three miles.

"Twenty-three!" called out the referee riding behind him.

Will's backers from Fort Hays cheered.

They went out twice more. The first time, the herd found them as they were sipping champagne and made a lively outing, as it consisted almost entirely of fleet cows and calves. Will made a poor job of his seventeenth kill, piercing a mother cow's stomach so that her entrails spilled out and she tripped over them. Bellowing, she struggled to rise. He drew a careful bead and shot her through the heart. She fell with a wheeze, shuddered, and sighed.

Silence, and then loud bawling from the half-grown calf Will had forgotten about standing over its fallen mother. He reloaded and blew its brains out. That put him four ahead for the round.

The afternoon was wearing down when they encountered a third bunch three miles from the last slaughter. Leaving behind his saddle and bridle— much to the delight and feigned alarm of the ladies (and a look of exaggerated tolerance from Louisa)—Will rode in windward of the buffaloes and destroyed thirteen as fast as he could feed fresh rounds into Lucretia's chamber. He sighted in on number fourteen, hesitated, then lowered the rifle and kneed the roan around the young bull's right shoulder. The buffalo snorted, feinted with its horns, and swung left. Will stayed with it, pressing closer. Again it corrected course. He had the beast heading straight at the spectators' wagons now.

The ladies shrieked as the brute bore down on them. There was a frenzied creaking of springs as the men piled to the ground and reached up to help down the women, their petticoats fluttering like white flags. Will led the buffalo with his sights to within fifty yards of the wagons before dumping it. The echo of his last shot broke against the distant hills.

The score was Cody 69; Comstock 46.

The spectators applauded when the contestants shook hands. Comstock then left Will to have his back slapped and his shoulders pummeled by the men from Fort Hays and rejoined the subdued crowd from Fort Wallace. A cloth sack containing twenty-five twenty-dollar gold pieces was eventually delivered to the victor, and Comstock corrected people who called him Buffalo Bill within his hearing until the day a Cheyenne bullet entered his back and burst his heart at the age of twenty-six.

The track foreman on the Kansas Pacific graveyard shift was a smiling Irishman with great shoulders and a shaggy blond mop that he swore was growing curly on the company's unchanging fare of hump steaks and buffalo jerky. He confided to his men that he sometimes found himself gazing at cows with indecent intent and maintained that his stool burned with a blue flame like prairie chips. Interrupted in the course of a new variation on this same theme by a cry from a fellow gandy, he lowered his hammer and squinted against the rising sun. Pasted on its face was the purple outline of a tall man driving a wagon mounded over with a tarpaulin-covered load. Flies swarmed over it.

"Well," sighed the foreman, "here comes this old Bill with more fucking buffalo."

CHAPTER FOUR

Razor flakes lanced out of a low iron sky, pecking hats and pricking unprotected skin. Savage gusts tore at brims tied down with scarves and seized and shook coattails in their teeth. The horses moved through mounting blue drifts in lunges, resting in between, their sides bellying and emptying like sails, their breath damp white tissue shredded by the gale. There was no horizon, just a dizzy swirl of white and gray, like spit in a puddle.

General E. A. Carr—fur-hatted, icicles in his beard—spotted a lone horseman, his mount standing perpendicular to the trail ahead, buried to its chest in snow. Then the wind changed directions again, obliterating the shadowy vision. The general circled wide to place his back to the wind and drew rein, tugging down the bandana he had tied over his nose.

"Anything?" he shouted. Snow flew into his mouth.

"I think so." The other rider was visible once again. His hat was secured over his ears bonnet-fashion by a scarf, and his eyebrows and goatee were stiff and white, tacking thirty years onto his appearance. Dark brown hair hung unfettered almost to the middle of his back. "We found an old camp and followed the trail up the west bank of the Cimarron."

"Penrose?"

"I have hopes. I left the others behind to mark the spot."

"How's the going for wagons?"

"There isn't any. But you'll find the way easier up the east bank."

Carr nodded absently. "What's the chances General Penrose and his men are still alive?"

"Hickok's his chief of scouts. As chances go, that's as good as you'll find."

"Very well, lead the way."

Will touched his hat and gathered up his reins.

The relief train, made up of ambulances, pack mules with bundles like camels' humps, and seventy-five wagons drawn by six-mule teams, leaned into the thickening weather. The men of the 5th Cavalry rode with their chins tucked into their throats and their eyes nailed to the ground, faces muffled against frostbite as they steered their mounts—mostly mules again

—along the line of rapidly filling depressions left in the snow by their youthful guide and the riders in between. The temperature huddled around thirty below.

The command "Halt!" bounced back through the ranks like a scrap of litter blown along the ground. Leather creaked and bit chains jingled.

Will doubled back on his trail to find General Carr glowering from the back of his big gray down the forty-degree slope that knifed from the Raton tableland to the snow-covered frozen hollow of the Cimarron River.

"You didn't say anything about this," Carr remarked.

"Figured you'd find out for yourself when the time came."

"We'll never get the wagons down in one piece."

"Just get your cavalry down, General. Let me worry about the wagons."

The riders picked their way down one by one, leaning back on the reins, the mules sliding and balking, legs stiff, their brays torn by the wind.

"They don't make wagons with wings," a driver told Will, watching the last of the mules crossing the ice at the base of the slope. "And that's the only way they're going to get from here to there."

Will said, "Down's the easiest direction there is. Run down, slide down or fall down—just get down. There's four companies of the 10th eating mule on the other side of that river, and we're going to get these supplies to them before they turn cannibal."

"You don't know nothing about wagons and mules."

"Only everything there is to know. You, there! Bring that mess wagon up front."

The team was coaxed to the edge of the decline. Will called for chains and crawled underneath the wagon. When all four wheels were locked tight, he rolled out and got up and dusted off and took the driver's place.

"Watch careful." He slipped the whip from its socket and uncurled it with a bang over the team's backs.

They started down, the frozen wheels grinding on the hardpack foundation under the thick wet surface. The mules tried to balk, but the wagon crowded their heels and the reports of the whip shattered their determination. Their breath drifted back and enveloped Will's face like warm wet wool. He screwed up his face against the slicing wind, feeling the regular drivers' eyes hot between his shoulder blades. His shirt was soaked through despite the cold.

The wagon wrenched sideways whenever a wheel found an irregularity, panicking the team. But Will kept a firm grip on the reins and continued the cursing litany that was like a lullaby to the veterans in the lead. Their calm spread to the others. Near the bottom Will took up breathing again, realizing only at that moment that he had stopped.

That was when everything broke loose.

The wagon had been pressuring the animals all the way down, but as the descent steepened, the leaders gave up straining against it and broke into a gallop. Will hauled back on the traces, standing with his feet braced against the board. He could as well have tried to slow down the wind. The wagon jounced and chattered and rocked from side to side wildly, its wheels lifting so high off the ground that when they slammed back down only his grasp on the reins and the forward pull of the mules prevented him from tumbling off. Pots, skillets, tin plates, utensils clattered around in back. They hit the river hard enough to crack the ice and skidded across, the terrified team clawing for traction on the slick surface, bounced up over the opposite bank, the wagon hanging in the air for a sickening eternity before coming down with a bang, and bolted across a field of snow toward Carr's camp.

A pair of troopers carrying a heavy tree limb for firewood across the wagon's path looked, let go of their burden, and dived in two directions. The mules leaped over the limb, the wagon slammed over it, and Will choked up on the reins and strained back with everything he had, shouting "Whoa!" at the top of his lungs. The mules slowed, braying, and the wagon dragged to a racketing halt, sluing around sideways, smoke pluming from the wheels. It tilted for a precarious moment, then righted itself with a crash. A broken chain link clanked and was silent.

The driver breathed some air. He unwound the reins from his burned and swollen hands, took his feet out of the floorboards, and bounded to the ground in the midst of a crowd of troopers. Among them was one of the foragers he had forced to vacate his path. "Where'd you come from?" demanded the trooper. The front of his uniform was covered with snow.

"Straight down."

All the essential wagons were in camp within the hour.

The shortcut whittled days off the rescue party's schedule. The weather cleared as if to show its approval, and from the river onward Penrose's trail was obvious, marked by the remains of old campfires and dead mules butchered almost to the bones. Strips of hide had been torn from the carcasses to patch the stranded soldiers' boots. One morning Will was riding near the rear of the train, joshing the driver who had doubted his knowledge of wagons and mules, when a trooper cantered back with a summons from General Carr. The scout found the commander on foot, conversing with a trio of Negro soldiers whose uniforms hung on their emaciated frames. Their eyes were like hard-boiled eggs.

"These men are with Penrose," Carr told Will. His expression was grim.

"They's terrible bad off, suh," reported one of the three, squinting at Will in a way that said he was almost blind from the snow. Dark blood caked his face from frostbitten cracks. "They ain't but a few mules and horses left un-et, and they was a-chawing at each other's manes and tails when we left to fetch help."

He was out of breath. His companions were in even worse condition, leaning on each other with chilblains on their cheeks and their hands and feet wrapped in filthy rags. Carr ordered them taken to the rear for food, rest, and medical attention. As they were leaving, supported by members of the 5th, the general turned to Will.

"It's a week's trip anyway for a train this size," he told the scout. "Cut out two companies and fifty mules and load them with emergency supplies. We'll be along later."

The snow blazed under a dead white sun like a bullet scar. Will advised his cavalry escort to keep their eyes down and refrain from staring at it directly for more than a few seconds at a time. After three days he spotted smoke, and by dusk his party came upon their first member of Penrose's command, a slat-sided mare wandering loose, with glassy eyes and a bloody stump of tail. A few hundred yards beyond that crouched a rag-clad figure with a hat pulled low over a tiny blue buffalo-chip fire, massaging red and peeling hands in the meager warmth. When Will was almost on top of him, he turned up a stubbled face with a ragged moustache, sunken eyes, and a sour look. The horseman grinned suddenly.

"What you doing, Wild Bill?"

"Well," drawled the other, "when they got hot enough I was fixing to eat my fingers. But yours are fatter."

Will found a warmer welcome in the main camp.

Hickok, thawed out and healthy, his spare waistline swelling to fill out fresh winter buckskins made soft as butter by a squaw's strong teeth, lay quiet on his stomach, only his eyes moving, quartering the snowy banks angling down to the sluggish gray waters of the Canadian River. After five minutes he picked up his hat, swiveled around, and slithered back down his side of the ridge like some great tan lizard. When he was well below the crest he got up, swatting snow off his front with the hat, and strode the rest of the way down to where Will waited, holding the horses.

"Let's head downriver," said Hickok.

Twice more he made the journey to the top of the ridge. Each time they remounted and worked their way south. On his third trip, Hickok placed his thumb and little finger in his mouth and whistled. His partner left the horses to forage for grass under the snow and joined him, sinking down on all fours as he neared the top.

"There." Hickok pointed.

Sunlight struck blinding sparks off the snow. Will lowered his eyelids until the lashes formed a gray screen, through which he eventually picked out a line of irregular shapes moving like a troop of ants along the riverbank.

"How you want to do her?" asked his companion.

"That's up to you. I never robbed a wagon train before."

"When you're with the Army, it's called commandeering."

They waited in silence as the wagons drew near. When the lead team was below them, Hickok sent Will down for the horses, dragged up his rifle by the barrel, and fired a shot over the mules' heads. One of them brayed and tried to rear but was defeated by the harness. The driver hauled back on the reins. Men scrambled out of the wagons, waving rifles and shouting in Spanish.

"Who's in charge?" Hickok's bellow caromed between the banks, losing shape as it bounded downriver.

The driver of the lead wagon, a tubby Mexican with a curling black moustache and a bearskin hat and coat, waited until the echoes ceased before answering.

"No hablo inglés!"

"Buffalo shit." Hickok spanged a bullet off the wagon rib directly over the driver's head.

"I am in charge, señor!" he shouted, ducking.

"What's your cargo?"

"Broadcloth and gingham. Dress material for the officers' wives at Fort Lyon."

This time he aimed more carefully and snatched off the driver's hat.

"Cerveza, señor! Beer. For the Colonel Evans and his cavalry from New Mexico Territory."

"That's what I heard too." The gunman dug his poke out from under his skins and held up a gold coin, turning it so that it caught the light. "I'm commandeering those there emergency rations in the name of the U.S. Army and General E. A. Carr."

The Mexican squinted at the flashing bit of metal. His round Basque face split into a slow grin in which there was nearly as much gold as in Hickok's hand. "Put away your weapons, *muchachos,"* he told his crew. "They will only get in the way of the talking."

Two hours later the scouts accompanied the wagons into camp on horseback, flicked quirts at the troopers who tried to clamber aboard, and after much pushing and many threats succeeded in forging the thirsty manhood into a grumbling line with their tin cups in hand.

"Penny a cup; keep it lively." As each coin clanked into the bucket he had standing next to the first upended barrel, Hickok filled a cup from the tap, returned it to its owner, and reached for the next.

"Hey, there's ice in this beer," one trooper complained.

Will said, "What'd you expect, eggs?" and plucking a red-hot picket pin from among the several he had in the campfire, plunked it hissing into the man's cup.

Some of the men were on their third trip through the line when General Carr appeared with a lieutenant in his early twenties.

"There they are, sir," reported the lieutenant. "That train was meant for Colonel Evans."

Several soldiers melted out of the line. Others, more determined, moved up to take their place.

Carr faced Will. "Cody, are those the wagons Evans is expecting?"

"We heard something on that order, General, but being as the report came from Mexicans we didn't credit it." The scout's eyes shone from the taste he and Hickok had shared along the road to camp.

The lieutenant snorted. "He's trying to weasel out of it, sir. He's a liar as well as a thief. Hickok too."

"Your time's coming, little brass buttons," said the gunman.

"There is no doubt in my mind as to the ownership of those wagons." Carr hooked his thumbs in his belt, patting his middle with his fingers. His glare swept the culprits and the men holding their empty cups and landed on the young officer at his side. "Lieutenant, have them unloaded and see that they're delivered to Colonel Evans. Go with them and report back to me when they reach their destination."

"Sir—" he began, astonished.

"Dismissed, Lieutenant."

He closed his mouth and snapped off a smart salute. When it was returned, he spun on his heel and left, trailing whoops and whistles from the enlisted men in line.

"I seem to have left my tent without change," Carr said. "I seldom request credit. However—"

Beaming, Will took a full cup from Hickok and handed it to the commander. "It's on the house, General."

The long bitter winter ended in wrath. Reports reverberated in the mountains as shelves of ice and snow as large as houses cracked apart and tumbled end over end in slow motion, splintering trees and trappers' shacks like twigs and melting into shrieking torrents that sucked roots and bushes loose from the banks and swept the legs from under helpless animals, their carcasses battered and bloody by the time they reached the foothills and drifted in slow circles into a roof-high plain of water dotted with uprooted trees and blasted muskrat huts. Flies laid their eggs in the jellied hides, and magpies and buffalo birds tore at their eyes. Death and rebirth and the frank glare of morning exposing the crimes of the long night.

Other truths floated in on the thaw. Black Kettle, mighty chief of the Cheyennes, was dead, awakened by the whirl and crash of the "Garry Owen" and killed with his young squaw while fleeing Custer's attack on the Washita in the predawn November gray—killed, some claimed, by a single thrust of Wild Bill Hickok's bowie knife in hand-to-hand combat. But at the moment Black Kettle's body was floating downstream, the scout was eating mule among his stranded fellows in General Penrose's 10th Cavalry, waiting for Will Cody and the 5th and thawing his gunslinger's hands over a tiny fire. When the fight was over, Custer had the village burned and the captured Indian ponies shot. There were hundreds of them and the reports continued late into the night. The Cheyennes, who had a name for everything, called it the time of the Red Moon.

Will saw in the last year of the decade at Fort Lyon, where he had returned with the 5th. The blizzards of January blew themselves out into the false spring of February while he was riding dispatch between Carr and General Sheridan in the field. Just in from his latest errand, he awoke in fat sunlight pouring in through the window of the scouts' barracks to a babble of voices outside. From reflex he grabbed Lucretia Borgia first and tugged on his winter moccasins on the way to the door. He was wearing only buckskin pants and his gray flannel underwear.

Blue uniforms crowded the gate. At first, he thought it was just the wood detail returning from its morning forage. There was too much excitement for that, however, and he stepped out for a closer look.

"Who is it?" someone asked.

"Hell," someone else responded, "don't you know Wild Bill?"

"He dead?"

"He don't look none too alive."

The scout bulled his way through to the center. There were complaints and curses, then someone whispered his name and silence fell. A pair of troopers were supporting Hickok between them, his flaccid arms across their shoulders. His chin was sunk on his chest and his buckskins were filthy, as if he'd been crawling through dirt and manure. Dark blood slicked his left leg from thigh to boot. His face was slug-colored.

Will looked hard at the trooper to Hickok's right, who said, "We went out looking for wood and found him."

"He was using this here for a crutch." His companion held up a Cheyenne lance stained dark back to the haft.

"Get him to the sawbones."

They hammered on the door until the post surgeon opened it in his nightshirt, then tramped through the office into the living space in back and deposited their burden in a bed that was still warm from their host's body. Will cleared the room of everyone but the surgeon and remained to assist. Hickok flinched but didn't regain consciousness as his gore-plastered trouser leg was cut with scissors and peeled away from the wound. Unstopping a bottle of alcohol, the sawbones sponged down the leg gently with cotton, then instructed Will to grip the patient's shoulders as hard as he could and poured clear liquid directly into the ragged hole.

Hickok's howl rattled the bottles on the shelves of the cabinet in the office outside. Will leaned his weight onto his friend's shoulders, astonished at the strength he had left after losing so much blood. Meanwhile the surgeon resumed cleaning the flesh around the wound.

"Hang on," he said. "It's deeper than I thought."

More alcohol was introduced. Will struggled to maintain his grip. Then the patient lapsed back into unconsciousness. The surgeon went into his office and returned after a long time with a sterilized needle and suture. At his request, his assistant removed the shade from the coal-oil lamp and held it up while the older man's deft fingers manipulated the thin steel rod with a seamstress' skill. Finally a cotton pad and gauze bandage were applied. Hickok's chest meanwhile rose and fell in even rhythm. His face was peaceful under a sheen of perspiration. The surgeon covered him with a blanket and crooked a finger at Will, who followed him through the door into the consultation room. Still in his nightshirt, the professional man resembled an old woman from behind, with his thin hairless legs and varicose veins exposed and the soles of his slippers slapping his feet. He opened a door in a cabinet next to his desk, filled two glasses with copper-colored brandy from a cut-glass decanter, and handed one to Will, who put down half its contents in a gulp. Warmth spread through his system like a fist opening.

"He'll make it," the surgeon announced. "He's lost a great deal of blood, but if they survive the alcohol, they're damn near indestructible."

"Aren't you supposed to put him out with chloroform or ether or something like that?"

"In most cases. But I got out of the habit at Shiloh, where a clean scalpel was a luxury."

"When you reckon he can get back to scouting?"

"Never."

Will stared.

The surgeon touched his lips to the edge of his glass and made a face. It was a long face, with muttonchops whose gray hairs curled in on themselves. Thick bifocals straddled his veined nose. "He's no longer young as scouts go, and the older he gets the more trouble he's going to have with that leg. There was muscular damage. Muscle doesn't replace itself like most tissue, and surgical thread can't put back what's lost. He'll always have a limp. If he tries to sit a horse too long, he'll wish he was back here with the alcohol. A true friend would advise him to seek another line of work. Indians smell out weakness like wolves. The frontier is a place for young whole men. Unless you're a damn fool or a doctor."

"He won't like hearing that."

"That's why I'm counting on you to be the one to tell him." He lifted the decanter. "Refill?"

The next day orderlies moved the patient to a bed in the post infirmary, where Will visited him that afternoon, pulling a quart of whiskey out of his coat when the men in white smocks were engaged elsewhere. After the bottle had passed back and forth a couple of times, he told Hickok what the surgeon had said. His friend nodded distractedly, as if the news concerned someone he knew by name only.

"It was a running fight," the patient explained. "They was doing all the fighting and I was doing all the running. Shook myself loose from all but one. Bastard unhorsed me with a lucky throw and left me for dead."

Exhausted from just that short speech, he rested his head on the pillow wedged between his back and the brass bedstead. His pomaded curls and sunburned face were as dark as old wood against the striped ticking and starched white of his nightshirt. "I'm an old man, Will."

"Buffalo shit, Wild Bill. You can't be thirty."

"I'm thirty-one. My pa was thirty-six when I was born and he was an old man as far back as I can remember. All the scouts I started with are dead or retired."

"What you going to do?"

"Go back home and work my ma's farm, I reckon, or help my brothers in the store."

"You wouldn't stick six months."

"I sure don't want to stack peach tins the rest of my life. Or walk behind a mule neither."

"What about marshaling? There's a lot of new railroad towns need a fair hand with a pistol."

"I never heard tell of any thirty-year-old marshals."

"You could be the first."

"Ten dollars a month and a nickel for every rat and stray dog I shoot inside the town limits? Forget it." He stroked his injured leg absently. "I could play cards for a living."

"That's no life. Spend half your time broke and the rest sneaking out of town on a stole horse."

Hickok nodded, sighing. Then he opened bright eyes and turned them on Will. "But not if I'm marshal too."

"Wild Bill," his friend said, smiling, "you are a one."

Heat ribbons crawled over the sand hills, reflecting blue sky like pools of water always atop the next rise. Through them, like shadows on a wavy mirror, waded Carr's 5th Cavalry and companies of the 10th and 7th, the white regiments burned as dark as the black, faces breaded with sand and sweat. The horses' sticky coats glistened like powdered glass under the white sun.

Carr paused atop a high mound to blow his horse while the men took position, tracking their progress through his glass. The maneuvers were carried out in silence but for the tinkling of bit chains, an eerie noise in the empty desert. From time to time the general trained his glass on the ponies grazing the bunch grass at the top of a bluff to the west to assure himself that the Cheyennes were still camped on the other side. As the dust drifted and settled he folded the instrument and returned it to his saddlebag.

"Bugler, sound charge."

The corporal mounted behind him raised the bugle to his lips—and paused.

Carr twisted in his saddle. "What are you waiting for? Sound charge."

"I—I disremember it, sir." The youth's face was flushed to the hairline.

"I suggest you start remembering."

The flustered bugler started to blow recall.

"Quartermaster!" shouted the general.

"Yes, sir." A beefy sergeant trotted forward, tore the bugle out of the corporal's grasp, blasted the proper call, and, flinging away the horn, drew his side arm and put spurs to his horse.

They caught the enemy sleeping. Two wings of regular cavalry and a third of Pawnee scouts under Major North—the latter stripped to their drawers so that their wounds would bleed clean and riding bareback—converged on the village, slithering sabers from their scabbards and creaking revolvers and rifles out of leather with a racket like tortured buggy springs. Will's Springfield roared against the crackle of lighter fire between the camp and the river. The surprised Cheyennes yelped and hooted and scrambled for their mounts. Bullets plucked them off their feet and flung them like loosely baled rags to the ground. Stinging blue smoke fouled the air.

The fighting crested in the first five minutes, subsided to isolated reports, and ended on a solitary shot that laid down a crisp period to the day's bloodletting after a quarter of an hour. After that a man with imagination could hear the shadow of smoke skidding along the ground. Carr strode through the vanquished camp afoot, upwind of the crackling tipis and Indian corpses already stinking in the heat. Shards of broken pottery crunched under his boots. The squaws' wailing made a weird rhythm, like wind rising. There were no Army casualties.

"They killed one of the white women, sir," reported an officer, saluting wearily. "The other one's pretty badly used, but the surgeon says she'll pull through."

The general nodded grimly. "Anything else?"

"Their chief, Tonka Haska, was killed. Major North says that translates into Tall Bull."

"Who killed him?"

"No one seems to know. But that's his horse Cody's riding."

Carr glanced at the frontiersman, maneuvering a big bay between rows of prisoners seated glumly on the scorched earth. "Write it up that way, then. Cody killed the chief."

"Yes, sir."

CHAPTER FIVE

"*Colonel* Judson, did you say?"

Major Frank North, chief of Pawnee scouts under General Carr at Fort McPherson, Nebraska, the 5th's new home, stared dubiously through the sun cracks in his leathern face at the little round man in a raveled brown suit smeared with dust. A gray hat clung to the back of the newcomer's shaggy head, and the prairie sun found whiskey welts among the pouches on his face and gray hairs in his wilting moustache and an ugly red scar that might have been an old rope burn around his neck. He looked like a drummer fallen on evil times.

"The title is a battlefield gesture, conferred upon me during the all-but-forgotten unpleasantness in Mexico," explained the little round man in his lecturer's voice, throwing it away with a theatrical flip of his oddly beautiful left hand. "We are all civilians in the sight of God. Edward Z. C. Judson awaiting your convenience." He bowed, snapping out his expansive rear under the tails of his claw-hammer coat.

"I think you want the chaplain. You won't find much God around my outfit."

"To which my very good friends in the clergy might respond that He is everywhere. However, while your recommendation convinces me that your chaplain is an exemplary fellow worthy of any man's time, it is you, Major, whom I have journeyed four hundred miles by rail to see."

North suppressed a sigh. They were standing in the midday heat, twisting and shimmering from the bare, trampled surface of the compound. "What can I do for you, Colonel?"

The man thus addressed beamed. "Rather, the question is what service I can render you. My sources have provided me with an account of your company's recent action at Summit Springs, most particularly the death of the Cheyenne chief Tall Bull. It is, I feel most strongly, my honorable duty to bring to the attention of our brothers and sisters in the East the details of your personal bravery in that stirring duel. In short—"

"You're a journalist."

"An humble biographer, sir. A minstrel *sans* music, a prose troubadour if you will, destined to wither in the shade of that same history shaped by the men whose exploits I am called to chronicle. My readers know me as Ned Buntline."

"Dime novels, Colonel?"

"Popular literature, Major. In the hallowed tradition of Homer and the Bard of Avon, if I may be pardoned the comparison. Millions who have never ventured west of Chicago look to myself and my colleagues for an example of the rugged American. I offer you immortality in exchange for a few hours of your time."

The chief of scouts cast a disgruntled glance around the post and grinned suddenly.

"You're talking to the wrong man, Colonel. If you want a fellow to fit that bill you'll find him over there under that wagon."

Judson followed the direction of North's pointing finger and frowned at a long pair of buckskin-clad legs protruding from under half a ton of stacked cartridge boxes.

Stretched out in the shade of the heavy Army ammunition wagon with flies on his face, Will dreamed that renegades had overrun his camp, barking like feral dogs and splitting skulls with the heavy trade axes the missionaries had given their grandfathers. One of the savages, a lean buck with his face painted to resemble a death's head and wearing a necklace made from

brown shriveled human fingers, seized Will's shoulder and swung a tomahawk. Will snatched up Lucretia Borgia and prepared to blow out the
Indian's brains.

"Easy, lad. What do they call you?"

He hesitated with his finger on the trigger, blinking sleep out of his eyes.
Squatting with one hand still on the young man's shoulder and his back to
the light, the round man looked like an enormous sage hen sitting its nest.

"Will Cody, sir."

The sage hen scowled thoughtfully. "It has a ring. It needs something,
but it has a ring indeed. Come out from under there and we'll talk."

Funny, fat Ned Buntline. That day Will invited him on a scouting expedition, not telling him that the Indians had withdrawn from the region for
the present, and smiled at the journalist's exaggeratedly furtive behavior,
coughing to cover a snicker when his companion stood in his stirrups to
survey the surrounding terrain with a hand shielding his eyes like a paunchy
cigar-store chief. The scout lent him his war-horse Powder Face and rode
the big bay he had named Tall Bull for its late master. Buntline's borrowed
buckskin jacket and slouch hat with the brim turned up in front added to
the element of burlesque.

"The corpses were piled knee-deep like felled trees and the blood on the
ground splashed up to the ankles." He uncorked his canteen, took a pull,
and handed it to Will, who sniffed at the mouth before partaking. The
potent odor took him back to that long-ago wagon train and young Hickok's
surreptitious gesture to celebrate the boy's first Indian. "I scurried up the
ladder even as the Roman Catholic devils were pushing it clear of the wall,
gained purchase of a battlement, and shot the first six Mexican faces that
showed themselves with my reliable Colt Paterson. Encouraged by my success, the siege crew redoubled its attack; by nightfall Montezuma was ours."

"What did you do when your pistol came up empty?" Will asked.

Buntline cleared his throat loudly. "I turned it around and used it as a
club until reinforcements arrived. But I am not here to discuss ancient
history. How did you come to shoot the chief?"

As daylight retreated, they adjourned to nearby Cottonwood Springs,
where as Colonel Judson the easterner was scheduled to deliver a temperance lecture later in the week, and took a back table in a dim saloon. There
they drank red whiskey and laid out the book from the first scalp to the last
gunshot. The unlikely pairing of the schoolmaster's aging son gone wrong
and the loose-limbed frontiersman drew stares and whispers from the drinkers at the bar.

"How old are you, Will?"

"Twenty-three."

"A lad in truth! Tell me, did anyone ever call you Buffalo Bill?"

He jerked down the contents of his glass and laughed. "Me and every runner I rode with for the KP that chanced to be christened William, and a fair number that didn't."

"When I am finished there will be but one. 'Buffalo Bill, the King of the Border Men.' The wildest and truest story I ever wrote, by God! I know an editor who will swallow it like strawberry jam and cry for more."

"I got to say some of those tales I told are plenty tall."

"Literary license, lad. The sum total of the difference between a democratic free press and Old World totalitarianism."

"You're the writer."

"Biographer," the other corrected. "A troubadour *sans* music, a prose minstrel if you will, destined—"

"Don't you have that backwards?"

"The sword cuts both ways." He raised his voice. "Innkeeper! Another flagon of this devil's milk. Now, lad, it would be advisable, purely in the interest of story value, to add another thousand buffalo to that Kansas Pacific score."

"Every time you take a drink a thousand more buffalo die. If we stay here much longer there won't be none left."

"Isn't that the way of it, though?"

Dusk met evening. Walking to Will's horse, the scout breaking stride from time to time to avoid outdistancing his hobbling companion, the two embroidered an unsteady line between yellow oblongs of light scalloping the dark street from windows on both sides. The air had a snap to it, the day's heat having drained into the sand hills. Will's head felt hollow and his feet didn't seem to be touching earth.

"Been meaning to ask, Colonel. How'd you come by that limp?"

"A misunderstanding involving a woman's husband slain in a fair duel and a large gathering of displeased citizenry in my improvident youth." The large words were somewhat slurred. "Seriously wounded and compelled to seek refuge in a Nashville hotel, I subsequently gained egress through an upstairs window and bounded forty-seven feet three inches to a broken leg, whereupon I was seized and hanged from an awning post."

"What happened then?" Will asked breathlessly.

"Remind me to send you the account in which I treat with that episode in my mobile and variegated, sometimes triumphant, often tragic, but always fascinating forty-six-year existence on this sadly benighted planet."

"Life you've led, I don't see why you got to go looking for stories."

"I am written out on the subject of one Edward Zane Carroll Judson. It falls to me to preserve on tame foolscap the living history of God's earthly

Eden in its pristine state. An Herculean task and well-nigh impossible for a lone mortal, but a just one and necessary."

"I like the way you talk. Just like a novel."

"You must live your books, lad, or your books will most certainly live you. Remain faithful to your ideals, respectful of fair womanhood, and touch not the brew that boils up from the pit of hell." He belched pleasantly, releasing a sour stench of fermented grain.

"A good deal of truth comes out of your mouth, Colonel."

"I have an ulcer. A handsome beast, by the by."

The scout untethered the bay. "Cheyennes don't have any ugly ones." He mounted. Tall Bull grunted and shook off a cloud of flies that buzzed about its ears and lighted. Powder Face was back in the Fort McPherson stable, Buntline having ridden his buggy into town.

"Where can one get in touch with you?" asked the journalist.

"At the fort, or if I'm not there, they'll send messages on to me or to my wife in St. Louis. She'll know where to reach me. She always has."

"What do you do when you're not chasing savages?"

"Drive coach or guide hunting expeditions through Indian territory, provided they pay in advance. Whatever needs doing and pays. I get by." He gathered his reins. "Thanks for the drinks, Colonel. Reckon I'll see you."

Peering up at him in the light from an upstairs hotel window, Buntline's eyes reflected a red glint. "I hold the conviction you will, lad. As surely as the moon sees the stars."

December. Cheeks and nose gnawed by bitter cold, whiskey in his belly and heat starting the slow crawl through his veins, Will leaned the leather-hinged door shut against the wind and peeled off his gloves to rub dry palms together over the black iron stove. The shack smelled of boiled coffee and steaming wool and man. Outside, a fresh gust hurled grainy snow against the building, making the oiled paper over the single window snap and rattle.

"Listen to this here." Lute North, brother of Frank, winked broadly at the other two scouts who shared the shack. They were sitting on their cots on the edge of the yellow oval of light shed by the coal-oil lamp on the table. " ' "Better son never blessed a mother, wild as he was. Rough he may be to others, but to us he is kind and gentle as the breeze of a summer eve." ' "

"Who's that, the Pope?" asked Will, shucking his bearskin.

A hoot of laughter went up from the others.

Lute grinned and continued reading from the thick paperbound periodical in his hands. " ' "Yes, ma'am," answered Wild Bill, "as good as ever made, no matter whar you find him. There isn't a bit of white in his liver, nor black in his heart." ' "

"If that's Hickok talking, you can bet it's about some poor bastard he just skinned at stud."

"You'd know better than me." Lute rolled the magazine into a tube and flipped it at Will, who caught it against his chest. It was the December issue of the *New York Weekly*, with a black-and-white lithograph on the tan cover of a long-haired, chin-whiskered dandy in ornate buckskins gripping a needle gun in both hands. His nickname was circus-lettered into the title, twice as large as the legend "By Ned Buntline." He opened it at random to find himself quoted:

> There is more fight, more headache—aye, more *heart*ache in one rum bottle than there is in all the water that ever sparkled in God's bright sunlight. And I, for the sake of my dear brothers and sisters, and for the sweet, trusting heart that throbs for me alone, intend to let the rum go where it belongs and that is not down my throat.

"That rum's devilish stuff," Lute commented. "Good thing you and me drink whiskey—right, Will?"

"Son of a bitch." Awed, he turned the coarse brown pages, admiring the lithographs, including one of himself slaying Chief Tall Bull at Summit Springs just as the Indian was about to scalp the remaining female captive.

"Them's some fine things your ma said about you," Red, a Pawnee half-breed, observed. He had knife scars on both cheeks. "How long's she been dead?"

"Six years this month."

Lute said, "That there stirring adventure come for you in the mail packet while you was cutting the bear loose in town. Frank'll be interested to hear you was the one dropped that chief last June. All this time he thought he done it."

"It was Lieutenant Hayes," Will replied. "But he wasn't there when I talked to Buntline."

"Something else come for you too." Red drew a yellow telegraph envelope from inside his grimy shirt and held it out.

Will opened it and unfolded the flimsy. "It's from my wife."

"She's expecting a kid," Lute told Red. "I got a month's night duty saying it's a girl."

The young scout whooped and directed a mighty openhanded blow to the broad back of Tiny, a hulking expert tracker from Wyoming. Tiny staggered forward two steps before reclaiming his balance.

Lute said, "Shit."

The boy had the Cody brown eyes and Louisa's square jaw. He grasped his father's fingers in a surprisingly strong hand for its size and lifted them over his blond head, smiling and showing his gums. His cheeks were round and glowing.

"He knows how to Indian wrestle!" exclaimed Will, holding the baby.

"He just started doing that. I thought the midwife taught it to him, but she denies it." Louisa was wearing a black skirt and stiff white blouse closed at the throat with a brooch, and had her hair done up the way it had been the day they met. They were standing in the parlor of her parents' home in St. Louis.

"Kit Carson Cody." He tasted the name. "It will sound good with 'President' in front of it, by God."

"William, don't swear in front of the child."

He stayed a week, taking long walks with her about the growing city, helping the Fredericis look after the children when she was out visiting, playing with little Arta, a toddling, chattering blond beauty now in pink satin ribbons and pinafores, and spoiling them all with presents bought on his scout's salary. To please Louisa, he donned a morning coat and striped pants she had bought and altered for a reception she was giving to introduce him to the friends she had made in his absence, but when she saw him with his hair tumbling over the black broadcloth she made him take it off and put on his best buckskins instead. Thus attired he stood out from the subdued party frippery like an Indian at a Presbyterian wedding. More than once in the course of the evening she found him surrounded by tittering women listening to his frontier stories with enraptured upturned faces and shining eyes. Usually she placed a proprietary hand on his arm and steered him away to meet someone she had just that moment thought of; the last time she brought out Arta, barefoot and in her nightgown, to kiss her father good night. Returning after tucking her in, Louisa saw him sighting down an imaginary rifle at an invisible buffalo for the edification of yet another giggling bevy. For the first time in their marriage she wondered if this was how it was when they weren't together, and what came of it without her sobering presence. More doubt trickled into the barrel.

When he was getting ready to report back to Fort McPherson, she presented him with her surprise, two new buckskin outfits she had made to his measurements, along with a startling crimson shirt and yellow silk kerchief "for dress occasions." She was an excellent seamstress. Touched by this proof of at least partial acquiescence to his unconventional lifestyle and deaf to her protests, Will picked her up and whirled her around, displacing knickknacks from tables to the shrill delight of Arta, who immediately did the same with one of her dolls with results less destructive. It was a habit Louisa fought hard to break in the weeks succeeding her husband's departure.

The Indian crisis had abated. Will filled the long periods between campaigns outfitting and guiding hunting parties bent on returning to civilization loaded down with buffalo robes and antelope heads. At the special request of General Sheridan he led a band made up of the general, other high officers, and a group of Easterners headed by Commodore James Gordon Bennett, Jr., flamboyant publisher of the New York *Herald*, and other prominent millionaires across the Nebraska plains, where they shot buffaloes and drank champagne and listened to Will's stories around the campfire; and when they parted at the North Platte railroad station, the Commodore shoved a fistful of money at the guide and shouted an invitation over the racket of the departing train to visit him in New York. Will smiled and waved and forgot the other's gesture as soon as it was made.

Another winter. A tall young man in a tight-fitting black uniform with gold trim under an ermine coat stepped down into the bracing Nebraska cold of the North Platte station, accompanied by several dramatically moustachioed and bearded men in similar dress. He had a gentle face under a queer cylindrical fur hat, thick burnsides to the angles of his jaw, and his moustache was trimmed into a neat inverted V with the ends hanging over the corners of his mouth. His clear blue eyes quartered the platform, then passed beyond the line of bareheaded natives standing along its edge to the street and the man seated there astride a white charger, and for the first time in his long journey delight transformed his features.

The horseman was as tall as he and quite lean, attired in soft bleached buckskins trimmed with fur and a brilliant red shirt, the whole topped off by a broad-brimmed black slouch hat with a snakeskin band cocked over his left eye. Thick brown hair fell to his shoulders, gleaming auburn in the sun. A small spray of beard gave him the look of a Shakespearean player. Then a short fat man in an American general's uniform came across the platform, obscuring the view. The visitor recognized him and nodded politely.

"It is good to see you again, General Sheridan." He had a deep voice and a pleasant accent.

"An honor as always, Your Highness," said the fat man, whose manner and smart bow were as polished as his figure was comical. He glanced over the young man's shoulder at another American officer alighting from the private train and dipped his chin. "I see you've met General Custer."

"He has been fascinating me since your Omaha with his adventures fighting the red Indians," he acknowledged, smiling at the man with the sad eyebrows and matching moustache.

"You'll find few more expert upon the subject than Curly." Sheridan turned his head. "Will!"

The man on the white horse dismounted with a fluid dexterity the visitor had previously seen only on the western steppes of his homeland and bounded up onto the platform, removing his big hat with a flourish.

"Your Highness, it is my privilege to present William F. Cody, otherwise and universally known as Buffalo Bill. Will, this is His Royal Highness Grand Duke Alexis, third son of Czar Alexander II of Russia."

"I am glad to see you," said Will, speaking slowly, as he did when addressing an Indian in English. "You have come out here, so the general tells me, to shoot some buffaloes?"

"Yes, and I hope to have a good, fine time. I heard of you before, and I am glad to meet you here." The grand duke's expression was more reserved now, but his eyes were animated, the eyes of an excited child.

"I took the liberty of giving His Highness a number of Ned Buntline's published accounts of your experiences on the prairie when we were both in New York," Sheridan explained. "I can't tell you what a sensation they've caused back East."

Will's smile broadened. "Thank you, thank you. If the weather holds good, we'll have one of the finest hunts that there ever was on the continent."

"We'll discuss details on the way to Camp Alexis. Your Highness?" The general swept an arm toward an open Concord wagon and four matched grays waiting at the edge of the platform.

"General," said Will as Custer approached on the heels of the rest of the party.

The commander of the 7th Cavalry nodded, amusement sparking his gray eyes. He was wearing his dress uniform and red Michigan Brigade tie. "And how is that mule of yours these days?"

The blue drifts surrounding the camp named for the imperial guest cast a phantom glow under a soap-sliver moon. Womb-red firelight writhed over the glistening, nearly naked bodies of Spotted Tail's Sioux braves, their war chants torn from their throats in guttural exhalations to the visceral pulse of tom-toms. Sitting cross-legged on a buffalo robe on the edge of the light, Alexis watched mesmerized from the center of a half circle with Will and General Sheridan at his elbows and the others, including the grand duke's Russian escort and Custer and Colonel Michael Sheridan, the general's

brother, forming the horns. The Indians' flesh steamed in the crisp cold air
of night.

"Magnificent!" exclaimed Alexis as the dancers drew blankets over their
streaming shoulders. "The Cossacks would be hard put to equal it."

Will loosened his vocal cords with champagne from the duke's private
stock and told of his rescue of General Penrose and Wild Bill Hickok at the
Canadian River. The bottle made the rounds, clanking against silver-plated
cups.

"How does one hunt the buffaloes?" Alexis asked the scout when the
story was finished.

"Ask Curly," said General Sheridan, and laughed. His eyes were bright
from the champagne. The other military men chuckled.

The grand duke looked at Custer, who moved his shoulders around under
his buckskins and said nothing. He wore a black fur hat like the Russian's.

Sheridan said, "Come on, Curly, don't be modest. He's developed his
own personal method," he told Alexis. "First he confuses the buffalo by
shooting his own horse. Then when he's on the ground he stares at it until
it gives up."

"The horse panicked when the bull tried to gore him." Custer's voice
rose above the guffaws. "His head got in the way of the revolver. It could
have happened to anyone."

"You tried to shoot a buffalo with a revolver?" Will pressed.

"The idea seemed sound at the time."

After a moment Alexis joined in the raucous laughter.

Custer waited until it had died down, then: "It's a fair night for a snipe
hunt, wouldn't you say, Cody?"

"Well, now, it does seem like one, come to study on it."

"Fellows," the general admonished.

The grand duke looked from one face to another. "What is this snipe
hunt?"

Sheridan said, "Nothing you'd be interested in, Your Highness. Sorry,
fellows, but I'd hate to have to think of what to say when the State Department asks why we left the third in line to the throne of Russia in the middle
of the wilderness holding a sack and waiting for a nonexistent creature to
come along and leap into it."

"Who said it was going to be him?" returned Custer, winking at Will.

Eventually, Sheridan laughed too.

From a distance their first herd resembled the shadow of a low-hanging
cloud moving slowly across the dazzling noon whiteness. Will, who had
described his "surround" technique to the Russian the night before, pro-

vided a practical demonstration, dropping half a dozen buffaloes in as many minutes. Then Custer took a turn, his six staghounds flying like gaunt ghosts behind his piebald as he galloped up to within arm's length of each target before emptying his side arm into it just to show that it could be done. In this manner he killed three, reloading in between while steering with his knees. Then Will changed mounts and lent his new buffalo horse, Buckskin Joe, and Lucretia Borgia to Alexis. He and Custer attended the grand duke, who drew his Colt revolver as he had seen the lieutenant colonel do and fired six times at the hump of a pitching bull. The beast didn't miss a step. Holstering the colt, Alexis hoisted the heavy Springfield. At that moment Will smacked Buckskin Joe's rump with the ends of his reins. The horse whinnied and plunged through a hole into the herd.

"Shoot!" Will directed.

Alexis fired. The bull grunted and fell rolling.

"Champagne!" The grand duke drew rein and weaved frantically at a member of his suite, who obediently opened a large basket bristling with green glass necks wrapped in gold foil.

While the party was celebrating the guest of honor's first kill, Will quietly walked his horse up to the panting bull with pink bubbles in its nostrils from its pierced lung and slammed a slug into its brain.

The hunt lasted five days, at the end of which Will presented the grand duke with eight handsomely mounted buffalo heads. While servants were engaged in placing them in the baggage car of Alexis' train, he invited the scout into the brass-and-red-plush splendor of his private coach.

"For you," said the grand duke.

Will accepted the jeweled box his host extended, mumbling an astonished thanks.

"Open it."

He obeyed. Twinkling inside were a pair of diamond-encrusted cuff links and a matching tiepin in the shape of tiny buffalo heads with gold snouts.

"Your Highness, I can't accept anything so expensive."

"Riches are nothing if they cannot be shared with men you admire. Do not insult a visitor from a friendly nation." He summoned Sheridan. "I will say good-bye to the red Indians now," he said. "What gifts should I give them?"

"Nothing grand, Your Highness. They wouldn't be able to appreciate it. A couple of your red blankets would make them as happy as if you gave them gold."

Alexis sent an aide to fetch the blankets and led the party outside, where Spotted Tail and his braves were waiting beyond the platform. The Sioux chief was in full headdress, and his pony was painted in barbaric colors from mane to tail.

Sheridan whispered, "Will, I received a message this morning from our friend James Gordon Bennett."

"How is the Commodore?" He fingered his jeweled box.

"Still talking about last year's hunt. He and his friends are still eager for you to be their guest in New York."

"I'm needed here."

"The Indian situation is under control at present. We can spare you. It's high time you and civilization made acquaintances." He patted Will's arm. "Bennett's an excellent host. Think about it and wire him when you've reached a decision."

The Sioux party accepted their gifts with grave gratitude and straddled their mounts.

"There goes a load," muttered Will, distracted still by his lavish gifts and the invitation from New York. "I never could get next to the notion of Spotted Tail standing behind me with a loaded rifle. He and Sitting Bull are too close."

Custer, who was standing close by, blew air. "Lighten up, Cody. If there's anything on this green earth that's predictable, it's an Indian."

DENVER, COLORADO

JANUARY 8, 1917

The old man is dying.

Fat yellow light slides politely into the bedroom like a mortician and rests on the printed amber wall. The old man lies on the lukewarm edge of awakening. Present and past tramp in and out of the space behind his eyelids, the long dead mingling with the new living, names of men and horses years forgotten coming to his dry lips. Dr. East, a young man with a round face and black-rimmed pince-nez on a ribbon, flutters pale brown double shadows across the blanket as he returns instruments to his bag with efficient little clinks, his starched sleeves rustling like leaves in a gust. His presence nudges gently but insistently into the old man's conscious. He tastes the words before giving them voice.

"Where's this?"

"You're in your sister May's home, Mr. Cody." The doctor's tone has a polished hush. "You were moved here from the sanitarium after the mineral-water cure failed."

"I know all that," snaps the old man. "I just woke up fuzzy. Don't talk to me like I'm senile. How's it look?"

"You have a severely inflamed prostate and I don't even want to think about your liver. Your condition, moreover, is being weakened by an eclipse of the moon."

"Save that for the newspapers. What are my chances?"

"There is a time when the greatest of physicians must commend his patient to a higher power."

He closes his eyes and breathes. Just as the doctor thinks him asleep he opens them. "How long?"

"The sand is slipping slowly . . ."

"How *long*, damn you?"

"About thirty-six hours, sir."

He breathes again. "All right. Who's outside?"

"Your wife, your daughter Irma, May, and Lew Decker, her husband."

"I know who Lew is. Ask him to come in."

The doctor withdraws carrying his bag, his rubber soles insinuating on the plank floor.

Waiting, the old man considers the glob of yellow light on the blankets and wonders at its remote familiarity. Then he remembers that the sunlight lay like that in the room where his father died. Damn fool kid. He should have held his hand, and to hell with the bonnet.

He closes his eyes and is returned instantly to the plains. Not the scene of his youth, however, but a garishly lit circle with a painted canvas backdrop and an audience humming in the darkness around the edge and music that tingles the soles of his feet. Always this is the screen against which his best memories are projected, containing friends and enemies dead and buried before he ever set foot inside an open-air arena, orange and cracked and leaping jerkily like the images on his one and only film now crumbling away in some storage vault. The bloodsuckers have got their hooks into his dreams along with everything else.

Someone in the unseen bleachers calls his name.

"Will? You wanted to see me?"

At first, still under the influence of his dream, he thinks the voice is Ned Buntline's, come to awaken him in the cool shade of the Army wagon. Fat, funny Ned Buntline, Homer to a generation of moldering heroes. But Buntline's remains are pickled in alcohol, and the pages of his precious history have gone brown and flaking, as dead as Hickok, as dead as Custer. As dead as he. He looks at his brother-in-law's funereal face and gestures feebly at a deck of cards on the bedside table.

"The doc says I've got thirty-six hours. Let's play high five."

BOOK TWO
1872–1883

BUNTLINE'S SPECIAL

"Oh, Mama, I'm a *bad* actor!"
—William F. Cody, 1872

CHAPTER SIX

In spite of its foreignness (and to some degree because of it), New York City put Will in mind of the kitchen in his mother's old boarding house. In his youth he had experienced this same fifth-wheel sensation as his mother and his five sisters scurried from the stove to the table and back, stirring pans, fetching knives, and hauling smoking pots, exposing the young plainsman to the dangers of accidental stabbing or trampling or scalding. But there the resemblance ended.

A brief stopover in Chicago to visit Phil Sheridan had not prepared him for the splendor and terrors of the world's fastest-growing center of commerce, where spired towers pierced anthracite clouds and trains racketed along the Sixth Avenue elevated railway, showering sparks and soot to the macadam street. Handsome brownstone tenements containing the city's new rich sniffed at that new innovation, the apartment house, taking shape on East 18th Street and along Central Park, with its dubious promise of life on shelves like books and bottles of patent medicine. Horse-drawn cabs and trolleys clogged the avenues and boulevards. The lone horseman was rare, and was most often a police officer in domed helmet and uniform buttoned to the neck. And there were people, more in a single block than Will had seen in some whole towns on the frontier, their speech where they congregated in doorways and on corners a clangor of strange, unmusical accents. He calculated that there were far too many pedestrians to fit inside at one time, like eleven suits for a ten-suit closet with one always out being brushed.

J. G. Heckscher and Schuyler Crosby, veterans of the celebrated Bennett buffalo hunt, shared his cab. They called his attention to the creeping steel skeleton of the Brooklyn Bridge under construction and Boss Tweed's infamous quarter-million-dollar courthouse that thus far had cost New York taxpayers in excess of thirteen million. But Will was like a wolf cub on its first venture outside the den, dazzled by the world's immenseness and variety and unable to take it all in.

"Where is this charming Mrs. Cody we've all heard so much about?" Crosby asked.

"Home, looking after our children. St. Louis is civilization enough for her."

In fact, there had been quite an argument about it, Louisa maintaining that travel was dangerous for children and ignoring Will's rejoinder that he and his brother and sisters had made the journey by wagon from Iowa to Kansas without incident. The upshot of it was that he was made to feel like a deserter for taking Bennett up on his invitation and leaving his family behind.

The cab halted before the looming benevolent paternity of the Union Club. Meekly, Will followed his companions inside, and later, in an alcoholic fog, to Heckscher's tailor, where he exchanged his Chicago suit of clothes for a full dress suit. His reflection in the full-length mirror appalled him. He inquired after a barber to shear his suddenly conspicuous long hair, to the horror of his New York friends.

"All you need is a silk hat," said Heckscher, and snapped his fingers at the tailor, a small man with a natty moustache and narrow Eastern European features, who asked what size. The New Yorker raised his eyebrows at Will.

"I just generally keep trying them on till I find one that fits," the scout admitted.

"Seven," estimated Schuyler Crosby. "No, seven and a half if his hair's to fit inside the crown."

"Seven and a half," Heckscher agreed.

The hat was produced. Deftly the tailor scooped Will's locks inside and placed it on his head. Will tilted it in his rakish fashion and admired the result in the mirror. With his neatly sculpted goatee he looked like visiting royalty. His face and neck were very dark against the starched sterile whiteness of his collar.

"A transformation," said Heckscher.

"One wouldn't know you from any Fifth Avenue swell," Crosby chimed in.

"Just don't tip your hat to the ladies or you'll cause a riot."

The tailor said the suit would be ready tomorrow. Will changed back into his other clothes and accompanied his hosts to the ground floor via the perpendicular railway. His second ride in the cable-strung cage unnerved him no less than the trip up, especially when the car stopped and his internal organs were still moving. Crosby, noting the pallor under Will's tan, advised him to brace his back and shoulders against the frame next time.

He waved away the counsel. "I've felt the same astride a bucking horse, where there's no frame to brace yourself against."

He saw his first stage play that evening, a melodrama entitled *The Black Crook,* and joked during intermission that he was glad he'd left his guns in his hotel suite, or the actor who portrayed the villain so convincingly might have been dead many times over. Heckscher laughed—after a beat that made Will slap his back and roar. The other theatergoers in the lobby stared. Later the three retired to the club, where James Gordon Bennett, Jr., greeted them, his lively face flushed from drink, crumbs in his well-trimmed moustache. He pressed on Will a treacherous mixture of brandy, absinthe, and ginger ale, and gazed wide-eyed as the frontiersman put it down in a draft. Will was used to grain alcohol as strong as a randy buffalo bull. Afterward he switched to rye whiskey and the party sat in deep brown leather chairs with high backs recalling their excursion West with Will as guide and listening to his account of the hunt with the grand duke. At midnight he returned to his suite, threw himself fully clothed on his stomach on the bed, and fell asleep while still bouncing. Such late hours were unknown on the plains.

He awoke at eight and dined in the suite on steak and eggs and hotcakes and sausage and gallons of steaming black coffee, luxuries forgotten since his late mother's last big spread. Then he went out under a pale winter sky supported like a tin ceiling on the spires of the brown and gray buildings and walked clear down to the Battery, where he watched ships sailing into and out of the harbor, their sails bellying like laboring horses. He bought roast chestnuts from an Italian vendor and flipped them into a tin cup held by a shivering monkey attached by a silver chain to an organ grinder's instrument.

"You supposed' t'row pennies," the grinder complained.

"He can't eat pennies," replied an astonished Will. But he plinked a handful of coins into the cup.

He listened to a political speech for Horace Greeley in the park, then found a photographer's studio on Canal Street and had his picture taken for Louisa in his city clothes standing in front of a painted backdrop representing a landscape. He got lost on his way back but made no effort to ask directions. He had been lost before, and not where there were hundreds of people from whom to enlist aid and food and drink for the buying. He walked for blocks and blocks, gazing up at the rococo architecture, reading advertising signs, and ignoring the stares of passersby made curious by this giant with hair to make a woman envious and his overcoat hanging open on the coldest day of the year. Eventually, he spotted a landmark he recognized and wound his way back to the hotel to find a welcome familiar bloated little figure in a vest and cutaway waiting for him in the lobby.

"Colonel!" Will seized one of Ned Buntline's carefully tended hands and squeezed until the little journalist's eyes watered.

"You're looking well turned out for a rude hero, lad." Buntline kneaded his bones back into place with his other hand, admiring his friend's vest and tiny gold horseshoe hanging from his watch chain. The biographer's hair and moustache were a tad grayer and his eyes were unnaturally bright for the time of day. Tobacco ash rested in the creases of his paunch. He transferred a stack of periodicals from under his left arm to the scout's hands. "Just so you realize your Boswell has not been idle."

Will shuffled through the material. Each buff cover bore a different steel engraving of a sharp-profiled frontiersman in long hair, goatee, and buckskins, posed in various heroic attitudes. He read the titles: *Buffalo Bill's Best Shot, Buffalo Bill's Last Victory,* and *Hazel Eye, the Girl Trapper.*

"Who's Hazel Eye?" he asked then.

"You rescue her from savages in the last chapter."

He paused to study the last item in the sheaf, which was not a novel like the others but a slim playbill bearing the simple legend *Buffalo Bill* and a list of names opposite colorful western sobriquets, a few of which he recognized. The proper names were all unfamiliar.

"I thought that might arouse your native curiosity," Buntline observed. "I'll wager you had no idea you were this season's theatrical lion. Perhaps you and I can stroll over to Niblo's Garden and view it this evening."

Before Will could reply, the white-haired desk clerk addressed him obsequiously and handed him three messages. Schuyler Crosby had invited him to lunch at Delmonico's and his Union Club friends were holding a reception in his honor in the ballroom of the Fifth Avenue Hotel that evening. The third message was from Heckscher's tailor, informing him that his dress suit was ready. He itched to wear it in public. "Tomorrow night, perhaps," he told Buntline, and added quickly, when the other's face fell, "Is it too early to stand you to a drink?"

The journalist beamed. "When I was five it was too early. Had I but known of the dark abyss that awaited me at the bottom of that first bottle. But there is reason for everything on God's good earth, and who are we to question His vast design?" He took his friend's elbow. "The bar is this way. Mind the end stool; it has a short leg."

Will's grand entrance at the Fifth Avenue underscored his quasiroyal status, but he soon found himself undone on the dance floor by the new steps from Europe and fled to the bar, where he sat with his curls spilling over the sober black cloth on his shoulders and told stories to a growing crowd of listeners while the bartender struggled to keep his glass full.

He spent part of the next day at Central Park, which was still under construction, walking among trees already dwarfed by the buildings beyond while snow fell in flakes the size of gold pieces. Red-faced masons at work on the footbridges wondered at the foolhardy soul who scorned a roof and a fire without being paid to, but the bare ground felt good under his aching feet. His high-heeled boots, which he wore to spare his new patent leathers, were not designed for walking great distances comfortably, especially when those great distances involved many blocks of concrete and macadam. But a man who had hiked a thousand miles on the whim of a band of armed Mormons suffered less than most. Nevertheless, he took a cab back to his hotel.

More summonses awaited him, some bearing signatures he didn't recognize but assumed belonged to people he had met at the reception. This time he begged off, pleading exhaustion, and sent word to Buntline through a uniformed page to stop by the hotel that evening and they would attend the theater. He stayed in the rest of the day and wrote a long letter to Louisa.

The play was based on Buntline's books and featured a flamboyant actor named J. B. Studley as Buffalo Bill. Although Will failed to reconcile the brave youth he saw fighting back the deranged crowd of slavers intent on murdering his father at the Salt Creek Trading Post with the terrified little boy he had been on that occasion, he blinked back tears of anger as the actor portraying Isaac Cody was "stabbed," and stamped and applauded along with everyone else in the audience when the hero bested border rough Jack McKandless in a duel with yard-long bowie knives, despite the fact that the latter incident was borrowed from Wild Bill Hickok's inflated memoirs. He had to keep reminding himself that that was he, Will Cody, facing death between the flickering footlights and the painted backdrop. It sickened him slightly for unknown reasons. For the first time he understood the aversion of the Indians he had helped capture to having their pictures taken.

But he couldn't disown a tiny surge of satisfaction mixed with his embarrassment when he heard his own name whispered a few seats away and a young couple leaned forward, plainly staring at his profile in the light shed from the stage. He pretended not to notice as that same name buzzed down the row and across the auditorium, punctuated by nudges and womanly gasps. Buntline, enraptured with his own words as usual, sat slumped in his rolls of fat with his chin tucked into his wattled throat and appeared to take no notice of the growing excitement. But when the curtain came down and the lights went up and the audience demanded to see the hero of the drama, it was the journalist who clamped an iron hand on Will's bicep and pulled him to his feet.

The walk to the stage seemed interminable, and despite the thunderous applause pressing him from behind like a wagon on a downgrade, he considered the journey from Mormon territory back to Kansas shorter. The lights had dimmed again, but the naked white shaft of the calcium spot blinded him. The audience was standing now. He found the steps with someone's help and mounted the boards, terrified of stumbling and falling. But he made his way to center stage without incident. The cheers and clapping reached a peak and subsided. The spectators sat down. Someone coughed. Will squinted into the spot. He folded his hands in front of him, behind him, crossed his arms over his chest, thrust his hands in his pockets. They had taken on a life independent of his own. The silence grew painful. He cleared his throat, mumbled something, cleared his throat again, raised his voice. His speech lasted thirty seconds; afterward, he had no idea what he'd said. A pause followed his words, then more noise than ever. Someone took hold of his elbow and steered him toward the wings. His hand was seized and pumped, and as his eyes adjusted themselves to the dim illumination backstage he saw that the man doing the pumping was J. B. Studley, his impersonator. Up close the actor's makeup was as thick as bear grease on a Sioux brave and his long wig and pasted-on beard and moustache looked glaringly false. He was a half inch shorter than Will in spite of two-inch heels and lifts in his boots. Ned Buntline was standing next to him, beaming.

"You had them in the hollow of your hand, lad," he said. "If you were running for President you'd have the vote of every man in the theater."

Your mother is convinced you'll be President someday. I hold lower goals for you.

Others in the cast shook his hand. He experienced the semitraumatic sensation of exchanging polite words with Jack McKandless, miraculously arisen from the dead. The small, swarthy woman who had played the part of the Indian maiden said something pleasant to him in Brooklyn-accented English. One of the renegade Cheyennes had blue eyes and freckles under the walnut stain on his face. Will clasped hands with a tall bald man in a gray three-piece suit who introduced himself as the manager of the theater and offered him five hundred dollars per week to portray himself in the production. Astonished, Will politely declined.

"Wise decision, lad," whispered Buntline, propelling him toward the stage door. He had their coats on his arm and was carrying their hats. "Never take the first offer."

Six weeks swept past in a swirl of colors and glitter. Will saw his first opera, commenting to Commodore Bennett that while the diva's voice was impressive, he knew a Cheyenne shaman who could yell louder. He addressed the journalists who followed him all over town by their first names, and those whose names he didn't remember he called "hoss." He dined on enough banquet chicken to sprout wings and lay eggs (or so he swore), appeared at fancy balls for his customary one dance, then repaired to the bar and spun tales for his party, sent clippings about himself from the *Times,* the *Sun,* the *Post,* the *Journal,* and Bennett's *Herald* home to his sisters and Louisa. For a masked ball held in his honor at the Academy of Music, he donned a Musketeer costume and watched enthralled as a group of actors dressed like bears towed a six-foot cotton snowball across the dance floor to the frenetic strains of the saber dance. The snowball split open and the Grand Duke Alexis strode out in full uniform. It was another actor, of course, but Will cried out in recognition just the same and embraced the impostor as if he were the genuine article.

He reserved a more sincere embrace for Ned Buntline a few nights later, when the journalist presented him with a handsome new Remington rifle at a reception Buntline gave for him. The initials "W.F.C." were engraved on the brass backstrap.

"You'll not have to stand so close to your next Indian," said Buntline, visibly touched and embarrassed by his friend's display of emotion.

Will laughed. "I'll have to charge it with rock salt, or any game I bring down will spoil by the time I reach it."

The next day the rotund biographer accompanied Will via the New York Central Railroad to Westchester, Pennsylvania, where they pulled at the bell of a large brick dwelling off the main boulevard and handed their cards to the black maid who answered. She showed them into a comfortable drawing room lit by a brass lamp and asked them to wait, withdrawing on silent crepe soles.

Buntline toyed nervously with his fob. His usually rumpled hair was pomaded and parted in the exact center and his high stiff collar was plainly cutting into the folds on his neck. "What sort of fellow is this uncle of yours?" he asked his companion.

"I have no idea." Although equally cowed by the unfamiliar surroundings, Will appeared to have reached accord with his heavy winter suit and maroon necktie. He was studying a large hunting print on the wall over the mantel. "Colonel Guss married my mother's sister, but she has been dead for some years and we've never met."

"I am to be your artillery support, is that about the size of it?"

"That's exactly the size of it." Grinning.

After a few minutes, a tall man with softly graying hair brushed carefully over the tops of his long ears entered the parlor. His light-colored eyes were set in a thicket of creases carved by wind and sun, the paleness contrasting sharply with the hue of his skin, which was nearly as dark as Will's. They went to Buntline first, lingered on him for a brief, polite moment, then moved to the scout. The smile behind his military-cut moustache was reserved but warm.

"William? I'm your Uncle Henry."

They clasped hands. The older man's grip was dry and firm.

"My friend, General E. Z. C. Judson," said Will, indicating Buntline. "General."

Buntline, preening at the promotion, accepted Guss's hand.

Their host was saying something gracious, but the nephew didn't hear his words. He stared at the young woman who had come in on the other's heels. She was a brunette of medium height in a ruffled beige dress that set off the deep brown in her eyes admirably. Will was face to face with his mother as she had looked in an old portrait that had hung in the boarding house for as long as he could remember. She colored under his frank scrutiny and smiled a lovely, embarrassed smile.

Guss noticed the exchange of glances and swiveled aside. "Lizzie," he said, "this is your cousin, Will. My daughter, Elizabeth."

He accepted her raised hand as if it were blown glass, saying, "I'd know a Cody anywhere."

In St. Louis, Louisa Cody looked up from their four-year-old daughter's sewing lesson and shuddered.

"I've arranged a fox hunt for later in the week," Guss told his guests. "Surely you'll stay and take part."

Will stopped looking at his cousin. "I've never heard of anyone eating fox."

"The hounds find it a delicacy. Mainly, it's an excuse for a group of otherwise sane grown men and women to climb on horseback and risk broken necks. If what this fellow Buntline writes about you is true, I think you'll enjoy the experience."

"Oh, he's quite a liar," remarked General Judson.

Will put on a scarlet coat and joined the hunt, tales of which a gifted storyteller could wring free drinks with to the end of his days. The newspapers devoured the spectacle of the buffalo killer riding to hounds, detailing the event as if it were a decisive battle in an important war, in the grand phrases and curling metaphors that Ned Buntline's fans had come to recognize as an art student recognizes the brush strokes and signature of his master. Buntline meanwhile depleted their host's stock of brandy and scribbled dispatches without once looking up at his inspiration.

Back in New York at the end of the week, Will presented himself in his friend's hotel room and found the journalist, collarless, suspenders hanging, rehearsing a temperance lecture in front of his dressing-table mirror. The scout's face reflected over his shoulder was visibly distressed. Buntline stopped in mid-hyperbole and turned.

"Trouble at home?" he asked.

"I've been recalled by General Sheridan, but my trouble is here." Will held out a square of paper.

Buntline hooked on a pair of wire-rimmed spectacles and studied the scrap. "It appears to be a bill from Delmonico's for six hundred dollars and change."

"I treated Commodore Bennett and eleven others to dinner last night. Where I come from you can get a meal like that for the price of a bullet. I have exactly fifty dollars with me, not counting train fare back home."

"Civilization comes dear." The journalist folded the bill. "My editors will stand to it. I am into them for my next three books and they will hardly notice the extra."

"Thanks, Colonel. I owe you."

Buntline grinned. "You needn't worry, lad. I shall collect."

They shook hands.

"You been East too long, Will. We stopped wearing them things on the scout months back."

Jim "Buffalo Chips" White—long-haired, buckskin-clad, a mirror image of Will if the mirror were pockmarked and shrunk its reflection four inches —frowned up at his idol, the latter straddling his horse Buckskin Joe in full dress suit with tails, his silk hat tilted back on his head, thumbing the cork loose from a bottle of champagne and pouring its contents into a stemmed glass. This was certainly not the rough-hewn frontiersman Chips had been emulating since the day they had met.

Will laughed and handed him the brimming glass. "Tell that to these strawheads," he said, waving a hand at the large party of fellow scouts and pioneers who had accompanied him from Omaha to Fort McPherson, guffawing and swigging more of the champagne he had brought with him from New York. "They're the ones wanted to get a look at me in my city clothes and then went and left my traps back at the hotel. Where's General Carr?"

"In Arizona with the 5th Cavalry. We're scouting for General Reynolds this trip. He's waiting on you west of here with the 3rd." Chips put down his champagne in a gulp and belched loudly, surprising himself.

"Well, what are you doing standing around guzzling spirits? Mount up and we'll see can a party of fifty trackers find one general and a whole army."

"In them duds?"

"It's this or naked. I told you my gear's in Omaha."

"Wait while I fetch my horse," said the other, handing back his empty glass. "I missed Sam Grant's inauguration, but I sure won't miss this." He struck off toward the stables, his swagger an exaggerated copy of Will's.

In Reynolds' camp, T. B. "Texas Jack" Omohundro, round-faced and clerical-looking but for hair longer than Will's and exotic buckskins strung with Indian scalps, glanced up from the rope he was splicing at the sound of hoofbeats, stared, rubbed his eyes vigorously with thumb and forefinger, looked again. He got up from his canvas stool. The rope, forgotten, slid off his lap to the ground.

"Howdy, Jack." The silk-hatted vision aboard the familiar tan buffalo horse slouched past, trailing Chips and a motley mounted band big enough to relieve a platoon of cavalry. As the last horse filed by, an empty green long-necked bottle fell from its saddlebag and plopped into the dust at the scout's feet without breaking.

Jack got in line behind the procession. Others in camp joined him. By the time the horsemen drew rein in front of command headquarters, everyone was present but the troopers on sentry duty, who had let the bizarre visitors pass only because Chips was with them.

A goggle-eyed corporal stationed outside the tent ducked through the flap, reappearing a moment later with General Reynolds hard on his heels.

The tall, gray-bearded commander scraped granite eyes over the dandy who had swung down from his saddle to stand before him at slightly lopsided attention.

"Who in thunder are you?" Reynolds demanded.

CHAPTER SEVEN

Texas Jack's grin was broad under his clerkly moustache. He had his sombrero on the back of his head, revealing the pale stripe just under his receding hairline where the tan stopped. His small black was winded but far from spent, switching its tail angrily at the cloud of flies around its glistening rump.

"Horses on one side of the creek, injuns on the other," Jack reported.

"Bastards never learn." Will glanced around at the five mounted troopers with whom Reynolds had entrusted him. Their blue uniforms were dusty and fading under a white summer sun. "We're seven against thirteen. I don't know what that does for our luck, but they'll spot us sure if we head back for camp."

Jack said, "Let's get back some Army property."

They got to within fifty yards of the Cheyenne camp when a brave spotted them and let out a whoop. The others sprang to their feet and splashed across the shallow creek to where the horses were grazing, among them the mounts they had stolen from Reynolds' cavalry. Will led the charge. Blue smoke slid along the ground before a stiff wind. The Indians returned fire. The reports were hollow pops in the vast vault of the plains. One buck threw a leg over a chestnut gelding, reversing the movement almost comically when a bullet shattered his sternum in mid-swing. Will dashed through the water on Buckskin Joe and caught the gelding's hair bridle while the Indian was still falling. Five others who had succeeded in mounting fled downriver, pursued by a storm of lead. One shrieked, slumped, and tumbled off. The riderless horse cantered for another hundred yards and drifted to a halt. The rest kept galloping, out of range now.

Jack and the troopers caught up with Will. Their horses' sides heaved. One trotted on ahead to claim the abandoned mount.

"The other seven lit out west," said the other scout. "I think we wounded a couple. You all right, Will?"

"Don't I look all right?"

"Your head's bleeding."

Startled, Will put a hand to his forehead. It came back stained red. A bullet had torn a three-inch gash along his hairline.

"Damn! If there's a scar, Lulu'll have the rest of my head."

Reynolds' 3rd Cavalry continued the pursuit and captured two hundred and fifty Indians in the main camp, after which a stunned sort of peace settled like dust over that vicinity. Texas Jack braided rope and the troopers gambled and wrote letters home. The days shortened, imperceptibly at first, then shedding minutes in clumps, like buffalo hair. The first frost shocked the prairie grass from vivid green to dead yellow overnight. Caked with sand and sweat and sporting a blade-thin scar on one side of his brow, Will returned to Fort McPherson in the fall at the end of a quiet scout to find a sheaf of messages waiting for him. One was a wire from the U.S. State Department informing him that he had been recommended for a Congressional Medal of Honor for his part in the skirmish that had led to the recovery of two Army horses and the subsequent imprisonment of a large band of outlaw Cheyennes. Other telegrams carried congratulations from friends in Omaha upon Will's election to the Nebraska legislature.

"When you fixing to start speechifying, Will?" asked an awed Buffalo Chips, drawing a needle and sinew through a split in the knee of his buckskin trousers.

"Never. Politics is one trail with more cactus burrs to the square inch than any I ever rode out here. But I believe I'll hold on to the 'Honorable' in front of my name. I do like an impressive title."

He opened the last envelope, containing a three-page letter written in Ned Buntline's flowing hand. For some minutes he concentrated on the journalist's grandiloquent terminology, then laid the pages carefully on his knee. "Chips," he said, "I want you to take a good look at me."

His friend glanced up from his sewing. "I'm looking."

"You see an actor?"

"I don't know. What's one look like?"

Texas Jack entered the scouts' quarters and placed his sombrero upside down on a table covered with empty brass shell casings and loose tobacco. The leather sweatband was dark. "Chips, you better see to your horse. Someone went and tied pink ribbons in its tail again."

"Tarnation!" It was as close to a real oath as the junior scout ever uttered. He'd pricked himself with the needle. "Last time he wore it clear into town." He tied off the sinew hurriedly, bit through it, dropped the needle on the table, and went out, snatching his slouch hat off the peg next to the door on the way.

"That ought to keep him from checking the stirrups I shortened for him," Jack told Will, chuckling. "He'll swear he growed an inch overnight."

Will said, "Ned Buntline wants me to meet him in Chicago and go on the stage."

"You going to?" The other hitched a leg over the chair vacated by Chips and sat down with his arms folded over the back.

"Hell, no. Can you see me painted up like a St. Louis whore?"

"Don't you owe this Buntline fellow some money?"

"I'll get it some way."

"You ought to at least try her, Will. This here work can't last forever."

"I figure to go into ranching when it's done, not playacting."

"What you figure to use to lay hold of land and stock, you can't scrape up six hunnert to pay your restaurant tab?"

Will, who had told him about the disaster at Delmonico's, fingered a corner of the letter. "I don't reckon I'd have to stick with it long."

"I hear Wild Bill took a shot at the show business, though it didn't work out too good."

"You really think I ought to?"

"Worst you can do is make a damn fool of yourself in front of several hunnert people," said Jack with a grin.

The other scout leaned forward, his face alight. The mark on his forehead stood out dead white against the flushed skin. "I'll go if you'll go with me."

Jack's heavy-lidded eyes opened slightly. Then his grin broadened. "We can take Chips along for laughs."

Will thought about it, then shook his head. "He wouldn't make it past his first ride on the perpendicular railway. What about it?" He proffered a callused hand.

His friend hesitated, then accepted it firmly.

"Where are the Indians?" Buntline asked.

Will and Jack looked at each other guiltily. The three were standing in the lobby of the journalist's hotel in Chicago, a narrow entryway with bare yellow-papered walls, an ancient concierge snoring behind a desk with a finish like dead skin, and a broken-backed settee with a stain on the cushion. Buntline's fortunes had soured since New York. Will said, "We forgot to bring them."

"You fight them daily. How could you forget? I promised the manager of the theater twenty real Indians."

"Maybe there's some around town you could hire," Jack suggested.

"Yes, you can find a full-blooded Sioux chief operating any streetcar in the metropolis, feathers and all." The little biographer spoke acidly. Broader than ever—improvidence had a strangely contrary effect upon his girth—he had circles of sticking plaster on his cheeks and chin and his clothes reeked of moth powder and whiskey. He heaved a theatrical sigh. "Well, I am delighted to see you both nonetheless. Perhaps the discovery that this production will have two authentic prairie scouts in the cast when only one was expected will quell the protests. Have you cash with you?"

Jack said, "Why?" suspiciously.

Will placed a hand on his partner's tense right arm. "We collected our pay before we set out," he told the journalist. "What do you want with it?"

"You must prime the pump if you expect to draw water." Buntline held out a pampered right palm.

Jack inhaled. Will slid an arm across his shoulders hurriedly and led him away. They walked across the lobby whispering, Texas Jack gesticulating furiously. His friend's tone was soothing. Jack fell silent, head down, nod-

ding from time to time. Buntline checked his watch against the clock on
the wall.

At length Jack reached reluctantly into a pocket of his tight suit and
handed something to Will. When they returned, the latter placed a fistful
of dirty bills in the journalist's hand.

"There's three hundred and fifty dollars there," he reported. "I reckon
this makes us partners in truth."

"You'll not regret it." Buntline folded the bills into a tiny square and
poked it into a vest pocket. "With the commission I made selling fire
insurance this past summer, we have enough capital to launch a most auspi-
cious venture. Come and see where you will make your debut and dramatic
history."

They took a cab to Nixon's Amphitheater, where Jim Nixon, the owner
and manager, greeted them in the deserted auditorium. He was a compact,
energetic fifty-year-old with gray in his handlebar and very bright blue eyes
like new bullets. He wrung both scouts' hands and laughed in short, hard
bursts when Jack remarked that civilization smelled like buffalo guts. When
the manager's mirth was spent he asked how the Indians were faring. Buntline started to explain about the Indians. Nixon's manner changed abruptly.

"No savages?" His voice quivered with rage. "You promised me savages.
We've been advertising savages for six weeks. Everyone has been asking
after savages at the ticket office. You'd better get me savages, by God."

"Arrangements are in motion even as we speak," Buntline said expan-
sively. "Surely you are aware, friend Nixon, that this most cosmopolitan city
fairly crawls with redskins. I was just saying something of the sort to Cody
and Omohundro, was I not?" He turned to them.

Will cleared his throat. "Yes, he told us you can't hardly board a streetcar
without knocking down a Sioux chief."

"Feathers and all," Texas Jack put in.

"I have yet to see one," grumbled the manager. But his anger seemed less
certain.

Buntline made one of his gestures. "Come opening night I shall introduce you. The Indians of whom I speak hail from the Blue Island tribe."

"Blue Island is where the out-of-work actors hang out!" Nixon colored.

"Exactly. Dress them in braided wigs and tan costumes and none will be
the wiser."

The manager breathed some air. "You try my patience, Judson. Let me
see the script and learn what is required of these bogus savages."

"I haven't it with me."

"Then I will send someone for it." He beckoned to a grip leaning against
the proscenium arch. "Is it at your hotel?"

"It isn't written yet."

Nixon cursed energetically. The grip stopped halfway down the aisle, hesitated, then discreetly reversed directions.

"There will be a script this weekend," Buntline assured the manager. "I am no stranger to deadlines."

"This is Thursday. You are scheduled to open Monday. *Were* scheduled. This production is canceled." He spun on his heels and headed toward his office on the other side of the auditorium.

"We have a contract."

Nixon called back over his shoulder, "Speak to my attorney. I am no stranger to lawsuits."

The journalist fumbled in his vest pocket. "How much to rent your theater next week?"

"Six hundred dollars." Still walking.

Buntline produced the folded bills and a wad from his pants pocket and counted them, popping the paper noisily. Nixon froze in mid-step, turned around.

"I reckon this squares my debt," Will muttered to Jack.

The other scout ran a finger around inside his stiff collar. "How come I felt safer in Cheyenne country?"

They shared Buntline's hotel room. There, overcome with fatigue from their long rail journey, the two frontiersmen stretched out fully clothed on their cots while their host turned up the single greasy coal-oil lamp on the desk and, pausing only to uncork a travel-polished flask and help himself to an inspirational sip, began scratching his pen across the top sheet in a stack of foolscap. Texas Jack started snoring the moment his head caressed the pillow. Will, slower to succumb, amused himself for a time watching Buntline, stuck for a device, pacing the cramped space between his "office" and the door, muttering lines and gesturing. The star attraction remembered nothing more until he awoke with a hand shaking his shoulder and stale liquor breath in his face.

"Time to rehearse, lad. The play is done."

On the *p* in "play," spittle flew into Will's left eye. He rubbed it and asked what time it was.

"Almost nine."

The scout blinked stupidly at the blackness outside the window. "Awful dark out for nine."

"Nine *P.M.*, lad. It is still last night, not tomorrow morning."

"You wrote a whole play in four hours?"

"Closer to three. I went out once for whiskey." Buntline thrust a sheaf of closely handwritten sheets at Will, who rubbed his eyes again and studied the one on top in the thick yellow light of the lamp.

The title was *Scouts of the Plains*.

"Looks kind of familiar. Didn't I hear these lines in *Buffalo Bill* last winter?"

"Call it a revival. The original story was mine to begin with."

"You got three scouts listed in the cast. Who's this Cale Durg?"

"I have scouted on occasion."

"You?" Will was wide awake now. His laugh shook the bed. Texas Jack, still sprawled on the adjoining cot, came awake in mid-snore and shot upright with an astonished profanity. "The only place you ever found without help was the unhappy end of a bottle," Will told Buntline, gasping.

"Perhaps so." The journalist drew himself rigid, his great belly describing an indignant arc between his suspenders. "But I was treading the boards when your stool was still yellow, and at my most intemperate I never tried to settle a six-hundred-dollar restaurant bill with fifty dollars and a handshake."

"You made your point, Colonel. What do I say first?" Will groped for his boots.

They rehearsed well past midnight, passing the flask and stopping only once, when Texas Jack choked on a healthy draft in the middle of a temperance speech assigned to his character, and picking their way laboriously through the late pages as Buntline's curlicues grew more exaggerated and difficult to decipher in direct relation to the volume of alcohol he had consumed to that point. The playwright demonstrated his dramatic abilities by assuming all the other roles, pitching his voice high to the scouts' vast amusement on those lines meant for Dove Eye, the beautiful Indian maiden of the piece. The next morning, clear-eyed and ruddy-faced after four hours' sleep and a shave, he left to deliver the script to the printers and hunt up props and scenery while his less adventurous fellow thespians negotiated an uneasy truce with their breakfast.

Dress rehearsal was Saturday morning. Will and Jack put on their best buckskins in the dressing room they shared, then threaded their way through stacked scenery and carpenters hammering and sawing onstage, where they found Buntline, looking surprisingly authentic in fringe and his favorite knockabout hat with the broad brim turned up in front, coaching a group of ten hollow-cheeked, potbellied extras in brown-dyed cambric with red bandanas tied around their waists to represent breechclouts, tiaralike warbonnets perched on their heads at various exotic angles. The journalist stooped to bend the knee of a brave with stubble on his cheeks and a short cold cigar clamped between his teeth.

"Higher," Buntline was saying. "Try to touch your chin with your knee. Remember that this is a war dance and that you're angry."

"I got a hernia," protested the Indian in an accent that suggested the South Side.

"Good. That should make you look angry."

Catching sight of the newcomers, he called a break and approached them, swamping his jowls and neck with a soaked handkerchief. "I'm beginning to understand why it is taking so long to subjugate the heathen," he said. "What do you think? Will they pass muster?"

"They're all chiefs," Jack pointed out. "Who's left to hold the horses?"

"Dramatic license, lad. The sum total of—"

Will cut him off. "Where is Dove Eye?"

"That's her coming in the door. Late, as usual. I have never known a leading lady to be on time for a rehearsal or a performance."

Buntline had indicated a small woman wrapped in furs proceeding in an unhurried gait up the center aisle of the auditorium. Her complexion was dark and she had high cheekbones and eyes as black and glossy as patent leather. She wore her raven hair in tiny curls framing her forehead.

"Nez Percé," Will guessed.

Jack grunted negatively. "Comanch'."

"Whose-a fault I no gotta the cab?" the woman demanded of Buntline, stopping with only her head showing above the footlights. Her nostrils flared.

"Zounds, but it slipped my mind completely." He waddled down the steps and took her hand. "Please forgive one who has been away from the theater far too long. From this time forward I shall place three conveyances at your disposal daily and you will have your choice." As he spoke, he walked her up the steps. "Mlle. Morlacchi, allow me to present the Honorable William F. Cody and Mr. T. B. Omohundro. Buffalo Bill and Texas Jack, your Dove Eye."

Will, who towered over her by twelve inches, removed his Stetson and accepted her imperiously upraised hand. He tried to say something gracious, but only laughter bubbled out.

She retracted her hand as if bitten. "Something is funny?"

"I'm sorry." He fought for control. "It's just that I wasn't aware there were any undomesticated tribes in Sicily."

"I am Neapolitan," she informed him coldly.

"Of course you are," Jack put in. "I was just telling Will that this lady looks as if she is Neapolitan. Wasn't I, Will?"

"Oh, yes."

La Morlacchi smiled radiantly, and touched Jack's palm with fingers greatly unlike a squaw's short strong digits. "Omohundro." She tasted the name. "Is that not *italiano?*"

"Well, it is so close it might as well be."

She made a hoarse sound of amusement in her throat. Her hand lingered a moment in his before she withdrew it. Will cast a sidelong glance at Buntline, the latter beaming from ear to greasepainted ear.

Opening night. Nixon's Amphitheater breathed nervously, its rafters humming like an expectant mother. The air was tinged with the odor of burning oil. Texas Jack removed his head from the aperture between the curtain and the proscenium and turned a stony face on Will, who was studying his script on his stool covered in papier-mâché bark to resemble a stump. Yellow straw littered the softwood boards at his feet and vague shadows writhed on the painted canvas landscape behind him. He had one moccasined foot propped up on a real log.

"Will, you seen how many people there are out there?"

"All of 'em, I reckon. Buntline said it was sold out." He closed his eyes and moved his lips silently.

"You praying?"

"Too late for that. I'm getting my cues down."

The other scout resettled his hat for the hundredth time. He was sweating under his greasepaint; flesh color stained the fur trim on his collar. "You recollect your friend Milligan?"

"Sure. I guided him on a buffalo hunt last year."

"He's out front."

"Thanks, Jack. You surely know how to put a fellow's nerves to rest."

"Five minutes to curtain," Buntline called out. He was helping the wardrobe woman adjust the headdress on one of the Indians. It kept sliding off his bald pate. Finally she took a tuck in the band and secured it with a safety pin.

With three minutes remaining, a pacing extra collided with one of the potted trees and knocked it over. Two grips hastened to right it and scoop dirt back into the pot. While they were thus engaged, a corner of the backdrop came loose. Buntline caught and held it until someone could erect a stepladder and nail it back in place. At one minute Mlle. Morlacchi was running around the stage in feathers and fringe, slashing the air with both hands and spitting imprecations in Italian at the makeup girl for some infraction no one quite understood.

The overture started. The mysterious frightening region beyond the hanging folds filled with brass and strings.

"Places, everyone," Buntline said calmly. "Curtain going up."

The playwright-director-performer took his position on Will's right, thumbs hooked in his belt and one foot planted next to the scout's on the log. Texas Jack stood on the other side. He put his thumbs in his own belt, saw that that pose was taken, then tried crossing his arms. Finally he just let his hands dangle at his sides. Will closed his eyes, mouthed something quickly, rolled up his script and dropped it behind the "stump." A grip hauled on a rope and the curtain rose.

An awed silence broke in applause. Under its cover the music subsided discreetly. The noise peaked, punctuated by hoots and whistles, then abated. New silence opened like a fan.

The first line was Will's.

The audience waited.

Will said nothing.

The three men dressed as scouts might have been fixtures. Someone in the auditorium coughed nervously.

Buntline coughed too, moved his shoulders, lifted and resettled his thumbs in his belt, cleared his throat. "What have you been about lately, Will?" he prompted.

Will made no response. A bead of sweat the size of a marble started through the grease on his forehead and crept down his nose, hanging from the end like an undecided suicide.

Jack said loudly, "You've been off buffalo hunting with Milligan, haven't you?"

The audience roared. Milligan was well known to Chicago. Will started at the noise and glanced around quickly as if roused from sleep. He started speaking then. The spectators shushed one another.

The words came haltingly at first, then with the mounting confidence of one who had told the story a hundred times. But none of them was in the script. He was recounting the details of his hunt with Milligan exactly as it had happened. The spectators hung on the quaint phrases and queer terminology. They laughed in the right places.

When the story was finished, Texas Jack leaped in with one of his own, again to the theatergoers' delight, and with a little help from Buntline's inexhaustible store of romantic fiction, the three groped their way through an impromptu first act. When it came time to close the curtain, Buntline signaled to the bogus braves offstage, whereupon all ten hurtled onto the set, swinging rubber tomahawks and shrieking like castrated mongrels.

"The Indians are upon us!" cried the journalist, unlimbering his pistol, which discharged its powder into the floor before he could raise it. In the smoky confusion following the eardrum-battering din, the untutored extras fell on their faces to a man.

"Damn good shooting, Durg!" shouted a wag in the back row. The curtain rolled down to tremendous applause and unbounded mirth.

Scraps of the original play found their way into the second act, in which Dove Eye was introduced and fell in love with each of the scouts in turn. Buntline was seized by the revived hostiles and bound to a potted tree while preparations were made to burn him alive.

"My candle gutters," he declaimed in his best lecturer's voice. "And yet there is time to deplore my dissolute life. In this miserable doomed sinner you see the sour dregs of that very first flagon of wicked rum I tapped as a callow youth of fifteen. Had I but seen reflected in that dark venom the pathetic and diseased creature I would become, I would have rammed the cork in tight and turned my back forever upon that empty, glittering existence from which my poor dead mother broke her heart and will attempting to dissuade me."

"Burn him!" rose a cry from the audience.

"What heights might I have scaled had I not given in to that base seduction?"

Someone in another seat offered the Indians a match.

A hearty cheer went up when a torch was finally applied to the dry kindling at Buntline's feet. Curtain.

"Cale Durg's" rescue in the third act, more Indian attacks, constant gunfire. Sharp-eyed extras stamped at the floor and slapped at scenery ignited by the powder flares while scalps were taken and lariats flew. Buntline's character took a bullet and expired after a brief temperance speech, a turn that brought the audience to its feet in an ovation that shook the theater.

The play ended, and even Buntline lost count of the curtain calls. Awash in the noise, Will shouted, "Sorry, Colonel."

"Sorry, hell! This is the biggest thing that's happened since Appomattox!"

"The newspapers'll eat us alive," muttered Jack.

"Let them. All of Chicago will come flocking here just to see how truly bad we are."

"That's the only way," Will conceded. "Words sure won't do it."

They linked hands with Mlle. Morlacchi and bowed.

Coals glowing in the fireplace shed red-orange light on the carpet and made looming dark things of the room's furniture. On the mantel a 365-day clock click-clunked against the sifting noise of snow floating down outside the frost-thick window. Drowsy from lovemaking, Will burrowed his back into the mattress and curled a hand around his wife's naked shoulder. "You haven't yet told me how you liked the play."

"I didn't think you wanted to hear about it." She was tense under the counterpane, straining to hear Kit's labored breathing through the open door of the next room, which he shared with his sister. The boy had a bad chest cold. "You stopped the play to call out to me how bad you thought you were."

"That's because when I spotted you I remembered I was just playacting. The audience appreciated it."

"They agreed with you."

"They know me in St. Louis, that's why. I think they liked the play even better than the audiences in Chicago."

"They liked that woman."

"Dove Eye?" He laughed. "She's the only woman in the cast. They had no choice but to like her."

"Do you?"

"I like you, Mama." He squeezed her.

"That's no answer."

"She dislikes me as much as she likes Texas Jack, and that's plenty. Not that you'd know it from the words Judson puts in their mouths during the love scenes." He snorted. "One of the Chicago critics found out he wrote *Scouts* in four hours and said he wondered why it took so long."

"I know. You sent me the clippings." She listened to the clock. "Is Elizabeth prettier than I am?"

He was silent for a moment. Then he swiveled to face her. "Christ, Mama, Lizzie's my *cousin!*"

"You wouldn't know it from the way you go on about her in your letters."

"I never did."

"You sound like a schoolboy in love with his teacher."

They were arguing when Kit started coughing, an alarming whoop with a phlegmy rattle. Louisa got up to give him codeine. The boy accepted the spoonful of thick syrup and fell asleep almost immediately. Will was snoring when she returned, or pretending. She watched his face in repose, so like his son's, the faint light glimmering on skin as smooth as a child's despite constant exposure to weather. She envied the Codys their perfect skin; her own was rather coarse and already drying out at twenty-four. Elizabeth Guss would have the Cody skin, she knew, just as Mlle. Morlacchi's trim figure accentuated her own thickening breeder's frame. And those were just the ones she knew about.

At length she took off her robe and slippers and climbed in beside her husband, where she listened to his heavy, measured breaths and the clock paying out time and the quietly hissing stream of snow and doubt piling up on the sill outside.

CHAPTER EIGHT

The passenger unfolded himself from the horse-drawn cab to an astonishing six foot two, resplendent in black cutaway, string tie, ruffled shirt, flowered vest, salt-and-pepper trousers, and high-sheen boots whose heels added yet another two inches to his height. The features under the broad brim of his Stetson were equally arresting: blue-gray eyes, large hooking nose, and a long upper lip pushed into a permanent pout under a flowing moustache that masked the beginnings of jowls where the ends hung down. His hair, darkened with pomade, spilled in perfumed ringlets to his shoulders.

"Five dollars," announced the driver, handing down the other's valise and carpetbag.

Their owner paused with his hand inside his coat. "I was advised to give you no more than two."

"No, it's five."

He produced a flat leather wallet and removed two singles.

The driver flexed the muscles under his tight coat. He was several inches shorter than the other man but built square and solid. His nose had been broken more than once. "Give me five dollars, you backwoods dude," he growled, "or I'll tan your hide for you."

Showing elaborate attention to detail, the passenger put away the bills and returned the wallet to his inside pocket. His teeth shone in a becoming smile.

Will pushed through the revolving front door of the Brevoort Hotel a few minutes later and shouldered his way through the hooting crowd that had gathered on the sidewalk. For a moment he watched the tall man in elegant clothes literally mopping the gutter with the bruised cab driver, holding him upside down by his legs and the seat of his pants and swishing his head around a brackish puddle.

"What you doing, Wild Bill?" Will asked casually.

"Just tidying up a little," replied the tall man.

"Figure to be done soon?"

"With you in a minute."

A red-painted trash barrel stood on the corner, half full of paper and fruit peels. Hickok hoisted the howling cabbie and dumped him seat-first into the barrel with his legs thrust heavenward. As an afterthought he got out his wallet again and stuffed the two singles into the stunned man's mouth. He stooped to wipe his boots with a white linen handkerchief, then picked up his bags and joined Will on the sidewalk.

"How was your trip, Wild Bill?" They were entering the hotel now, the crowd having parted for them.

"Boring as hell. The railroads sure took all the fun out of traveling."

Hickok signed the register with a flourish. While the bell captain was lifting his luggage, Will laid a hand on the shoulder of a fat man with muttonchop whiskers and longish hair in a Prince Albert and striped trousers, an exact copy of his own attire. "Wild Bill, this here is Arizona John Burke, my partner."

Hickok grasped the fat man's pudgy hand in his own corded one. "What happened to Buntline?"

"Oh, he's back doing dime novels," Will said. "Things got complicated after they arrested him on some old bail-jumping charge and we had to change the title of the play to keep the courts from attaching the receipts. He's out again, but if he comes near the theater and the detectives see him we'll all be working for free."

"I've followed your exploits ever since Hays City, Mr. Hickok," gushed Arizona John. "I'm delighted to welcome you to the show."

"Yeah. There a bar in this hotel?"

They adjourned to the dimly lit room, where Hickok and Will ordered bourbon and branch and Burke contented himself with bock. Hickok glared at a group of well-fed men in business suits jammed into a back booth until they stopped staring at the longhairs and busied themselves with their drinks.

"Arizona agrees with me that we got to sign some more famous names in order to keep this show popular," Will explained. "We were big in Chicago and St. Louis and Boston, but they've seen us here in New York. That's why I wired you to come join up. We've rewritten Buntline's old part to fit you."

Hickok bolted his drink and caught the bartender's eye. "I come to take a look-see, but now I'm here I don't know. Playing pretend just don't seem manly."

"Hell, Wild Bill, it's just like spinning a yarn, only bigger. I read that write-up of you in *Harper's* a few years back. I didn't notice you tripping over the truth."

"It ain't the same."

"Sure it is. I got plans. We're going to sign some real Indians, dress them in authentic warbonnets and buckskin leggings. Eventually we'll go outdoors, bring in some horses and buffaloes, make a real exhibition of it. Show folks in the East what it's like on the frontier. Arizona says there's never been anything like it."

"I done it two years ago in Niagara Falls."

Will peered closely at his friend. Age had caught up with the gunman, thickening his waist and scratching deep lines from his nose to his mouth. Flesh sagged under his chin. He was drinking as hard as ever, but without enjoyment, and there was something in his eyes.

"Goddamn injuns I hired didn't know the first thing about herding buffaloes," Hickok recalled. "Bastards got away from them while they was fixing to drive them into the arena, and we chased 'em all over town till they finally run up a blind alley. Meantime the grizzly busted out of the cattle car and went straight for the nearest hot-dog cart. By the time we got him back in the cage we had to sell the buffaloes to settle damages and raise train fare out of town. I recollected all that coming over, which is how come I'm thinking twice now."

"Then why are you here?" asked Will.

"I'm sick to death of marshaling. I had it with matching fire with every vagrant who ever read about me in Beadle's Dime Library and shooting stray rats and sitting with my back to the wall and a hideout derringer up my ass. I need a vacation, but I can't afford one. Pick out whichever answer suits you."

Burke said, "Does that mean you're in with us, Mr. Hickok?"

He looked at Will, cocking his head toward the third man. "What'd you say he's called?"

"Arizona John."

"He ever been to Arizona?"

"I never asked. John?"

Burke hesitated, then shook his head.

"I'll sign on one condition," Hickok said. "You keep him the hell away from me."

Will kept him the hell away. That afternoon, the bell captain delivered the new script of *Scouts of the Prairie*, formerly *Scouts of the Plains*, to the gunman's room. Hickok accepted it with a grunt and pushed the door shut in the hotel employee's face, ignoring his unobtrusively outstretched hand.

Finding his entrance cue, he pulled the cork from his traveling flask with his teeth and read while filling a water tumbler with the red liquid.

"Fear not, fair maid," his first line read. "You are safe at last with Wild Bill, who is ready to risk his life, if need be, in the defense of weak and helpless womanhood."

He cursed when the glass brimmed over and slopped whiskey onto the writing desk.

"Good house, Papa!" cried the little boy in the balcony, making a trumpet of his hands.

The audience laughed and beat its palms thunderously. Will paused in the middle of his first exit to smile broadly and wave at the child and his mother.

"That your boy?" Hickok asked backstage.

Will said it was, flushing proudly under his makeup. "He and his mother are here on a visit. What do you think of a four-year-old boy with that kind of gumption?"

The gunman, decked in frontier costume, grunted. He wore little greasepaint and no rouge, having threatened to geld the makeup man who had approached him with the jar. "You ought to cut his hair. He looks like a girl."

The audience gasped when Hickok stepped onto the stage. He had on his favorite buckskin shirt studded with turquoise and gypsum, cinched at the waist with a broad leather belt with a square buckle, the fringed hem hanging to his knees. A brace of revolvers closely resembling his famous pearl-handled Navy Colts rode in the belt with the butts turned forward, and his wealth of glistening curls threw off halos from the footlights. No one had yet accused him to his face of looking like a girl. He blinked in the glare of the calcium spot and strode away from it toward where Mlle. Morlacchi, attired as Dove Eye, awaited his opening line. The circle of light followed him.

He delivered his first speech, and his second and his third, not listening to the actress' responses, impatient to get his next line over with. As he spoke he paced, but the spotlight stayed with him. Someone in the seats tittered.

"That tears it." In the middle of one of Dove Eye's impassioned pleas he faced front, drew one of his revolvers, and hurled it at the source of the offending illumination in the balcony. There was an explosion, the light died, and bitter smoke rolled out into the auditorium. A woman who had been sitting in the shower of glass screamed.

Watching from the wings with Texas Jack, Will said, "I had a nightmare like this once, but I woke up."

For the campfire scene, the only lamp burning onstage was concealed in a "fire" rigged from strips of red and yellow crepe surreptitiously fanned into motion by a grip stationed under the open trap. The show's newest member had by this time settled into his role. Feeling in control now, Will passed the whiskey bottle to Hickok, who took a greedy pull, made a face, then spat out the mouthful and flung away the vessel. It bounced on the floor without shattering and rolled into the backdrop, jiggling the sky and hills.

"You think I'm the worst fool east of the Rockies," he accused Will in a voice that carried to the back row. "I can tell whiskey from cold tea. Give me real whiskey or I'll tell no stories."

The spectators laughed and applauded. Real whiskey was provided. Face flushed from the stimulation, the gunman glided weightlessly into his next scene with Dove Eye, with whom he promptly fell in love somewhat more energetically than the script demanded. Will sent in the Indians to rescue her from her rescuer. The instant the curtain fell she clawed her way out of Hickok's embrace and pelted him with curses in English and Italian.

"She's too little anyway," growled Hickok when she had stormed into the wings, leaving behind a respectful path cleared by the players assembled backstage.

"She's big enough to take you down a notch," Texas Jack pointed out.

Hickok lunged for Jack's throat. Will grabbed his arm. "They're engaged."

Arizona John Burke, standing nearby, slumped his fat shoulders at the announcement. Hickok noted the reaction.

"Well, well," he reflected. "I guess she ain't so little at that."

Scouts of the Prairie rolled into Titusville, Pennsylvania, on a glory road paved with Arizona John's eye-catching posters and columns of print in the local newspapers. Pirate editions of Ned Buntline's Buffalo Bill books and the Beadle chain of Wild Bill titles sprang up all around the nation's first oil boomtown, and a local dressmaker added fringe to a line of blouses she had despaired of selling and went out of stock six hours after placing a card advertising them in the window. A grifter claiming to be William F. Cody was arrested peddling hanks of hair said to be pieces of Chief Tall Bull's scalp on the main four corners after Will had complained to the police that he was a gentleman and not given to taking scalps. "Buffalo Bill's Scruples," ran the headline on Burke's subsequent press release. It worked. The company's first performance played to a sellout crowd of oil barons, field workers with black fingernails, and their families. Between shows, Will looked up from the stacks of slightly greasy bills he was counting on the desk in the theater manager's office to ask Burke what the commotion was outside.

"It's the supers," reported the publicist. "They're threatening to quit."

"Wild Bill again?"

He nodded. "He gets bored onstage and shoots at their legs because he likes to see them dance. They're refusing to lie down when they're supposed to be dead because they're afraid he'll blow their heads off."

"He doesn't have any bullets in his pistols."

"You ever catch one of those powder flares at close range?"

"I'll talk to him. Anything else?"

"Those oilfield roughnecks were by again this morning. They're wondering will you pay the hospital bills of the ones Wild Bill knocked down with that chair in the saloon yesterday."

"They started it. You don't whistle at Wild Bill and ask him does he wear hair ribbons on Sundays." He handed the stacked bills to the poker-faced manager, who banded them and squatted in front of the black metal safe behind the desk. The key on the end of his watch chain rattled in the lock.

"The ticket clerk's scared they'll burn down the theater if they don't get some promise of recompense. I'm not so sure he's wrong."

The manager glanced up, alarmed. "You pay damages. It's in your contract."

Will said, "Tell them to come by the hotel tomorrow morning and I'll see what I can do."

"I thought we were leaving for Rochester tonight."

"We are."

There was no sign of Hickok when the train pulled into the Rochester station. Will saw that his bags were delivered to the hotel along with everyone else's, turned in, and rose early to supervise the restrained chaos of staging at the theater. At a quarter past four he returned to the hotel to learn that Hickok still hadn't checked in. He went looking.

The bar he eventually entered was as dark as any adobe saloon in Arizona or New Mexico, but the air was damp and smelled of fish. A lone fog horn cleared its throat out on Lake Ontario, as isolated and hard to place as an owl hoot in the woods. Will ducked to avoid rusty hanging lanterns as he worked his way through the smoke and buzz of voices, squinting at the jowly, stubbled faces in the greasy light. He found the owner of the one he was looking for dealing stud at a back table ringed with huddled forms in peacoats and shabby wool jackets that smelled like uncured hides.

"Wild Bill, you are a hard man to locate," Will said.

Hickok skidded a card across a table. "That's the general idea. How come you did?"

"I'm a scout, or did you forget? You cut a pretty wide swath of busted windows and bloody noses along the lakeshore."

He plunked down the remainder of the deck and picked up his hand. "Jack opens."

The man with the designated card flipped a white check into the center of the table. Will said, "We got a show at eight o'clock. You missed rehearsal."

"I knew that. You didn't have to come tell me." He matched the bet and raised five.

His friend scooped a vacant chair from under the next table and spun it around. "You want to talk?"

"Sit at this table, you play cards," grunted a stevedore in a sweat-stiffened pullover to Hickok's right.

Will went to the bar and exchanged money for a stack of checks. Returning to the table, he sat down and watched the others play out the hand. Hickok raked in the pot, dealt a fresh round. Will opened.

"You changed, Wild Bill," he said, frowning at his hand. "I knew you to raise some hell out on the plains, but you been in civilization before. You know better."

Hickok said nothing. The man who had opened the last hand kicked up the bet. Reluctantly the stevedore saw the raise.

Will matched it. "I'm having trouble finding supers. It's hard hiring someone who's scared to turn his back on one of the featured players."

"I just like to hooraw them now and again. You get tired saying and doing the same things every night." He saw the raise and sweetened it another five. The player across from him hesitated, then met it. The stevedore folded.

"It ain't like you." Will added one red check to the pot and then another. The man who had seen Hickok's raise said something foul and threw in his hand. That left only the two plainsmen.

"Strutting around in front of all them people like a honky-tonk bitch. It ain't work for a grown man." The gunman met Will's raise. "Call."

His friend turned up a pair of tens and three odd face cards. Hickok had a queen-high straight. He scooped in his winnings.

"I don't think that's what's riding you," Will persisted.

The other refilled his glass from a bottle that was three-quarters full of red whiskey. His eyes flicked over the other two men seated at the table. "Clear out."

The stevedore glared. "Don't we get a chance to finish even?"

"You're even now. I been watching you two play partners all day. You're lucky you caught me in a generous mood."

"Hold on!" barked the other player, scraping back his chair. Hickok sat back, unbuttoning his Prince Albert with his left hand. The plain handle of a Colt showed above the red sash around his waist. The two men got up and left without further discussion.

The gunman drained his glass and set it down with a thump. Then he filled it again from the bottle. "You been hitched a couple years now, ain't you, Will?"

"More than a couple. I got a daughter seven and you saw the boy, and another daughter new as a shiny gold coin. Moving the whole kit and kaboodle out here to Rochester next season." He paused, wondering where the conversation was leading.

"What's it like?"

"Rochester? You're sitting in it."

"Bein' married."

Will shrugged. "It could be better. I've had it worse." Slowly he looked up from his checks, and his face split in a wide grin. "By God, you're on the scout, ain't you? Or maybe you got someone all picked out. How come hell froze over and nobody told me?"

"Just thinking."

"Since when?"

"Since I turned thirty-eight. I got one good suit and a saddle with a bad cinch. Seems to me a thirty-eight-year-old man ought to have more."

"You'd have more, you didn't spend all your time around saloons."

Hickok glanced up, startled. "I don't got to give that up, do I? If I get hitched?"

"Depends on who you get hitched to. Stands to reason you got to give up something. You can't just keep going on the way you been."

The gunman cut the ace of spades from the deck idly. "Well, I don't want to do that."

They took a cab to the theater, where a hyper Arizona John met them on the sidewalk and hustled them inside, chattering about Ned Buntline's genius in having written a play with scenes so easily rearranged while its two stars were off seeing the sights. Texas Jack was playing a love scene with Mlle. Morlacchi when they reached the wings. Will watched the betrothed couple pawing each other in the footlights for a moment, then turned to his friend with a smile. "They sure do put on that romance stuff with enthusiasm, don't they?"

Hickok was grim. "Ain't they foolish? What's the sense in getting out there and making a show of yourself?"

"Beats grading track." Will slapped him on the shoulder. "Let's go climb out of these city duds and get ready to make a foolish show of ourselves."

Finishing his first scene, Will strode backstage in costume to find Arizona John standing alone among the ropes and lumber. "Where's Wild Bill?"

Burke said, "I'll let you look. I'd rather go rattlesnake hunting in a dark cave."

A quick round of the dressing rooms failed to turn up the gunman. Finally Will buttonholed a pale-faced young grip and asked him if he'd seen Hickok.

"Yes, sir. He left while you was onstage."

"Did he say where he was headed?"

"No, sir. But he left a message for you."

Will waited. "Well?"

The boy scraped his shoe in the sawdust. "He said to 'tell that long-haired son of a bitch I am done with him and his show business for good.' "

Burke came in on the last part of the message. Will said, "Tell the others, will you, John?"

"They'll be disappointed," replied the publicist, deadpan.

Two days later at a rival theater an actor billed as "Wild Bill Hickok" felt a rough hand on his shoulder in the middle of a performance and turned in time to see the fist that unhinged his jaw and drove his front teeth down his throat. Other blows broke his nose and cracked two ribs. Witnesses described the assailant, who fled before security arrived, as tall and mean-looking, with hair to his shoulders and a slight limp.

Autumn dampened the air inside the cramped vault of the New York Central and Hudson River Station, its walls humming not with the prayers of the pious but the echo of hurrying footsteps and the shriek and bang of high-carbon wheels and loose couplings, muffled slightly by exhaling steam. Will and Arizona John Burke searched the faces of the passengers alighting from the train. The stream slowed to a trickle and stopped entirely, and they were still waiting. Will mounted the step and peered down the aisle between the two rows of seats. A colored porter was busy sweeping the runner at the other end of the car.

"Excuse me, but is there anyone else aboard this train?"

The employee stared at the long-haired apparition stuffed incongruously into city clothes. "Just the crew, suh."

Scratching his beard, Will stepped down to find a man in a conductor's uniform standing with Burke. "Is your name Cody?" asked the conductor.

Will said it was. The conductor jerked his head. "I have something for you in Baggage."

As he walked, the railroad man favored the outside edges of his feet, as if the soles hurt. He led the way to a boxcar just ahead of the caboose, undid the padlock with a key on a large ring taken from his belt, and heaved open the sliding door with a noise like coal skidding down a chute. Will peered through the gloom inside the car at the faces of the men getting up from the bare floor, shielding their full black eyes from the sudden light with callused hands. They had flat features and stoic mouths and their black hair fell in braids to the blankets drawn over their shoulders.

The scout whirled on the conductor. "These men had tickets to ride in the coach!"

"Complain to Mr. Harriman." He leaned against the side of the car and rubbed one foot through the thick leather Oxford. "On my train savages don't sit with the decent passengers."

"I'll take your advice when I dine with Mr. Harriman next week."

The conductor paled a little and stood upright, forgetting his feet. The Indians were standing at the open door now. They smelled of rancid grease and fresh sweat. "What you want them for anyway, kitchen help?"

"They're my actors."

"Oh." He stood around for a while as the cargo was unloaded, then left, hobbling and cursing under his breath.

Will escorted the Indians to a clothing store, where he made them take off their blankets and put on ready-made suits. They tugged at their crotches and muttered in broken English about cutting away the material there so their organs could breathe, but Will lectured to them through their interpreter that this was not a custom in civilization. At the hotel the clerk consulted briefly with the manager, then placed the Indians in one small room on the ground floor next to the kitchen. He charged Will double the regular rate and insisted that the guests enter and exit the building through the alley. They slept naked in the stifling heat from the kitchen and ate what their host ordered for them in their room because the restaurant refused to serve them. Will explained bitterly that this was a service due their high tribal standing. They listened to this diplomacy with no expression on their faces.

As supers they asked no questions and enlivened rehearsals with embellishments from their own ritual experience. Arizona John held his breath opening night, envisioning a massacre if the audience failed to appreciate them. But from the moment of their entrance—first to awed silence, then explosive applause, and even a cheer or two for the savages—their place in theatrical history was peacefully assured. One critic even remarked grumpily that it was the most well-behaved uprising in memory. Burke used the quote in his publicity, hoping by it to attract the more fainthearted women.

"How are the Indians?" Will asked him one night toward the close of the

1875–76 season. The scout was in costume, dabbing carefully at the beads of sweat blistering his greasepaint. It was close in the wings for April. Out front the professional actor Will had signed to fill the gap left by Hickok was delivering a moody soliloquy on the unpredictable nature of hostiles to a packed house. From here the speech sounded stagey and hollow.

Arizona John shrugged. His hair was nearly as long as his idol's now, accentuating his apple cheeks and fat neck. "They keep blowing out the gas light in their dressing room instead of turning it down. One of these nights we'll all go up in a roar. But next to Wild Bill they're Sarah Bernhardt." His voice was dull. The company had just received invitations to the wedding of Texas Jack and Mlle. Morlacchi.

"Good old Wild Bill. I hear he shed his new wife already and went prospecting in the Black Hills."

"Jealous?"

"A little." Will smiled. "A lot. But I'm thirty, and that's old out there. Here I'm just a whippersnapper."

"Still, killing Indians is heaps easier than looking after them."

"How would you know, John? The only Indian you ever killed was one you worked to death on your father's farm."

His cue was coming up. He tugged down the hem of his buckskin shirt, another work of art from Louisa's skilled seamstress' hands, drew his revolver and inspected the blanks. He had had two misfires that week.

"Oh, damn! This came while you were dressing. I forgot." Burke held out a Western Union envelope.

"Hold on to it, will you, John? I'll read it after this act."

"I was trying to make myself clear to one of the Indians when the boy delivered 't. I think he said it was urgent."

Sighing, Will accepted the envelope and opened it.

Burke was watching the play. "There's your cue, Will." Then he turned and saw the scout's face.

CHAPTER NINE

He left the cards and telegrams unopened in a big pile on the parlor table and had the flowers taken away, all but a modest spray of yellow roses from Texas Jack, who had taken time out from his wedding plans to send them along with a card bearing just his name. These he placed in their vase on the mantel next to Kit's picture. The boy had liked Jack.

Will studied the photograph in its frame of black lace. He had had it taken just last month, Kit leaning against a studio boulder in a little tailored suit, holding one of his father's rifles. His red-gold hair was arranged in sausagelike curls that hung to his collar. It was after that that Will had insisted his hair be cut, over Louisa's shrill objections.

"I'll not have a boy of mine scuffling in the schoolyard over something so inconsequential as his hair," he had said, and she had acceded then, horrified at the thought of anyone laying a hand on their son. Later she had blamed the haircut for the chill that had ushered in the illness.

Audiences in St. Louis, New York, and Rochester had claimed the boisterous child in the balcony as their own, and if the press had harbored any suspicions about Arizona John's story concerning the boy's daring escape from gypsies and return home using his inherent tracking skills last year, it had suppressed them and published the account faithfully. Reporters welcomed any fresh opportunity to remark on the boy's handsome brown eyes and ringlets.

"Good house, Papa."

"Were you addressing me, sir?"

Will looked away from the photograph to the colored butler in livery and white gloves standing in the doorway. He shook his head and the servant bowed slightly and departed on silent feet.

He topped off his glass again with sherry from the decanter and drank. It tasted like colored water. He wished it were panther piss from the filthiest bug-ridden saloon on the plains, that scorched and cauterized pain like a hot iron, two hundred proof clear or cloudy brown, anything but this scarlet that put him in mind of the killer that had entered his home on the fevered air.

A thin, tearing, nasal cry sounded from the upstairs bedroom. Orra, the baby, had awakened in her usual fashion. Will poured again.

Louisa entered as he was setting down the empty glass with a double thump on the table cluttered with unopened envelopes. She glared at the two-thirds-empty decanter but said nothing. She had lost a great deal of weight in just a few days. Her cheeks were shadowed and there were purple marks under her red-rimmed eyes. New lines forked up her neck from the collar of her black dress. She was just twenty-eight.

He shifted his weight heavily in his creaking chair. "What's wrong with Orra?"

"Nothing."

"How come she's crying?"

"Babies cry. It doesn't always mean something."

"Arta with her?"

"She's asleep in her room."

The 365-day clock grew loud on the mantel. It had traveled a thousand miles and been wound four times since Will's troupe first played St. Louis. He got up, swaying a little. "I'm going out."

"Where?" She was looking at the picture next to the roses.

"Wherever the air hasn't been breathed once already." He rang for the butler and demanded his hat and coat.

"It's late," said Louisa.

"It's just now got dark."

He saw the whiteness at her nostrils then and lurched forward, catching her just as she crumpled forward and almost losing his own balance under the sudden burden. The Negro came to the doorway carrying the master's outerwear, saw him holding his wife, started to withdraw.

"Turn down Mrs. Cody's bed," Will snapped, curling an arm behind her knees and lifting her. "She's fainted."

"Yes, sir." The butler's livery rustled.

As her husband was lowering her to the mattress, Louisa threw an arm around his neck, burying her face in his chest. "Oh, Will, he's dead. Our boy is gone."

Something in her voice cried out for him to contradict her. *Now, Mama, Kit's just playing one of his tricks; he'll pop in any minute now, grinning the way he does when he gets one past us.* But Will had seen them lowering the little coffin into the ground and heard the hollow thump of the first shovel-ful of earth striking the lid. He patted her back. "It's just us now, Mama. Just us and Arta and Orra." The baby had gone back to sleep in her cradle at the foot of the bed. He paused to listen for his daughter's faint breathing, then gently disentangled himself from Louisa's arms and unclasped the brooch at her throat. She was unconscious again, but her color was normal; he remembered then that neither of them had slept in days. He unbuttoned her shoes, feeling as he slid them from her slim, black-stockinged feet the familiar warmth that heralded the swelling at his crotch. Alarmed, he straightened, then swiftly drew the sheet and counterpane up to her throat and left the room. He found the butler sitting at the table in the kitchen. The colored man stood up awkwardly.

"Fetch the nurse to look after Orra and Arta while Mrs. Cody is sleeping," Will directed. "I'll be gone a spell."

"Yes, sir. May I inform Madam when she awakes what you'll be about?"

"Cutting the bear loose."

He left the servant standing in the kitchen with furrowed brow.

Elizabeth Guss lay awake listening to the Westchester town clock clanging out the small hours. Travel made her restless, and she and her father had returned only the afternoon before from Rochester and Kit Carson Cody's burial in Mount Hope Cemetery. She kept seeing Will's face at the funeral, wearing the expression of a boy whose father had just dealt him an unexpected blow for no apparent reason. At length she gave up on sleep, put on her robe and slippers, and padded downstairs to select a book from her father's library. She was passing the entryway on her way back to the stairs when she heard a strange noise outside the door.

Colonel Guss, who had led troops south near the end of the war on the heels of night riders and marauding rebel deserters, would never report what he had seen, but he had instilled in his daughter from childhood a healthy fear of curious sounds in the night. She seized a fireplace poker before going to the door. It was quiet outside. The air had an early-spring snap to it and it was too early for crickets. Nothing moved in the pale light from the gas lamp on the corner. She stepped back inside and started to close the door. An animal growled at her from under the porch.

She paused. The shadows were black in the foliage between the sidewalk and the house, but something rustled behind her rosebushes. The noise it made fell between a snarl and a moan. She choked up on the poker, walked to the edge of the porch, and peered over the railing. Her cousin was kneeling in the soft damp earth beside the steps.

"Will, what's wrong?" She lowered the poker. "Where is Louisa?"

"Sh. She's asleep."

"You'll catch your death."

"I'll have to. I waited for it, but it didn't catch me. Train was too fast."

He laughed and vomited down the front of his shirt. A rank stench of half-digested liquor rolled up into her face.

She put down the poker and her book and hurried down the steps, clutching her robe together at her throat. Cold air squirmed up her bare legs under her nightgown. In the light coming through the door she saw that Will's funeral suit was smeared, as if he'd been crawling around in the dirt for a while, and his glistening shirt was plastered to his chest. "Gimme a leg up, will you, Chips? My stirrup's busted."

Elizabeth had no idea who Chips was. She got her cousin's arm over her shoulders and a grip on his back and tried heaving him to his feet, but he wasn't cooperating and she had to half drag him to the foot of the steps. There she poked and pleaded and finally persuaded him to grasp the railing and raise himself semiupright, leaning on her. On the way up she stopped twice to rest. The railing creaked when she propped her burden against it. Inside she left the door open, struggled down the entryway and into the parlor, where she deposited Will on the settee, the oak frame bowing alarmingly under the impact. She hurried back out to retrieve the book and poker from the porch and close the door.

"Lizzie? Is that you?" Guss's voice floated sleepily down the stairs.

"Just securing things, Father," she called back.

"I thought you did that hours ago."

"I came down for a book."

She pulled off Will's coat and sodden shirt and got a blanket from the hall closet and put it over him.

"Who's got the watch?" he inquired.

"That's all taken care of. You sleep now."

"You're a good scout, Chips, but your voice is too high. A body'd think . . ." He snored.

She looked at him, at the smooth youthful features of the boy caught writing his name on a wagon sheet. "You should be West, Will," she said. He went on snoring. She went back upstairs, forgetting her book. Hours later she told her father that Will had probably contracted some sickness on the train coming over from Rochester.

"He'll be a lot sicker when he wakes up," said the Colonel, buttering a morsel of toast the size of his thumbnail.

The world turned an angry face to the sun. Bismarck rattled the German saber at France and France rattled hers back. Alexander II, Czar of Russia and father to the Grand Duke Alexis, watched unrest spread through the Balkan slaves in the land of the enemy Turk and stroked his beard in thought. In the States, authorities followed the trail of New York rascal and fugitive from justice Boss Tweed south toward Cuba. President Ulysses S. Grant, his sad bearded visage dragged long by the weight of half a dozen Congressional probes into charges of misconduct, opened the Centennial Exposition at Philadelphia with an entreaty "to appreciate the excellences and deficiencies of our achievements," then yielded the floor to an artillery salute. George Armstrong Custer, having earned Grant's disfavor for testifying against his Secretary of War, was denied the supreme command of the first all-out offensive against the Plains Indians but tossed the bone of his old regiment, the 7th Cavalry. Sitting Bull, the great Hunkpapa Sioux medicine man, announced that the seven lodges of the Sioux tribe were gathering at the Powder River and issued a blanket invitation to the Cheyennes and Arapahos to leave their reservations and join them in the last holy war against the white Long Knives.

The telegram from General Sheridan's headquarters caught up with Will Cody in Wilmington, New York.

Wilmington theatergoers were jolted out of their willing suspension of disbelief when the star of the drama vaulted onstage in the middle of a love scene, decked in a striking Mexican-cowboy ensemble of gold-embroidered black velvet and hat with a red plume and waving a yellow Western Union flimsy, bellowing, "I'm through playing at war! I'm going West to take part in it!"

He read the wire aloud in his powerful baritone, pumping such emotion into Colonel Mills's orders in cold print that when he finished, the audience leaped to its feet, applauding mightily. Flushing to his hairline, Will bowed deeply and exited. When the excitement faded, his fellow players resumed the scene where they had left off. It was only after the last curtain that some of the spectators wondered what that bit of business with the telegram had had to do with the rest of the play.

Days later, the conductor on the Chicago-to-Omaha run fetched his apprentice from the caboose and took him through the last day coach to prove he'd just punched a ticket for a man in a suit that looked like a widow's hat with trim.

"Takes all kinds to keep the rust off the rails, boy," the conductor said later. "That's a fact you won't learn in no school."

The Mini Pusa, or South Fork of the Cheyenne River, had been nicknamed the Dry Fork on a day like the one the 5th Cavalry began its march through that valley in June 1876; grass grew through cracks in the yellow bed and varmints had honeycombed the banks with their burrows. Distant buttes swam in the heat of the Wyoming sun, under which the waist-high grass covering the bluffs had burned to match the bronze of the sky. Horseflies lapped blood and sweat from the necks of men and mounts alike. In camp the troopers on sentry duty listened to their flesh bake and gazed enviously at the trapezoid of cool shade where the officers had gathered under the canopy in front of the commander's tent. Had they been able to hear the conversation, they would have been content to remain where they were.

General Wesley Merritt glowered down at the two messages spread side by side atop the map on his folding camp table, a lock of his carefully brushed hair falling down to uncover his balding pate. He had a large head with eyes sunk deep under a brow like a carapace and a satanic moustache whose tips swung below his chin.

"Carr's original orders, and mine when I assumed this command," he said, "were at all costs to prevent the Cheyennes from joining with the Sioux. Now I have a conflicting directive to return to Fort Laramie for fresh supplies and then proceed by way of Fort Fetterman to join General Crook, who has got his ears pinned back by the Sioux at the Rosebud in Montana."

"The Sioux are fighting?" asked an astonished Colonel Mason above the excited babble that followed the announcement.

"We all knew they would when they stopped running." Merritt looked up from the map, supporting himself on his fists. "Our orders are clear. We are to cut across the Cheyennes' line of march in the south and turn them back whilst simultaneously reinforcing Preacher George against Crazy Horse in the north. Gentlemen, I'm throwing it open to discussion."

Mason snorted. "What's to discuss? We're to be in two places at once as usual."

"Faced with conflicting orders, obey the most recent," declared Lieutenant Hall. "That's the Army line."

"The desk cavalry in Washington knows nothing of the situation out here," the colonel argued. "We know the southern Cheyennes are moving to hook up with Sitting Bull. Where they go, the Arapahos are certain to follow. I say we go on as arranged."

"And risk court-martial if we fail," finished the general. "They broke Custer once for doing much the same thing. Still, I'm convinced that in that direction lies the success of this campaign. Shall we put it to a vote?"

"Rider coming, General." One of the other officers pointed.

The newcomer leaped down before the sentry post, exchanged words with the trooper stationed there, and entered camp on foot leading his lathered buckskin. A sergeant who knew him whistled at his Spanish-looking outfit of black velvet under a layer of dust and plumed hat ruined by sun and sweat. He waved back good-naturedly. Sunlight caught his long copper-colored hair and Merritt said, "It's Cody."

"How come he's dressed like that?" Lieutenant Hall sounded indignant.

"He's in the show business. What have you got for me, Will?" The commander stepped out of the shade to confront the scout, who drew a dispatch pouch from his shirt and handed him a wilted fold of paper from inside.

Merritt read swiftly. He turned bright eyes on his officers. "The Red Cloud agency reports that eight hundred Cheyennes are leaving the reservation tomorrow morning for Sitting Bull's last known camp on the Rosebud. General Crook will have to bank his fires for the present. We will proceed as originally ordered."

Forward, ho. Keep moving. Cover eighty-five miles before the renegades make thirty. Borrow a leaf from Bonaparte: substitute pack mules for supply trains where possible, jettison the hospital train and take along only the surgeon and a skeleton staff of medics with just the instruments they can carry on horseback. If you're too sick or too hurt to ride, fall out and get better or die. Keep moving. Snap jerky and bolt warm water in the saddle. Urinate and defecate in your pants, no time to find a bush, much less dig a latrine. Keep moving. Ignore the heat, sleep in snatches while riding, let that horsefly on the back of your neck draw his fill and keep moving. Stop once, you're on report. Stop twice, you're shot for a deserter. Keep moving or get out of the way.

Rider coming. A small scout on a mustang with no saddle to slow him down and only one revolver, no other weapons, trotted down the moving line of horsemen until he found the general and handed him a scrap of dirty paper. Seven words scrawled in travel-blurred pencil:

Custer and five troops, 7th Cavalry, killed.

Tight-faced, Merritt gave the message to his aide. "Spread the word back through the ranks. From here on in we make speed."

The news sped from regiment to regiment with telegraphic rapidity. When it reached Will, his first thought was of a mouse-colored mule.

Dawn peeled the sky away from the horizon like a scalp, opening a raw gash that bled over the shadowed bluffs grading downward from Warbonnet Creek and tinted the waters pink. At the base of the grade lay Will and Lieutenant Charles King of Company K on their stomachs on a small grassy mound with mosquitoes singing in their ears and the bluffs rearing behind them, the expanse looking from a distance like clear even ground but concealing seven companies of the 5th in the pockets and creases like flakes of tobacco on Ned Buntline's swollen vest. It was precisely this deceptive terrain that had enabled Crazy Horse and Gall to rout General Crook and cut Custer and the 7th to pieces.

"There's another bunch," said King, pointing.

Will nodded. He had already observed the party of Indians on horseback three miles to the south moving west. Their horses were gaunt and grass-fed, reservation ponies and not stolen Army mounts. "That makes six," he remarked. "I wonder what's drawing them."

There was no reply, nor did he expect one. King had posed the same question last time.

The gash opened slowly, sending streaks of bright yellow lancing out over the plain. They overshot the feathered braves moving into and out of sight among the long rolls of ground and touched a broken white line crawling along the western edge of the circle of earth and sky.

Will said, "That would be Lieutenant Hall and the supply train."

"Now we know."

The scout crawled back down to the bottom of the mound and straddled his buckskin. Zigzagging to keep the bluffs between him and the Cheyennes like a dog quartering a corn patch for grouse, he approached General Merritt and the main body of cavalry massed in a depression invisible from the south. The commander was sipping coffee from a smoking tin cup. Will reported what he had seen. Merritt nodded. "Keep me informed."

Will returned to his post beside the lieutenant. The sun was visible now, brick-red but turning golden in the center. Its rays flashed off the distant braves' war regalia of copper and polished bone, silhouetted the trailing ends of their warbonnets like devils' tails, and caught fire on the bright colors painted on their buffalo-hide shields. The six bands had grouped to form a formidable force.

"Jesus Christ." The scout observed them through King's glass. "I haven't seen them this gussied up since before the war."

"*Which* war?"

"Pick one. They must have looked something like this when they came to sign the big treaty at Fort Laramie twenty-five years ago." He handed the instrument to King, who focused on a splinter of seven warriors that had split off the main shaft, then tracked ahead to a pair of uniformed troopers riding well ahead of Hall's train. The braves were moving to cut them off along a route that would take them close to the observers' position. The lieutenant described the scene.

"That's it." Will withdrew again to fetch his horse.

Merritt's cavalry was mounted now and strung along the ridge behind the observation post. The general heard Will out, then watched the predatory band for a while through his glass, admiring the colored streamers flying from their lances as they broke into gallop.

"By God, they're almost beautiful," he said. "Like a pack of wolves on the scent. And they're all yours. Give 'em hell." He folded the glass decisively.

The scout stepped into leather and joined his little command, made up of six troopers and fellow scouts John Tait and Jim "Buffalo Chips" White, and waited for Lieutenant King's signal from the mound. The morning dampness had evaporated; the spreading heat drew steam from the horses' withers.

The lieutenant had put away his glass, which he no longer needed to see the light glistening on the braves' naked chests and the gash of white in their mounts' muzzles when they bared their teeth against the hackamores. He heard the pounding hoofs and then the terrific explosion of spent animal breath. He raised and lowered his arm. A cry went up from Will's band and they tore down the hill bound for the Indians' flank.

The first shot came from the main body of cavalry on the ridge. A lone brave who had drawn rein and fallen behind the party of attackers-turned-victims disappeared from his horse's back, and King thought he had been hit. Then flame spurted from under the neck of the frightened animal, followed an instant later by the crack of a rifle. The Indian had swung behind the horse without relinquishing his seat and fired from cover. More shots sounded. Merritt's cavalry was moving.

Down below, the original seven Cheyennes reared their mounts and wheeled in confusion. The eighty-five-mile "lightning march" had caught them flat-footed. Then beyond them the horizon bristled suddenly with scores of feathered braves on horseback.

King's warning was drowned out by the bugle. The first wing of cavalry broke forth like flushed game, flying the guidon of K Company, the lieutenant's own outfit. He sprang to his feet with a yell and ran back down the hill for his horse. But the beast had broken away, dragging its picket. Clucking and cooing, King maneuvered it against the incurving side of a bluff, lunged for the bridle, almost missed it, got a hand on the bit chain, and swung a leg over the saddle. He reeled in the trailing reins, shook loose the picket, and took off on the heels of the last straggler, whipping the ends of the reins quirt-fashion across the horse's flanks. He caught up halfway down the hill and charged past a strange figure in some kind of Mexican dress standing over the body of a fallen Cheyenne.

"First scalp for Custer!" the man was shouting over and over.

Lieutenant King made another fifty yards before his excited senses arranged themselves and he realized who it was in the theatrical costume waving the ghastly thing over his head.

The "battle" was anticlimactic. Stunned by the unexpected enemy numbers, the Cheyennes broke and fled for the reservation at Red Cloud, where by the time Merritt caught up with them at nightfall, they had cast off their war dress and mingled with the Indians who hadn't left. The oft-heard complaint "You can't tell the good redskins from the bad ones" was just as often met with General Sherman's notorious caustic comment on good Indians being dead Indians. But after that first brief clash at Warbonnet Creek no more blood was spilled. The frustrated command set up camp on agency grounds.

The scalp Will had lifted from the Cheyenne he'd slain, a minor chieftain whose name was first translated as Yellow Hand (later amended to Yellow Hair and attributed to the long blond scalp he'd worn), made the rounds of awed scouts and troopers at a celebration held around a blistering bonfire in honor of the symbolic victory. Several offers to buy it were turned down.

"What you fixing to do with it, Will?"

"I got a neighbor in Rochester who'd admire to display it in his clothing store till I come to collect it. Believe I'll send it to him for safekeeping, along with Yellow Hand's headdress and bridle and such."

"Hell, why'n't you stuff the bastard and be done with it?"

The men laughed and pummeled the guest of honor.

He left early. Chips White, going off to search for his idol, almost bumped into him in the dark. Will was standing on the edge of the reservation, his tall bulk punching a starless hole out of the sky.

"Celebration's just getting started, Will."

"One's pretty much like another. Best I ever was at had just one sip of whiskey to it. That was a long time ago."

"Heck, we got lots more whiskey than that. There's always plenty to be had on a reservation if you know where to look."

"Thanks just the same."

"No one ever seen you take hair before today. Lieutenant King says you done it on account of that white woman's scalp the injun had."

"I didn't even see it till I had my knife out." He chuckled dryly. "I thought at first it was Custer's, but his hair wasn't any yellower than mine."

Chips smacked a fat mosquito on his cheek. "What you doing out here all by yourself anyway? It ain't safe."

"Something I don't believe I'll be doing again for quite a spell," Will said after a moment. "And maybe not ever."

The wind freshened, combing the grass with a noise like surf. Under a beaded sky the earth rolled.

CHAPTER TEN

"Scissors, please, Arta."

The little girl seated at her mother's feet handed up the pearl-handled scissors from the wicker basket in her lap and resumed her study of the pattern in the carpet. Eight now, she had grown into a serious child—no more swinging dolls for her—with her mother's brooding eyes and square jaw, and auburn hair like her father's. Since her brother's death she had not laughed, and spoke only when addressed. She seldom played, seeming to exist only for errands.

Louisa snipped the thread on the shirt she was brocading and worried about her children. Orra was a sickly baby; her sister would watch her for hours sleeping in her cradle, waiting. Alarmed, Louisa had asked Will to explain death's random nature to the child. He had tried, but his many absences had made him a benevolent stranger to his daughter and it was clear—astonishingly so, in view of the loss of his parents, two brothers, and a sister in rapid succession, and his violent life on the plains—that he had yet to accept it himself. His close brush with death in the Cheyenne skirmish of '72 had made him a believer in destiny, though he never confided as much to his wife. So Louisa made pretty clothing and watched the girl withdraw further inward each day and waited for the year of mourning to end.

The shirt's red and blue beads were startling splashes of color in a parlor made drab by grief. The work was flawless. She had a callus on the tip of the third finger of her right hand as thick as a sailmaker's palm from years of pushing needles through tough buckskin, and she could embroider or brocade an entire outfit in an hour. The results were satisfyingly gaudy and the work took her mind off Kit. She had been intensely annoyed to learn that her masterpiece, the black vaquero ensemble she had carefully patterned for

Will from a picture in a book, had been ruined on the plains, whose rigors it was scarcely designed to withstand. Even the ignorant heathens he acted with changed their clothes before leaving the theater.

He strode in from the hall, buttoning his collar. His force filled the somber room like an explosion of light. Louisa's scissors slipped, puncturing the fleshy mound on her left palm. A rill of blood appeared. She exclaimed in French and sucked it.

"How is the world's youngest seamstress?" He scooped Arta off the floor. She gasped, clutching his arm tightly as he hoisted her to his shoulder. Her fear unsettled him. He kissed her on the cheek, his beard scratching her, and set her back down. She knelt and started scooping buttons and spools of thread back into the spilled sewing basket. He noticed Louisa's injury then and seized her hand to kiss it too.

"It's stopped bleeding," she said, withdrawing the hand. "There are other ways to enter a room than at full gallop. Hold still." She stood and held the shirt up to his torso, aligning the shoulders with his. "I may have to let it out around the waist." Her tone was accusing. Unlike hers, his appetite had not suffered in the past few months.

"No time, Mama, if you're expecting me to wear it in California. My train leaves in twenty minutes."

The colored butler appeared in the doorway. "Your cab is here, sir."

Will threw him the shirt. "Pack this and have him load my traps." When the servant had gone with the garment: "Mama, a child shouldn't fear her father." He spoke low, watching the grave little girl arrange the items in the basket on the floor.

"Sometimes you forget how big you are. She was afraid of falling."

"Heights don't scare kids. When I was six I climbed trees I wouldn't now if Crazy Horse and the whole Sioux nation were on my heels."

"You were a boy." She reached up and tucked the ends of his black bow tie under his collar. He was wearing his traveling suit over a plain white shirt. "Maybe you wouldn't frighten her so if you were home more."

"I've a family to support. Sitting Bull is in Canada and the rest of the renegades are back on reservations or on their way there and there's no work for me on the frontier. But they want me on the Pacific Coast, and I go where I'm wanted."

"Don't you find it strange that you moved us East so you could be with us, and that ever since you've spent more time in the West?"

"Why don't you come with me?"

"Who'd look after the children?"

"Bring them along."

"No. Orra is sick."

"She's always sick. I've a hunch she'll grow up healthier than all of us put together. I just looked in on her upstairs and she seemed all right."

"The girls are staying here and so is their mother," she said firmly.

He glanced down at Arta and turned his back to her. His voice dropped. "I want another boy, Lulu."

"Not another Kit." They had discussed this before.

"We'll call him James. That was Wild Bill's right name."

"I'll not have my son named for a killer."

"He was my friend."

Hickok was dead, shot from behind in the Black Hills of Dakota by a saloon swamper named McCall just six weeks after Custer fell at the Little Big Horn. The murderer had been freed by a vigilante court in Deadwood, arrested again when he left town to avoid the dead man's friends, tried in Yankton, pronounced guilty, and hanged. Will remembered the death in his friend's eyes the day they were reunited in New York City.

"Your bags are loaded, sir," the butler reported.

Louisa said they'd talk when Will returned from his tour. He kissed her, disregarding the needle pricking his back where her hands held him, and left with a promise to Arta to bring back enough seashells to fill her room to the ceiling. She replied gravely that one would do.

The new play, *Life on the Border*, introduced fellow scout-turned-writer Captain Jack Crawford, a long-haired, goateed dandy like Will with girlish features, in whose mouth Ned Buntline's leftover temperance speeches found a natural home. The Irish-born veteran of Spotsylvania Courthouse and the Indian wars kept his promise to his mother on her deathbed never to touch hard liquor, and while Will enjoyed his company and envied him his superior acting ability, he ducked him from time to time to visit the gin mills along the Barbary Coast with Arizona John Burke. The drama swept through San Francisco and finished the season before a sellout audience in Virginia City, Nevada, against a boomtown background of hammering and sawing that brought back bittersweet memories of Rome, Kansas. Will wrote on board the train between engagements, scribbling freely and without regard to capitals or punctuation, about massacres and buffalo hunts— borrowing liberally from tall tales he had heard around campfires and in the dank dimness of saloons, for he had run low on material from his own experience. His sister Helen would then correct his grammar and spelling back East and turn the amended scrawl over to Buntline or (increasingly, as the rotund journalist passed beyond Will's ken aboard his steam yacht on the East River) Arizona John, who would give it a literary twist before delivering it to the publisher. The stories appeared in the *New York Weekly* and the *Saturday Evening Post* and, expanded to book length, through Beadle's Dime Library, and sold in the millions of copies. There seemed to be no bottom to this well. And he hated it.

He visited his sisters in Leavenworth, shaking hands all around with the husbands and introducing them to Arizona John and a new partner, Major Gordon W. Lillie, "Pawnee Bill"—yet another Cody imitator in silken tresses and magnificent handlebar—who was currently negotiating with tribal elders in Oklahoma Territory for Sioux supers to use in the show. Helen—married now, Cody-eyed but in posture and deportment the image of their mother—came to see the play afterward and found the star combing greasepaint out of his beard in his dressing room, with Burke standing by looking fat and preposterous in his scout's getup. Members of the Buffalo Bill entourage tended to dress and look alike.

"Oh, Nellie," Will said, catching sight of her in the mirror, "don't say anything about the show. If God will forgive me for this foolishness I promise to quit it forever as soon as this season is over."

"What will you do, Will?" The question was resentful. She had enjoyed the play.

"Take the prairie and the Indians and everything else East. There's not room on a stage to do anything worthwhile. But there would be on a big lot where we could have horses and buffaloes and maybe the old Deadwood coach. That'd be something they'd never seen before. That'd be showing them the West!"

Burke rolled his eyes ceilingward. He had heard all this before.

"But didn't you once tell me Hickok tried the same thing and failed?" his sister reminded him.

"Wild Bill was my friend. But he knew guns and very little else."

That subject depressed him. With Hickok's murder and the death of Buffalo Chips White at the hands of the Sioux at Slim Buttes that same bloody summer ("Oh, my God, boys!"—blood pumping between the fingers clasped over his breast—"Good-bye, Will!"), the frontier was swiftly becoming a place without old friends.

"Well, call on me if there is any spelling to be done," said Helen.

But there were more seasons, other dramas. In the summer of 1877—still waiting on a son from Louisa—he took time out to clasp hands with one of the few remaining links to his recent but fading past, Major Frank North, he of the impish sense of humor who had foisted Ned Buntline off on the youth sleeping under a wagon at Fort McPherson, over the ownership of a vast cattle ranch at North Platte, Nebraska. Together they rode over the thousands of acres where they had once tracked Cheyennes, discussing irrigation now instead of Indian signs.

"Too expensive," said North of Will's plan to divert some of the Platte onto the ranch.

Will said, "Let me worry about that part."

Gone were the flamboyant locks and dress of the major's scouting past; his hair was cropped close about the ears and combed across his forehead to cover the thin spots, his moustache trimmed in a conservative droop. He wore a black suit like a banker's. Next to him Will felt painfully conspicuous for the first time since his initial New York visit—out here, where he grew up, and where long hair and buckskins had always been as common as bunch grass.

"I was stuck between floors once on the perpendicular railway," he muttered. "I'm commencing to feel like that all the time now."

Red Right Hand, or Buffalo Bill's First Scalp for Custer, Will's first attempt at playwriting, opened in New York with the 1877–78 season, recreating Custer's Last Stand for the first time on any stage and climaxing with the scout's victory over Chief Yellow Hand at Warbonnet Creek. To avoid confusing the audience he substituted buckskins for the theatrical costume he had actually worn that day. Many years later even eyewitnesses to the duel would remember it only as it appeared in the theaters, including General (formerly Lieutenant) Charles King, whose account would be immortalized on canvas by an artist who had never traveled west of State Street. The few balding veterans of the skirmish who recalled the absurd tight vaquero pants and plumed hat would tell their stories in the dark on front porches to snickering grandchildren.

A castlelike headquarters building rose on the Cody estate, dubbed Scout's Rest Ranch, and in town a great ridiculous Victorian jungle of gables and spired turrets dripping with gingerbread like white frosting made its presence known under the name Welcome Wigwam. The design was Louisa's. Will moved his family to Scout's Rest from Rochester while the house in town was under construction. Immediately upon arrival, Arta fled inside the house and one week later had not ventured out. When her parents asked what was wrong she made no answer. Asked to help bring in the wash or fetch water from the well in back, she would complain that it was too hot out or that the bucket was too heavy for her to carry. "Why can't the maid do it?" she whined. Will said the child was spoiled and should be punished. Louisa demurred. Then she observed that Arta left the room hurriedly whenever a blind was raised in the morning, and confided to Will that their daughter was terrified of the featureless Nebraska terrain.

She had grown up around buildings and felt naked and vulnerable in the empty vastness.

"She'll have trees," he decided.

He put Bill Goodman, his sister Julia's husband, in charge of landscaping. After experimenting with several varieties of trees, Goodman shipped in cottonwoods and box elders by the carload and hired laborers from North Platte for the massive project. The trees flourished, and as the ranch acquired a skyline, Arta's fears subsided. Against her mother's wishes, she took her first riding lessons from Will—Louisa, familiar with the fate of young Samuel Cody, crushed under a rolling mare, gnawed her nails—and soon the workers digging and lowering the bagged roots into the holes grew accustomed to the sight of the little girl astride gentle, aging Buckskin Joe, led by her proud father. But they never saw her smile.

While her sister rode, Orra grew from a sickly baby to a sickly child and died at the age of five. Texas Jack, starting his own family now, sent roses.

The year of mourning had not ended when the wild corners and stairwells of Welcome Wigwam rang with the cries of another Cody. The unsettled argument between Will and Louisa over whether to name their son James proved unimportant; the child was a girl. Will overcame his disappointment and christened her Irma. Arta, no longer a grave little girl but a grave young woman of thirteen, was by this time a better rider than a seamstress. When school ended she would race home and change into her riding clothes and saddle the pinto her father had given her for her twelfth birthday, canter off across the ranch, and not return until sunset. Will told Louisa, who considered this curious behavior for a girl, that he had done the same thing at her age. It was a mild fib; he had been a Pony Express courier at thirteen and paid to spend hours in the saddle.

Meanwhile, readers across the nation who had given up waiting for Buffalo Bill's autobiography to return to the library formed lines to order copies at bookstores. *White Beaver* was then establishing new records on tour, with Will fighting real Pawnee braves onstage. And still hating it.

His corps of female players had expanded from one to several, and every one of them in love with the star. His thirties were running out on him, but he was tall and straight and when he smiled his teeth shone and his eyes crinkled becomingly. His rough maleness excited the younger actresses resigned to effeminate leading men, and his naughty boyishness, which manifested itself in outrageous practical jokes on his fellow performers to ease tension, made the older women want to mother him. One small brunette, a bit player with one line, teased him mercilessly all through the season until after the last performance at the end of the run in Omaha, when she ran into him by a carefully contrived accident in a hotel corridor. Without saying anything he took her arm and steered her down the hall into his room.

They kissed good-bye in the open doorway. She traced the white scar on his forehead with her fingertips. "That must have been nasty." She had a stage-trained pseudo-English accent her friends in the company had worked hours with her to eliminate for the purpose of her brief speech.

"Cheyenne bullet. It bought me the Congressional Medal of Honor."

He kissed her again, as no one had done in the troupe since the day Wild Bill Hickok drank too much whiskey before his love scene with Mlle. Morlacchi. When Will straightened, he saw Louisa watching him from the end of the hall.

She had come from North Platte to take him home. Oddly, her emotion as she turned on her heel and hurried toward the stairs was neither hurt nor anger, but satisfaction, even relief. She had not worried away the past fourteen years in vain. He caught up with her on the landing, panting and talking at a pace that made his sentences run together without pause the way they did when he wrote. Theater people are close, he said. I can see that, she retorted. No, you don't understand, he explained; you don't live and travel with someone for six months and then just say good-bye, it's been fun. *You* don't, apparently, she said. He spoke to her on the way down the stairs and across the lobby and in the carriage on the way back to North Platte, forgetting his luggage, but she didn't pretend to be listening.

She said nothing more to him all that summer, and she gave him no more children.

"Mr. Burke?"

Arizona John Burke—*Major* Burke now, according to the advertising sheets waiting for him at the printers whenever he could get up the cash to ransom them—sat slumped in his rolls of fat, Buntline fashion, in the first row of seats at the New Orleans racetrack, moodily contemplating the drizzling rain stitching up a puddle the size of a small pond in the center of the grounds and Captain A. H. Bogardus' rifle-barrel back heading toward the exit. The crack shot had quit the show a few days short of the scheduled opening.

Burke looked at the couple standing at the railing. The man who had addressed him was well built and compact under a shining oilskin and hat with a curled brim. The woman, standing a bit behind him lifting her skirts clear of the wet grass, was small and plain, her cape soaked through, bonnet wilting. The man held a rifle. More auditioners, thought the publicist sourly. "I'm Burke."

"My name's Frank Butler. This here's my wife Phoebe Anne. We just left the Sells Brothers Circus because we heard you was hiring. We're trick shots."

" 'We'?" Arizona John studied the woman. Her shy, serious expression under the dark hair plastered to her rather bulbous forehead put him in mind of Will's daughter Arta.

Butler said, "She's as good as me. If you got a minute, we'll show you."

She was far better than he, as Burke saw when he had escorted them reluctantly to the target range where young Johnny Baker, Will's new protégé, was practicing. Butler hit the bull's-eye as often as his wife, but she was surer of herself and took less time aiming. When he finished reloading after his turn and handed her the rifle, her hands went to the grip and forepiece like young animals to their mother's teats and she worked the lever and fired as fast as anyone Burke had ever seen—maybe even faster than Will when he shattered the blue glass balls Johnny tossed into the air during rehearsal—and he fired sand, not bullets. The boy's face as he watched the exhibition was all eyes and open mouth.

"What do you say, Mr. Burke—Major?" asked Butler, while the echo of his wife's last shot was fading. His grin was open and infectious, like Will's when he watched his daughter exercising her pinto. The air stank of spent powder.

"Mr. Butler, if I thought I could pay you, I'd hire you both right here." He scraped mud off his heel on the edge of the plank the young woman was standing on. He'd been debating with himself whether they were entitled to the truth; now he made his decision. He told them how the show was jinxed. At Hartford, Connecticut, Major Frank North, whom Will had persuaded to put aside ranching temporarily for a spot with the show, had been badly broken up when his horse trampled him after a fall; he had died at Scout's Rest, the victim of a joke he'd played fourteen years before. Then unseasonably cold and wet weather had forced the company south, only to find the same conditions prevailing there. Then the riverboat carrying the animals and equipment down the Mississippi had sunk, taking with it all but the horses, the Deadwood coach, and the band wagon. When last heard from, the locals were still fishing debris and drowned buffaloes out of the river. "Right now Buffalo Bill and his new partner, Mr. Salsbury, are in town trying to raise money enough to pay those we have on salary. Come see us in Louisville in the spring and we can talk business then."

The disappointed couple exchanged polite farewells with Burke and left. Mrs. Butler's hesitant speech displayed a slight Midwestern twang. Johnny and Arizona John watched them picking their way through the puddles on their way out.

"Sure hope we see them when we get to Louisville," said the boy.

"I hope we still have a show when they get there," said Burke.

Smarting as he was from his sudden demotion from partner and publicist to just plain publicist, Arizona John didn't know he was selling his energetic replacement far short.

"The goddamnedest thing about Nate Salsbury," one of his many friend-enemies once remarked, "is you can't never tell whether the bastard's eating wallpaper paste or shitting diamonds."

And it was true. Down to his last copper or sitting on a billfold thick enough to fall from and hurt himself, the natty new manager of Buffalo Bill's Wild West was always turned out in spotless charcoal-gray with the jacket buttoned almost to his starched white collar and an immaculate derby set square on his handsome head, black beard trimmed and brushed to perfection, and a shine on his patent leathers that someone else once said could cause a buggy accident on a busy street in bright sunlight.

But he was as prosperous as he looked the day he swung his gold-headed walking stick onto the exhibition grounds in Louisville, Kentucky, leased from the money he had managed to raise from friends and family. The performers and roustabouts were paid and happy and for the first time there was cash in the strongbox in the wagon Salsbury used for an office. He paused in jaunty mid-whistle to watch Phoebe Anne Butler target practicing with her husband.

She was wearing a western outfit of pleated dress and white Stetson with yellow gaiters on her boots, her rather flat bosom crusted over with county and state sharpshooting medals. She held a plain hand mirror in front of her with her rifle barrel resting on her right shoulder and pointing backward. Butler, standing thirty paces behind her, asked if she was ready.

"Ready!"

He rotated his right hand, feeding out string in an ever-widening circle, the blue glass sphere attached to the other end whistling faster and faster, the pitch heightening as it orbited, a flashing blur describing a circle ten feet in diameter. When the shrill whirr was almost too much to bear, the rifle cracked. The golf-ball-size globe exploded in a shower of glittering dust.

Salsbury applauded, joining the others who had witnessed the spectacle. The performers flushed. The manager transferred his stick from his armpit to his left hand and approached them, removing his hat. He introduced himself, shook Butler's hand and touched his wife's small gloved palm. She was barely five feet tall.

"Where did you ever learn to handle a rifle like that?" he demanded.

"I used to shoot game on my father's farm in Ohio." She spoke quietly, her eyes meeting his for an instant, then darting away. "I never thought it was anything special till they asked me to take part in county turkey shoots."

"A born markswoman! Tell me, can you shoot from horseback?"

"I have."

"At dead gallop?" Dubiously.

She nodded, looking him in the eye now. She wore her dark hair brushed behind her ears, and her serious expression impressed Salsbury.

Butler said, "Annie don't brag. She can hit anything from anywhere. Her specialty's splitting a playing card at fifty paces."

"Annie?"

"She don't like Phoebe."

The manager stroked his beard. "Well, Annie, we'll not have you splitting anyone else's playing cards while I'm in charge of this exhibition."

"I thought Buffalo Bill was in charge," said Butler.

"On the plains, yes. Come with me to the mess tent."

They were getting comfortable at one of the long tables when the show's star entered, accompanied by three men with long hair like his, dressed in less expensive imitations of his best yellow buckskin jacket with Louisa's needlework on the front and a red silk handkerchief knotted at his throat and fixed with the grand duke's diamond buffalo-head stickpin. Arizona John was one of the three. A pair of Sioux Indians on loan from the Standing Rock Reservation in Dakota, squatting at the rear of the tent, glanced up at the newcomers briefly, then returned their attention to the game they were playing with the bones of some small animal at their feet. Will swept off his Stetson in a graceful bow before Mrs. Butler, who blushed prettily. She looked tiny standing in front of him.

"They told me about you, little missy," he said. "We're glad to have you."

The papers were signed then, on that table in that tent. The new act was billed as "Butler and Oakley," but from that moment on Annie was Little Missy to everyone who knew her.

DENVER, COLORADO

JUNE 3, 1917

The old man is dead.

With the dead's infinite patience his body has been awaiting burial since the simple funeral services were held in the Elks' Lodge in January, the bronze casket cluttering the vault of Olinger's Mortuary while crews hired by Harry H. Tammen, owner of the Sells-Floto Circus and Buffalo Bill's last contract, blasted a steel crypt into Lookout Mountain west of Denver, the walls doubly reinforced to discourage rival promoters from stealing the remains. Although Cody's will has requested interment at Cedar Mountain overlooking the Wyoming town named for him, Tammen has opted for Denver, home of the circus and his own Denver *Post*. As he is paying for the burial, Louisa, the widow, has voiced no objections.

The procession up the mountain is long, jammed with automobiles like black iron beetles with ticking engines and the tall, square rocking boxes of horse-drawn circus wagons. It isn't the first for Cody. In the bitter January cold a similar parade accompanied the casket from the rotunda of the state capitol (where thousands had filed past the showman's bier to the litany of a silk-hatted master of ceremonies: "Step lively, folks; big crowd behind") to the lodge, led by a squadron of infantry, a regimental band, and an aging white horse identified by the newspaper as McKinley, Cody's last mount. But it wasn't McKinley, just an old horse procured from a local stable at the last minute. This pilgrimage, like the first, includes Boy Scouts in uniform and wearing the yellow neckerchief inspired by Buffalo Bill, brothers of the deceased's own Elks' Lodge, dozing Civil War veterans and Spanish-American War volunteers with graying hair and paunches, Shriners, and members of the Showman's League of America among the estimated twenty-five thousand mourners, some of whom as children rooted for Buffalo Bill in his carefully choreographed duel with Yellow Hand and race to foil the robbers of the Deadwood coach. Tammen's publicists have been advertising the event for days and the reading public has not disappointed them.

In the spring cool of the shaded mountain, the family and friends of the deceased repair to their folding chairs and campstools while the soldiers in dress khaki are barked through precision maneuvers and the onlookers scramble for positions that will enable them to see into the tent and the waiting vault—an activity that in itself takes more than an hour despite the organizational abilities of circus veterans supervising the operation. The band plays Custer's "Garry Owen," that whirling, crashing mock march that spelled doom for Black Kettle at the Washita and saw the bold 7th off on its fateful trek to the valley of the Little Big Horn. A quartet sings Cody's favorite hymn, "Tenting Tonight on the Old Camp Ground." Dignitaries he didn't know deliver speeches, one of them a call to arms against Germany in the European war.

As the hours wear on, spectators who have brought flasks and bottles to the obsequies sneak off to relieve bursting bladders into the undergrowth. The ammonia smell sparks a small flurry of lifted handkerchiefs and hurried exits among the women. Some of the males admire the black-netted ankles of the six women dressed in elegant mourning weeping on campstools by the casket; Cody's old girlfriends, come to have their pictures taken and their names mentioned in the press. Louisa Cody, seated in the front row, never looks their way.

The final speech sputters to a patriotic close. The first line of infantrymen takes two steps forward. Their rifles rattle. Eleven shots crackle against the wall of the Rockies. The wind snatches away the blue smoke.

"Brigadier General William F. Cody, Buffalo Bill, rests in a tomb splendid," writes the correspondent for the Denver *Post* that day. "Human hands today placed him on the crest of Lookout Mountain, on the dividing line between the wild and the tame. . . ."

I was stuck between floors once on the perpendicular railway. . . .

". . . There in the light of the setting sun are the memories of his achievements."

Write it up that way then. Cody killed the chief.

"There to the east, where the first gray dawn sets the wheels of commerce in motion, there lies a city, a dream come true! . . ."

We're laying out a city on the west bank of Big Creek and reserving corner lots for ourselves. I figure if we sell them for two fifty each we'll be sitting on two hundred and fifty thousand easy.

". . . The 25,000 citizens who saw them press the earth over the sleeping form of Pahaska, the trailblazer, this afternoon were touched by the romance, the thrill of it all. . . ."

If you want a fellow to fit that bill, you'll find him over there under that wagon.

". . . No President could have been more honored by the presence of thousands. . . ."

Your mother is convinced you'll be President someday. . . .

". . . Pahaska, farewell!"

By nightfall the last mourner has left, leaving behind an uneven pavement of paper, cigar butts, broken glass, and trampled plants. The tent is folded away and returned to the caretaker's shed in the churchyard from which it was borrowed, the folding chairs and stools to Denver Lodge No. 17, BPOE. Tomorrow fresh sod will be laid on the mound of raw earth covering the vault. Deer and rabbits come around to inspect the invasion site, lick the candy wrappers, and sniff at the acrid stuff in the discarded bottles. Then they too depart.

Encouraged by its proprietors, the *Post* speculates what sort of inscription should be placed on the monument to be erected over the tomb.

" 'Property of H. H. Tammen,' " suggests a wag from the Contests section.

BOOK THREE
1883–1917

THE COLONEL

"I have been spreading it ever since."
—William F. Cody, 1898

CHAPTER ELEVEN

Posters large enough to cover pastures and small enough to fold and put in a pocket, plastered on barns and silos and telegraph poles and the brick walls of banks, splashing yellow and red everywhere and lending town and country the look of false autumn. THE ONLY REAL NOVELTY OF THE CENTURY! THE AMUSEMENT TRIUMPH OF THE AGE. THE ROMANTIC WEST BROUGHT EAST IN REALITY. EVERYTHING GENUINE . . . A YEAR'S VISIT WEST IN THREE HOURS. ACTUAL SCENES IN THE NATION'S PROGRESS TO DELIGHT, PLEASE, GRATIFY, CHAIN, AND INTEREST THE VISITOR . . . AN EQUINE DRAMATIC EXPOSITION ON GRASS OR UNDER CANVAS OF THE ADVANTAGES OF FRONTIERSMEN AND COWBOYS! NO GILDING, NO HUMBUG, NO FREAKS. At the bottom an endorsement, signed in facsimile by the Honorable William F. Cody: "A true rescript of life on the frontier as I know it to be, and which no fictitious pen can describe."

In Chicago the first Sunday, buggies and traps funneled into the streets bordering the West Side Driving Park, disgorging forty thousand eager spectators between noon and four o'clock, ladies' flowered hats blossoming in a field of derbies. Boys in pomade and knickers chased squealing girls in ribbons and pinafores between and around adult legs. Pickpockets, scalpers, and peddlers worked their way through the press at the gates, the last hawking souvenir tomahawks and programs and copies of Buffalo Bill's autobiography. Uniformed city policemen briefed by Nate Salsbury confiscated the wares of peddlers not sanctioned by the exhibition and ran them off with their nightsticks. The shrill of their whistles splintered the sabbath peace.

The week before the opening had been an organized man's nightmare, the final few hectic moments before a theater curtain's rise multiplied by a thousand and spread out over days. Salsbury had listened to, and politely refused, a stern request by a pince-nez-wearing delegate from the Chicago Reform Alliance to abandon the Sunday performances. The fellow had huffed from there directly to the office of Mayor Carter Harrison, who explained that if he withdrew the Wild West's license, he would also have to close every theater in the city on Sunday. An impatient buffalo bull had battered its way through the side of a cattle car in the railroad yard before it could be unloaded, breaking its neck and forcing one of the cowboys Will had hired to drive the livestock to shoot it. When Alliance members picketed the entrances to the park, Con Groner, a former cowboy and North Platte sheriff with a reputation for settling points with gunplay, had suggested "busting a few caps," but Salsbury had dispersed the protesters by handing out free passes to the weekday performances.

For this and other reasons, not the least of which was his partner's propensity to hire old pards for jobs wholly unsuited to them—one, Bob Haslam, a friend from Pony Express days, had set the company back hundreds of dollars when he rented an empty lot in New Orleans that quickly became a lake under the heavy rains and forced Will to lease the race track for the exhibition—Salsbury had assumed veto power over all the frontiersman's personnel decisions. The dapper manager recalled Will's story of how he had come to engage Bronco Bill Irving's services:

"Where were you born?" he had asked the cowboy.

"Near Kit Bullard's mill, on Big Pigeon."

"Religious parents, I suppose?"

"Yes."

"What is your denomination?"

"My what?"

"Your denomination."

"Er, Smith and Wesson."

The anecdote, which seldom failed to elicit a chuckle from listeners, made Salsbury shudder. He had offered his imagination and ability to conjure money out of tight purses to Will at the end of his first two disastrous seasons, when he had found the star dead drunk in a plug hat and thousands of dollars in debt, with a written provision that Will would avoid liquor on the job. The scout, scratching his flamboyant signature across the bottom, had muttered, "I put my mark to a paper like this when I was twelve." But he had promised to stop drinking and assured Salsbury: "Your pard will be himself, and on deck all the time." The show's new manager had said something flattering and folded away the pledge in his wallet.

He had begun by pruning deadwood. His experience as a comic in vaudeville had taught him that most people in the show business were drawn there less by a need to display their minimal talents than by the prospect of easy money; very little dross escaped his first glance and none at all the second. The only problem among those who hung on Will's buckskins was where to start.

Arizona John Burke—Salsbury could never quite bring himself to call the fat blowhard "Major"—was an exception to the rule, a canny publicist who was quick to recognize the same virtue in the men he chose to assist him in

the massively important enterprise of informing people of the show's existence. He had hired Prentiss Ingraham at the start of the new season on the
basis of his hundreds of dime novels, a third of which dealt with Buffalo
Bill. The novelist, a soft-spoken Briton who unlike his employer seldom
talked about himself, had once written thirty-five thousand words in one
eighteen-hour period while a boy kept him supplied with freshly dipped
pens. His prose filled the columns of every local newspaper for weeks before
the Wild West's scheduled appearance, and his storytelling talent found its
way into all the souvenir pamphlets sold in the grandstand during performances. With his efforts and those of an uninhibited staff of poster artists
whose bold, sweeping reds and brilliant yellows affixed hordes of painted
savages and valiant frontiersmen to every vertical surface for miles around, a
person had to be blind and friendless not to know that America's National
Entertainment was coming to town.

Will led the grand entry into the arena, an arresting figure in white
Stetson, bleached doeskins, and mirror-finish black boots to his knees,
astride Old Charlie, a magnificent half-bred Kentucky stallion on which he
had once ridden a hundred miles in nine hours and forty-five minutes on a
bet that he could not do it in ten. Behind him, high-stepping to the strains
of "The Girl I Left Behind Me" from musicians wearing the uniform of
Custer's regimental band, rode the Indians in feathers and paint, scouts in
buckskin, John Nelson driving the Deadwood coach, Bronco Bill, "Cowboy
King" Buck Taylor, ex-Sheriff Con Groner, young Johnny Baker, Frank
Butler and Annie Oakley, and dozens of supers, from vaqueros in black and
silver mounted on swift little mustangs to cowboys in Stetsons and woolly
chaps straddling big American studs. The procession circled inside the
bleachers while the applause swelled and receded and then peaked, threatening to drown the flatulent tubas and insolent flutes, the famous leader
sweeping off his big hat as if to scoop up the noise for later consumption.

The applause slid down behind the last rider to exit and died on a
crackle. An island of silence, and then a small young woman in a pleated
skirt and hat with a curled brim entered with twin Colts on her hips,
followed by a young man in a Western-cut suit carrying a rifle and a leather
pouch. From the pouch he drew a blue glass ball, and after a walk around
the arena, holding it aloft for all to see, he looked at the woman and
launched the sphere underhand into the air. She drew one of the Colts,
cocking it in the same motion, took aim quickly, and fired just as the ball
reached the top of its trajectory. It burst glitteringly. Polite applause
started, only to be lost under more gunfire as two more balls were launched,
then three, then five. When one revolver was empty she holstered it and

drew its mate without missing a beat or a target. Sunlight twinkled on fine blue dust drifting down.

Gradually, as the audience grew accustomed to the reports, Annie increased the charges and then switched to the rifle. As her range lengthened and the feats crowded incredible, the applause became sincere, and when she split a playing card at forty paces with her back to the target and a hand mirror in front of her, the cheers nudged the white clouds sliding overhead and the seats swayed under pounding feet. She joined hands with Butler and curtsied, her accolade buffeting her ears like a hot wind. Will, watching from behind the bleachers, shouted to cotton-bearded John Nelson, mounting the Deadwood coach, that he'd heaps rather send him into a real Cheyenne massacre than ask him to follow Little Missy.

But the Indian attack on the coach had the audience rooting wildly for the driver with his exploding whip and powerful lungs and its valiant defender firing blanks from a rifle at the pursuing band. When the rocking vehicle glowed with red fire, suggesting that its occupants were roasting alive, there was the kind of eerie stillness that sets in only when twenty thousand tongues are paralyzed. At this point Arizona John scanned the rapt faces closely. A woman had collapsed from the suspense at Louisville, but he hadn't learned about it until it was too late to interview her, and he was loath to pass up the opportunity a second time. But Chicago bred stouter stock; when the scouts arrived to drive away the savages and rescue the passengers, relieving the tension, he said, "Shit," and went back into a huddle with Prentiss Ingraham over a new biography they were constructing for Annie Oakley. With the exception of Buffalo Bill's, the publicist had yet to find a life that wouldn't benefit from a little extra juice.

"Whoop 'er up there, Jim!" urged the tough West Siders, laughing at the Pawnee war dance. "Dosey do!"

Said Salsbury, "They're not impressed."

Will grunted. "I'd admire to see how loud they'd laugh when one of those pained faces stuck itself through their wagon sheet some night on the South Platte."

Johnny Baker's marksmanship, brought along by Will and remarkable for a lad, sparked appreciative applause, but the crowd had seen far more spectacular stunts performed by a mere girl and looked to their programs for the next act. The pageant showing life in an Indian camp gave them a chance to rest eardrums ringing with gunfire. Then a buffalo hunt, the braves donning robes and horns to infiltrate the herd, then yelping and shrieking and turning the great dumb beasts with their lances until they had a proper surround, the earth growling under the drumming hoofs before they turned them over to trained cowboys who drove them out of the arena toward the corrals.

The climax, recreating Buffalo Bill's desperate duel with Yellow Hand, was played out in tense pantomime, broken only by grunts and blows as the star and a formidable Cheyenne from the Powder River reservation lunged at each other and grappled, their wicked knives catching the sun. The collective sigh that went up when Will pretended to thrust his blade into the Indian's rib cage and his opponent gasped and buckled was like a sudden break in the weather. Then he bent over the body of his vanquished foe, and as he came up with the victim's warbonnet in one hand and his "scalp" in the other, the band jumped in with a victory sting that blew the audience to its feet, beating palms and shouting.

Again the grand parade, Indians and cavalrymen who had died in the arena resurrecting themselves to join their fellow performers. At last the star claimed the grounds alone for a bellowed "Hail and farewell!" and with a final wave of his hat cantered back the way he had come under a brassy canopy thrown up by the band.

As the spectators filed out to take advantage of the souvenir items for sale in the smaller tents, Salsbury moved among them smoking a cigar and inhaling superlatives. But for a moderate nod to the vices, this pastime was his main diversion, and his wife's one rival. On this occasion he found it more satisfying than at any other entertainment with which he had been involved, and almost as satisfying as the sound of Jule Keene counting the take in the treasury tent.

Between shows Will and Arizona John Burke invited the Chicago press to a beef barbecue in the arena. The derbied journalists squatted on the ground with the Indians and walked around gnawing great black greasy hunks in their fingers while the sweet aroma mingled with the manure stench that overlay the exhibition grounds and Bronco Bill rode a steer borrowed from the Union Stock Yards between the grandstands, whooping and sending reporters diving for cover under the seats and trestle tables holding up champagne buckets and kegs of foaming beer.

"Make certain you write 'Buffalo Bill's Wild West,' the whole name at all times," a cigar-chomping Burke advised a pale young man with a pubic moustache writing furiously in a pad. "It's copyrighted. The Wild West has gone generic and fallen in with some hard company."

"Speaking of Doc Carver," said Will, approaching with his entourage and Nate Salsbury, "I hear the Evil Spirit of the Plains is touring the Southeast, mostly on borrowed steam from our brief partnership."

"That peacock." Salsbury, who in Eastern togs stood out from the group in long hair and buckskins, had spent all spring and most of the previous fall expunging all trace of the trick-shooting dentist whose irresponsible arrogance had come near to aborting the show in its first season.

"We showed a sixty-thousand-dollar loss last season," the star told the reporter, "but we'll not be in the red long. We've been turning them away since Louisville."

"How do you respond to P. T. Barnum's charge that you stole the idea for the show from him?" asked the young man.

"If he thinks we've one of his freaks, he's free to buy a ticket like everyone else and see for himself."

"What about the rumors that Annie Oakley is really a man in disguise?"

"Highly unlikely," said Will with a twinkle. "She shoots better than any man I ever knew."

He finished the interview after a few more questions by thrusting a mug of beer into the reporter's hand while Arizona John poked a fistful of cigars into the man's breast pocket and, drunk with generosity, handed one to each of the men in the group. Turning away, he almost bumped into a tall Arapaho wrapped in a red blanket and stepped back involuntarily. In ten years of dealing with Indians he had never been comfortable in one's presence. Although as an accomplished liar he was adept at concealing his unease, the brave's stern copper features and lashless black eyes were not calculated to relax him.

"Good smoke?" inquired the savage.

"The best." Burke patted his pockets automatically. "I've run out, but I'll bring you heap big cigars when I get back from town this afternoon. A whole box."

Salsbury said, "He can have mine." He gave it to the Indian and lit it. The Arapaho withdrew, nodding and puffing great blue clouds.

"Grateful chap," remarked the manager dryly.

"The Indians have no word for thanks." Will shook hands heartily with the young journalist and drew Arizona John aside. The famous baritone sank to an earnest murmur, his breath redolent of whiskey. "Whatever you do, don't forget those cigars. Maybe you didn't mean it, but don't ever promise an Indian anything without delivering. Get a box of cigars in town and charge it to me. Don't forget."

"I won't."

"I hope not. If you break a promise to an Indian, you'll be no good to me or the show."

Burke pondered this advice on board a train across-country a few weeks later.

In a pleasant, book-lined office smelling of tobacco and leather bindings and sunlight at Fort Yates, D.T., James McLaughlin fingered his cold pipe thoughtfully and finally laid it in a brass ashtray with a buffalo embossed in the bottom. A clean-shaven man with very white hair and gray eyes whose lids turned down sadly at the corners, the Indian agent met Arizona John's gaze with the kind of directness that disconcerted the publicist almost as much as the nearness of the Indians themselves.

"You have to understand that he's coming on sixty if he isn't there already, which among the Sioux is very old, and difficult to deal with. He has the respect and fear of every brave on the reservation, and that makes him dangerous. Also he's as slick a swindler as you're likely to meet this side of St. Louis."

"An entire generation brought up on the legend of Custer is well aware of that," Burke replied. He tapped a thick forefinger on the letter he had placed on McLaughlin's desk, indicating the official seal. "But I have Secretary of the Interior Henry M. Teller's permission to exhibit the chief, and instructions from my employer, the Honorable William F. Cody, to secure him for the Indian Village portion of our entertainment."

"He's a medicine man, not a chief," McLaughlin corrected automatically. "As agent in charge of the Standing Rock Reservation all I can do is grant you an interview, as he is a ward and not a prisoner of the United States Government. If he doesn't want to go he can't be made to."

"That's fair."

"He'll be difficult to persuade. Last year Colonel Alvaren Allen came to him with a letter just like this and promised to arrange an audience with the President in return for his cooperation. He agreed, and got no closer to Washington City than a New York wax museum, where he was placed on display with the Napoleons and Simon Girtys. His memories of the experience are bitter."

"I shouldn't wonder. Breaking a promise to an Indian is unforgivable."

McLaughlin looked at the fat man in dandified scout's garb with new respect. "That's right. You've dealt with them before?"

"I'm an old campaigner." He pushed himself grunting to his feet and tugged the hem of his fringed shirt down over his paunch. A ruby cuff link glittered in a sunbeam slanting through the window behind the desk.

The agent got up and reached for his hat. "Just take care while you're talking to him he doesn't relieve you of those fancy studs."

A grim escort of Indian police on Army mounts accompanied Arizona John's buckboard on the half-day ride to Grand Camp, their features burnished copper under broad-brimmed campaign hats and their braided black hair hanging down the front of blue tunics, cleaving a raw gash between two worlds. The bleak scenery made the publicist sick at heart. Stories of blue-pine mountains in Montana and startling eruptions of raw color in the deserts of the Southwest hadn't prepared him for the sterile, treeless bar top that was southern Dakota Territory, baking dirty yellow under a June sun. The oven heat parched his lungs and made shimmering black ghosts of the false buttes on the horizon.

"Is it like this all summer?" he asked the agent.

"No, it starts getting hot around the end of the month."

At first, they passed many tipis with Sioux women and children sitting in their shade grinding corn and sewing cotton patches on old buckskin, the men in floppy hats tending burned-out gardens in back; when the Indians recognized McLaughlin riding with Burke they waved and called out affectionate greetings to "Father Whitehair." Then the signs of habitation grew sparse and finally vanished, and the visitor wondered if they had taken a wrong turn. But in a little while they drew within sight of the barely running stream that was Grand River, and the agent pointed out one of a pair of squat log cabins on the opposite bank.

An Indian boy of about twelve stood in front of the cabin, watching the small procession splash across the river. Naked except for a breechclout and moccasins, he had a man's strong features and the beginnings of adult muscles in his hairless chest and shoulders. His ribs showed clearly.

"Hello, Crow Foot," McLaughlin said, when they had come to a stop before the building. The escorts' mounts stood shaking off water and pulling at spidery clumps of dead grass poking through cracks in the hard earth. "This is Major Burke. He would like to speak with your father."

The boy studied the stranger without speaking, then turned and went inside. Waiting, Arizona John became conscious of eyes on him, and looked around at the graven faces of Sioux braves surrounding the party. Some of them sported glistening white scars like worms on their brown arms and torsos.

"They came down from Canada with the old man when he surrendered," explained McLaughlin quietly. "Most of them were at the Little Big Horn."

Burke's clothes felt clammy.

Three women swathed in blankets came out of the cabin, the third wearing a white man's Stetson with a butterfly pinned to the crown. Crow Foot followed on her heels.

"Seen-by-Her-Nation and Four Times," the agent murmured, removing his hat. "His wives."

Arizona John followed his lead. The air felt cool on his scalp with his hair plastered to it by sweat. "Who's the squaw with the hat?"

"That's not a squaw. That's Sitting Bull."

The revelation startled him. He looked closely at the Hunkpapa medicine man whose vision of soldiers falling upside down into the Indian camp had united the Sioux, Cheyenne, and Arapaho nations and led to Custer's massacre nine years before. Sitting Bull was small and slight, with hair dangling in graying, unadorned plaits and the puffed eyelids and fallen features of an old Chinese woman. He shuffled a little when he walked.

McLaughlin made introductions—the Indians looked at the stranger without speaking—and the two stepped down and followed Sitting Bull and his son into the cabin. The women stayed outside. Dismounting, the Indian police stood sentry at the door while the suspicious braves loitered out front. Inside, gray light fell on surprisingly handsome furniture and straw pallets on an earthen floor. There was a black iron stove, and the air smelled of wood smoke and stale grease. Still taking his cues from the agent, Arizona John sat cross-legged on the floor across from the Hunkpapas, ignoring the various chairs. Sitting Bull spoke briefly in guttural Sioux.

"My father wishes me to speak for him in the white man's tongue that I have learned in the mission school," said Crow Foot, when the old man had finished. The boy chose his words with care. "He says that Longhair Cody is welcome in his house."

Burke, whose hair was indeed as long as his employer's now, corrected the error in leisurely fashion. "You have to be patient when you talk to Indians," Will had tutored him. "They take a long time coming to the point and they hold it rude when you try cutting corners." He complimented the medicine man on his family and fine dwelling and agreed that it was hot outside, but not as hot as the year of the brown grass, and expressed delight that his host had dreamed of a gentle rain that would swell the Grand River and paint the fields as green as moss on the mountain pines. Crow Foot translated, betraying neither pleasure nor embarrassment at the publicist's comment that he was a handsome young brave. Finally he broached the subject of his visit, for punctuation opening a box the size of a cigar case to display its contents and explaining that there were many more such boxes and many red blankets in the wagon outside, gifts for the great Sitting Bull.

Will had decided that hard candy was best. "It holds up in the heat and even if the chief hasn't any teeth, as Indians seldom do past the age of thirty-five, he can still suck on it. They generally favor sweets ahead of women and horses." Arizona John set the box on the floor between them and waited for the boy to finish interpreting, searching the medicine man's oriental face anxiously for a reaction, but in vain. There was a brief pause, and then he spoke at length. Crow Foot translated simultaneously, in bursts of English.

"The day has gone when the red man will be bought with blankets and candy. The white father in Washington has said that the red man must learn to live in the white man's world. I have seen the white man's world, and know that money speaks there with the voice of eagles. If I am to live in that world, I must speak with this voice. With it I may buy all the blankets and candy I will ever want or need."

"I was coming to that. We are prepared to offer fifty dollars a week and living expenses to the great Sitting Bull if he will agree to tour with the show for four moons." Burke felt himself on firm ground now. Dealing with Indians was getting to be like dealing with everyone else.

"Here it comes," said McLaughlin.

The other white man glanced at him. The warning was so low he was about to ask him to repeat it when the old Hunkpapa started talking again.

"In your city of Bismarck I met Bluecoat Grant and took part in a ceremony to open a new trail for the iron horse," relayed Crow Foot for his father. "Photographs were made of me and the man who made them asked me to write my name on them. He said people would pay much money for them and promised to share the money with me. His tongue was straight; I came back to Standing Rock with much silver in a cloth bag. I will join Longhair Cody's show if he will promise me all the money from selling photographs of me. I will have this in writing, as words on paper are the only words the white man heeds."

Arizona John deliberated. The photograph concession was one of the Wild West's more lucrative sidelines. Nate Salsbury would be livid. But Will had been adamant about signing Custer's executioner. Finally he nodded. "I will add such a clause to the contract."

Before his son could translate this, Sitting bull smiled broadly for the first time, showing naked gums and substantiating Will's conjecture about his teeth. In English he said, "We have a bargain, Major Longhair Burke."

Burke wired the news to Will, who put Prentiss Ingraham to work on press releases, and by the time the pair boarded an eastbound passenger train with a band of braves selected by Sitting Bull, they were engulfed by reporters, who noted the contrast between the publicist's portly cheer and the grave taciturnity of the Indians. He handed out cigars and metaphors by the bushel.

The great Sioux and the famed scout met cordially in Buffalo, and if Will was disappointed by his new attraction's unprepossessing appearance he concealed it skillfully, actor that he was. Sitting Bull told more reporters through an interpreter that Buffalo Bill was a sincere man and recounted again the story of Custer's death: "The longhair stood like a sheaf of corn with all the ears fallen around him, and he laughed." Crowds in Buffalo booed him for the Little Big Horn when he appeared before them astride a sleek white stallion larger than any Indian pony, and again in Boston, but they packed the stands to see him and bought thousands of autographed prints of the medicine man in an impressive headdress of bleached eagle feathers Will had given him. When his hand grew sore from writing his name, the show's photographer demonstrated how he could reproduce the signature on prints and save him effort, and for this the grateful Indian dubbed him "Fire-in-His-Hand," a name the flashpan-using artist wore proudly throughout his association with the Wild West. During rehearsals Sitting Bull watched for hours while Annie Oakley practiced her marksmanship, standing on the back of a galloping horse and shooting doubles from a speeding bicycle. He called her Little Sure-Shot—a nickname not lost on Arizona John, who saw that it found its way onto posters—and adopted her as his daughter. Having discovered a new taste in Boston, he thereafter extorted oyster stew from Nate Salsbury along with the usual candy, meanwhile giving whatever cash he had on his person to newsboys and orphans he encountered on the lot and in the streets. In the society where he had come to manhood, there was always a place for homeless children; he himself had raised eleven of his own and yet still found room for others. Some journalists who had witnessed these flights of generosity expressed doubt in print that this was the same fiendish mind that had plotted the greatest defeat of American arms in their history.

Spectators cheered him in Canada, where a flattered Sitting Bull posed in feathers and brocaded shirt next to a towering Buffalo Bill while the photographer held a candle to the touchhole in his pan and the little heap of magnesium powder ignited in a burst of blue-white light.

"Caption it 'Enemies in '76, friends in '85,' " Will instructed Fire-in-His-Hand. He was wearing a very wide Stetson and a black silk shirt beautifully embroidered in gold by Louisa, his slightly spreading middle cinched by a belt with a big square buckle. Thigh-length black leather boots creaked when he shifted his weight.

The group of reporters, lacking the technology to reproduce pictures on newsprint, contented themselves with numerous questions about the disastrous campaign of 1876.

"Did you ever meet Sitting Bull in the field?"

"I don't think so. He was not much of a chief but more of a medicine man."

"Sitting Bull, do you feel any regret at killing Custer and so many whites?"

"I have answered to my people for the Indians slain in that fight. The chief that sent Custer must answer to his people." This through an interpreter.

Added the frontiersman, "The defeat of Custer was not a massacre. The Indians were being pursued by skilled fighters with orders to kill. For centuries they had been hounded from the Atlantic to the Pacific and back again. They had their wives and little ones to protect and they were fighting for their existence. With the end of Custer they considered that their greatest enemy had passed away."

"Defends slaughter," scribbled the journalists.

In St. Louis, traditional final stopping place for Will's tours since *Scouts of the Plains*, the star was approached in the midst of hectic arrangements in the hotel lobby by a stout, gray-bearded man with thinning hair and skin the color and texture of leather chaps left hanging on a corral fence, dressed in evening clothes. Will shook his extended hand, then recognized him and embraced him, roaring, "Come meet an old enemy." With a hand on the other's back he swept aside a crowd of reporters and autograph hounds clustered around the medicine man. "Sitting Bull, this is General E. A. Carr, late commander of the 5th Cavalry. It's high time you two old warriors shook hands."

"I'm proud to make your acquaintance under happier circumstances," said Carr, offering his hand.

The Hunkpapa looked at him from under the brim of his butterfly Stetson and kept his hands folded under his blanket. After a quiet moment Carr lowered his. He said something cordial to Will and withdrew.

"Chief snubs general," the reporters wrote.

A living waxworks exhibit, Sitting Bull bore the hisses and catcalls one last time and retired to his tent after watching Annie Oakley's act, a silent man insulated by his circle of loyal Sioux from his fellow players.

At a little ceremony on the exhibition grounds that was closed to the press and public following the last performance, Will led the white charger the Indian had ridden throughout the season into the calcium-lit arena and handed the reins to Sitting Bull, saying: "Mind you hold on tight if there is gunfire nearby. He is trained to rear and dance on his hind legs at the sound of it."

Sitting Bull's gray eyes glittered. For a moment he remained unmoving, the reins slack in his hand. Then he grasped the scout's forearm with the other, pressed and let go. Annie Oakley, her face still flushed from performing, came forward and threw her arms around the little warrior. Then one by one the other members of the troupe filed past to grasp his hand and wish him luck. When farewells had been said all around, the stallion was tethered to the back of a wagon stacked high with blankets and boxes of candy and tinned oysters and a driver climbed up beside the Hunkpapa and they left for the railroad station, surrounded by braves on horseback. Sitting Bull never turned around.

"Sure wish we could have talked him into another season," remarked Arizona John, watching the departing band.

Will said, "One more like this one and he could of bought back Manhattan."

The roustabouts struck the tents and booths for shipping back to the barns at Scout's Rest and Will shook the men's hands and kissed the women's cheeks and said he'd see them back there in May, then went home to his family, bringing along Johnny Baker, whom Arta and Irma had come to accept as a brother. Louisa no longer came into town to bring her husband back.

CHAPTER TWELVE

Will folded his napkin and laid it down beside his scraped plate. "Let's shoot."

Excusing himself, Johnny Baker, who had been looking for that familiar gesture, got up from the table and went out to fetch the Winchester '76 carbine Will had given him, narrowly avoiding a collision with little Irma, who was helping her sister and the maid clear away the dishes. On his way outside with the weapon he stopped as always to thank Louisa for the meal. She nodded without saying anything and herded her daughters into the sewing room for their evening lesson. Johnny was never sure if she approved of his spending so much time there. He was too young to suspect a mother's doubts about a boy in his early teens hovering near her girls, and in any case, five-year-old Irma and seventeen-year-old Arta were both beyond his grasp even if he cared to reach. Firearms were his interest, had been since he was ten and happened upon one of Ned Buntline's Buffalo Bill stories in a North Platte general store. When the Wild West was wobbling and jerking along under the Cody-Carver partnership, the boy had presented himself at the ranch and begged for an unpaid spot with the show. He had brought along his squirrel rifle, and when the scout hesitated, he had showed him how he could drive nails into a fence rail at thirty paces.

Declaring that he showed promise, Will had engaged him to toss the glass balls he had substituted for Doc Carver's nickels, meanwhile tutoring him between performances in what he called "the manly art of triggernometry." With a little help from Annie Oakley and Frank Butler, the boy was fast becoming the youngest crack shot on the fading frontier.

They rode out from Welcome Wigwam to Scout's Rest Ranch, Will aboard Old Charlie, Johnny on a fleet sorrel mare, another gift from his mentor and surrogate father. As always the boy's heart grew big in his breast as they passed through the gate onto the four-thousand-acre spread with its thousand acres of alfalfa shrugging in the wind and as much planted in corn twelve feet high, green as emeralds to the horizon, beyond which grazed cattle and buffalo and, in the great stands of trees grown for Arta's sake, bull-throated elk and deer whose soft brown eyes Will had once admitted he could never look into and pull a trigger at the same time. Here he and Texas Jack and Buffalo Chips and Wild Bill and Billy Comstock, who had competed with Will for the title Buffalo Bill, had chased and been chased by the wild Plains Indians who were now growing tattered and toothless on reservations. It all seemed like something that had happened a long time ago, and yet in the boy's own lifetime the prairie had gone from warriors to corn.

They stopped in at the castlelike headquarters building to pay their respects to Will's sister Julia and her husband Bill Goodman, supervisors of the ranch, and found ox-shouldered, honest-faced Goodman rubbing down his lathered chestnut in the stable.

"It's been awful dry," complained the brother-in-law after greetings had been exchanged. "I'm thinking we'll lose the northeast hundred and sixty if it don't rain soon."

"Irrigate," said Will.

"The Platte's down. It'll cost."

"It'll cost more to lose that much alfalfa."

"I don't know, Will. You put more into irrigation than you take out, and every time it gets to look like we might show black you add on, and then that has to be irrigated too."

"The show grossed a million this season. I can stand it."

"Colonel," Johnny put in apologetically, "we're losing the light."

They said good-bye to Goodman and rode out toward the south pasture, past corrals containing some of the fifteen hundred horses Will raised, the half-grown colts running in circles and tossing their dished heads, their unshod hoofs kicking up clods of earth and manure. Will ground-tethered the mounts in the open and walked away carrying a spring trap and an armload of clay pigeons. After a hundred yards he glanced back to see if

Johnny was ready, then loaded the trap and swung it back and brought it swooping forward side-hand, launching one of the black and yellow disks in a high wide loop. Johnny nestled his cheek into the Winchester's stock and led the pigeon for fifty feet before pressing the trigger. The carbine pushed at his shoulder and a piece flew off the target. The rest of it wobbled to the ground while the report shattered against the distant hills.

"Sorry, Colonel!" He levered in another cartridge.

"A hit's a hit. Let's try another."

This time his bullet struck the projectile square in the center, blowing it to bits. Will's whoop echoed the joy in the boy's heart.

Four more pigeons flew, the last two at once. He burst the first two, got a piece of the third, and missed the last entirely. It completed its arc with impudent grace.

He reloaded and tried again. The next set of doubles exploded obligingly, then a single, then a triple. Will varied the pattern cunningly, but Johnny had swift reflexes and a good eye. He finished with a score of seventeen for twenty. Then it was Will's turn while the boy acted as second. The scout started with Lucretia Borgia, the converted Springfield needle gun that had seen him safely through the Indian wars, then switched to the repeating Winchester for the multiple shots. He missed twice at the beginning while he was still getting used to firing bullets instead of sand, as he did in the arena. Glass balls were harder to hit than clay pigeons, and he was one of the few sharpshooters in the world who would admit privately that they were not as good as that female phenomenon Annie Oakley. While reloading he told of Hickok's putting ten shots through the *o* in a saloon sign at a hundred paces and piercing a knothole in a tree trunk while galloping past on horseback.

Johnny loved this last hour of daylight, when school was out and ranch business was finished and there was nothing for the men to do but shoot and tell stories. He wished he had his own to tell, and was acutely conscious that at his age Will had slain his first Indian, been ambushed by Mormons, and ridden Pony Express, but an evening with Colonel Cody was worth a year on the changing plains. He dreaded mealtimes, dominated by Arta's troubled silences and the tensions between Will and Louisa. It was a little better with Arta now that she was seeing that young Mr. Boal, but as she blossomed, the gulf that separated her parents seemed to broaden and deepen with the unspoken inevitability of ancient erosion. Shooting, there was just a man and a youth and targets to be destroyed, simple goals and instant satisfaction. Thus they spent the hour when the man-made forests to the west caught fire in the sinking sun and night hammocked down purple from above, and thus they spent the days of mellow reflection between the exhausted rage of summer and the narrow blind glimmer of winter. To breathe alfalfa on the Nebraska wind and shoot clay pigeons with Buffalo Bill: What other ambition could a boy have?

Winter came and stayed and blew itself out. Will and Johnny, wrapped in cowhide coats with the fur reversed, rode the snow-swept ranch and helped pull shivering heifers out of holes in the river ice, the scout cursing white vapor and recalling similar duty for Alexander Majors the winter he turned twelve. Nate Salsbury came to Welcome Wigwam often to discuss the coming season, those discussions usually taking the form of classroom instruction as the manager showed Will wardrobe sketches and equipment plans and new scripts already decided on and paid for out of net profits. At these times Johnny thought that the man for whom the exhibition was named looked more like an employee than a decision maker, nodding automatically at the other's recommendations as if they were commands. It bothered him to see his idol behaving in this meek fashion, like an idiot child in the presence of his master, and he generally excused himself from these meetings. The earth warmed.

May, 1886.

A white train, painting a ghostly streak through the cities of night, its mother-new cars shrieking BUFFALO BILL'S GREAT WILD WEST in arrogant gold and carrying 240 performers, bookkeepers, scribblers, and strong backs, a complete power plant, livestock, a painted canvas mural depicting a Wyoming mountainscape, band instruments, trunks of wardrobe, lumber, and enough weapons to wage a new war for the frontier. St. Louis, Terre Haute, Dayton, Wheeling, Washington, D.C., New York City. A new feature making its debut on Staten Island on the tenth anniversary of the annihilation of the 7th Cavalry, the Battle of the Little Big Horn: ululating redskins and wailing bugles and plunging horses, hissing arrows and stinging blue smoke, Buck Taylor standing six foot five in borrowed blond curls among the tightening ring of savages, then the final heart-shattering report and deadly silence while the naked white shaft of the spotlight followed Buffalo Bill onto the field carpeted with blue-clad bodies, head bowed, while the solemn legend TOO LATE flashed on the canvas backdrop.

The patriotic New Yorkers hurled insults at Chiefs Red Cloud and American Horse when they rode next to the star during the parade up Eighth Avenue and flocked around the feathered former warriors for their pictographs, stylized drawings of a cloud and a horse in place of signatures.

Fifth Avenue hotels put up the attractions, technicians, and roustabouts —suites with views for the Indians now, no more roasting in unpopular rooms next to the kitchen. Will and his party commanded a floor of the old Fifth Avenue, where he and Nate Salsbury received aristocratic Governor Hill, Mark Twain with his cigar and white suit, P. T. Barnum, limping and half blind, old jealousies forgotten, long-haired Henry Irving (Arizona John introduced the visitor, a decade away from knighthood, as "a British actor of no little note"), and Brazil's Prince Dom Augusta, whose battleship was anchored in the harbor near the blazing copper newness of the freshly erected Statue of Liberty. The dignitaries competed with a steady stream of bellhops heading for the presidential suite with chilled champagne and coming away with five-dollar gold pieces. Meanwhile the famous and obscure packed the Staten Island ferry to watch Buck Taylor invent bulldogging and hear Con Groner tell how he took Jesse and Frank James off the train in North Platte.

A month before the Madison Square Garden opening, Will, in his underwear and pinstriped pants, greeted Salsbury at the door of his suite. The manager frowned at the glass in the scout's hand.

"Steady, Nate," boomed his partner. "I'm not working today, remember?"

Salsbury shrugged and came in past him, removing his derby. His dark hair had begun to recede at the temples and his beard was powdered with gray. Three years of fourteen-hour days had aged him and made inroads on his iron constitution. He sniffed the air.

"I like your cologne. Lavender, isn't it?"

Will grinned sheepishly. "Come on out, missy," he called.

A girl in her middle twenties entered from another room. Her red hair was pinned behind her head and her pleated russet dress swished and rustled when she walked. Salsbury interested himself in a framed painting on the wall while his partner helped her into her wrap and saw her out the door.

"They're getting younger," the manager observed as the elevator doors clanked shut in the corridor outside.

"No, you're just getting longer in the tooth." Will uncorked a bottle on the serving cart.

Salsbury said, "If that's for me, no thanks. It's still daylight."

"It's not for you." Will topped off his own glass.

They sat on the satin-covered couch and discussed the Manhattan show. Salsbury was planning a "Drama of Civilization" that would chronicle the nation's development from the Pilgrims' landing to the present day. "We'll go deeper into American history, that being what they'll pay to see when we get to Europe."

"Europe?" The scout was coming back from the cart after a fresh refill.

The famous physique was much in evidence under the thin cotton of his underwear shirt, but without the restraint of a broad leather belt his belly was beginning to stick out. He was forty and looked a few years older, but in a way attractive to women, with laugh wrinkles at the corners of his eyes and flinty threads in his hair and goatee.

"Yes, we sail for England in the spring. We've discussed this before. A fellow named Robinson in Yorkshire is putting together an American trade exhibition, and I'm sending Arizona John over to iron out the details for including the Wild West. It will be the only truly American offering at Queen Victoria's Golden Jubilee."

"It will be a feat getting all those Indians and animals aboard a boat. Noah had it easy."

"It's just a big ferry like at Staten Island," said Salsbury, and allowed himself a rare grin. "The *State of Nebraska*. I think that's appropriate."

"I like it." Will drained his glass a third time and sprang up, no less steady than when he had admitted his partner. "Damn it, Nate, we've got to drink to it or it won't be any good."

The manager fingered the seat of his burgeoning ulcer uncertainly. "Oh, all right," he said at last. "The sun's down in England."

Attendance records shattered at the Garden, where the Park Avenue elite plunked down fifty cents a head to sit next to butchers from Brooklyn and watch Steele MacKaye's wind machine blow down an Indian village and hurl the Deadwood coach across the arena like a toy boat in a pond. Many of them were on hand in the Battery the following spring when Buffalo Bill's Wild West boarded the *State of Nabraska* for England while the band played "Oh! Susanna" and streamers flew like late snow. Some of the eighteen buffaloes in the hold bellowed a terrified response to the harsh stridency of the steam whistle.

The equinoctial gales struck in mid-ocean. The vessel pitched and yawed on a foaming sea, its decks slick with salt water. Buck Taylor—greenish, his shoulder-length hair hanging lank and wet, flannel shirt and jeans stiff— tapped on the door of Will's cabin and let himself in without waiting for an answer. He found the scout sprawled in his captain's chair with a glass in one hand and a bottle in the other. A Rochester lamp swung from the ceiling, slinging lariats of shadow up alternating bulkheads. Taylor, his long frame bent almost double under the low ceiling, gripped the door handle for balance.

"Colonel, the injuns is all sick as curs. I'm thinking they're getting set to throw theirselves overboard soon's they find where that is."

"Tell 'em to line up behind me." Will upended the bottle into the glass.

I may walk it, or bus it, or hansom it; still
I am faced with the features of Buffalo Bill;
Every hoarding is plastered from East End to West
With his hat, coat and countenance, lovelocks and vest.

Londoners accustomed to seeing the soot-blackened masonry of Picadilly and Whitehall papered over with Arizona John's riotous posters chuckled at the newspaper doggerel and chanted it on the Royal Albert docks at Gravesend, where helmeted bobbies pressed back the crowds while a tug towed the *Nebraska* toward shore. A small local band on board the tug struck up "The Star-Spangled Banner" and was answered by the Wild West ensemble with "Yankee Doodle," the result being an ecstatic and incoherent collision of brass. Will, in cocked Stetson and a chamois leather coat with a white fox lining, a quart of whiskey holding down his storm-tossed insides, stood waving among a colorful collection of green Indians and pale cowboys at the railing. The tribesmen swayed a little under their feathers. Chief Red Shirt, resplendent in a warbonnet whose train dragged the deck, leaned heavily on his lance, his faith in Sioux tradition restored. Superstition held that evil would befall those braves who dared to cross an ocean. Indeed, High Heron and Has-No-Horse had already given away their possessions so that they might enter the Land of Shadows without earthly encumbrance, and Sergeant Bates, late of the Bluecoat Army, had stopped talking about his part in the white man's Civil War (or about anything else) for the first time in living memory, preferring to remain below decks with his bottle and a bucket handy. The chief's skull rang with the exploding strains of the unfamiliar marches and the incessant yammering on shore. It seemed that the white man was noisy in all his lodges.

Mercifully, the music came to an end, uncovering the rusty squeaks of seagulls and whooshing crowd noise. When the gangplank was in place, Arizona John Burke, broad as a board fence in a ruffled white shirt and a ten-gallon hat, bounded aboard accompanied by a group of bewhiskered men in morning coats and silk toppers. Wringing Will's hand, the publicist introduced the directors of the American trade exhibition led by Lord Ronald Gower.

His lordship, tall and thin with a Vandyke beard like Will's, but jet black and waxed to a wicked point, shook the scout's hand warmly. "I welcome you on behalf of Her Majesty's government to the British Empire. Special permits have been issued to allow you to land your animals, and there is a boat train waiting to convey you and your company to the Earl's Court grounds in Kensington." He smiled engagingly, steely British nobleman's teeth glittering behind the waxed moustache, and the officiousness went out of his tone. "I should also be supremely honored if you would consent to sup with me at my estate this evening."

Will's grin reflected his. "Your Lordship, I can't think of anyone I'd rather strap on my first feedbag with in England." He introduced Nate Salsbury, turned out for the occasion in silk hat and cutaway, and ticked off the names of the longhairs in frontier finery standing around him. Buck Taylor cut a swath of winces among the welcoming party as he worked his way down the line of outstretched hands with his steel-corded grip. Presently, they were joined by a tall, dark-eyed woman with auburn hair done up becomingly on top of her head, in a blue silk gown that caught and threw back the light. Will touched her elbow gently. "My daughter, Arta Cody."

Lord Gower doffed his hat and declared that he was charmed. Still looking at her but speaking to Will, he added that she would of course accompany her father to dinner. Beaming, Will replied warningly that she was spoken for back in the States. Arta colored and shot him a glance that reminded him uncomfortably of her mother.

Earl's Court was a third of a mile in circumference, with open grandstands for twenty thousand spectators, sheltered stands for another ten thousand, and standing room for ten thousand more. The American trade exhibition occupied a row of long, covered buildings, with the rest of the area reserved and equipped, at a cost of $130,000 thus far, for the Wild West. All day, to the intense interest of gawkers and journalists from as far north as Edinburgh, cowpokes riding lathered mounts harangued and prodded queasy, frightened and stumbling livestock down a reinforced ramp into the arena toward special stalls, the Texas longhorns glaring red fire at the hooting East Enders lining the way. Chimney sweeps and lamplighters admired the richness of the Americans' profanity. One of the ten elk caused a minor panic when it sprang toward the crowd, nostrils quivering, sunlight glinting off the points of its antlers, but it rejoined the herd when a cowpoke cantered in and fetched it a sharp blow across the muzzle with his quirt. After that the watchers called him Disraeli. They cheered the "red Indians," and some of the braver souls asked Buck Taylor for his autograph, mistaking him in his long hair and drooping moustache for Buffalo Bill. He obliged, cheerfully signing "James Butler Hickok."

When the animals were in place and all heads had been counted, Will gathered the band and had them play "God Save the Queen" for the benefit of the spectators, who applauded and whistled when it was done. Then a gang of reporters broke from the crowd and made for the star, unlimbering their pads and pencils as they walked. Will's longhairs moved forward to head them off, but Will stepped around and faced them like Custer mounting his rise.

"Did you slay Chief Crazy Horse?"

"No, he was killed by a treacherous agency Indian."

"Whom do you consider the greatest Indian fighter?"

"General Nelson A. Miles."

"What was Wild Bill Hickok like?"

"He was a magnificent specimen of manhood and one of the most deadly shots with rifle or pistol that ever lived."

"What do you think of the Conservative Party?"

"Can't say. I haven't been invited to one yet."

The questions flew like Sioux bullets, so many and so fast that he could answer only one out of three. Asked if Annie Oakley had really single-handedly defended her Quaker family from hostiles during a day-long siege, as Arizona John and Prentiss Ingraham maintained, he advised them to put the question to her, "as she is standing over yonder." No, he wasn't planning to run for President in '88. Yes, Sitting Bull was his friend. No, he saw no conflict between that and his statement on record that he had been friendly with Custer too. They asked him what he thought of the Queen and he replied that he held her the greatest female since St. Joan and looked forward to entertaining Her Majesty at Earl's Court.

"Small chance o' that," scoffed the gentleman from the Manchester *Guardian.* "The old girl 'asn't attended a public function since Albert died in '61."

"Maybe no one's thought to ask her," Will considered.

As the rest of the company was sitting down to dinner at trestle tables in full view of their admirers, Will donned his best linen, tails, and white sombrero, linked arms with Arta in a satin evening dress designed and made by her mother, and took a waiting carriage to Lord Gower's country estate. There the scout was introduced as "Colonel Cody" to a dizzying succession of earls and dukes and duchesses and baronets and ladies, whom he started out addressing by their titles but after wine was poured and he forgot who belonged to which he ended up hailing as "hoss" and "missy," much to the delight of everyone but a group of browned officers just back from India. The men in dress uniform kept to themselves, slinging hard glances at the Americans and not speaking until a major seated next to Will turned blood-shot eyes and a grand nose raw with burst vessels on the frontiersman in the midst of an account of the Battle of Slim Buttes and announced, "I understand you're a colonel."

Will interrupted his story to respond politely that he had been commissioned a colonel in the National Guard by Governor Thayer of Nebraska. The other didn't appear to have heard the explanation.

"You Yanks are dashed fond of military titles. Sir, I believe we may have to come over and give you fellows a good licking."

"What, again?"

Listeners the length of the table hesitated, then guffawed and beat their palms, silencing the bewildered major. The other officers grinned and proposed toasts to the scout and his daughter.

After a nightcap of Napoleon brandy under a fierce tusked boar's head in his lordship's game room, Will yawned and shook his host's hand, reporting that dawn comes as early in England as in America, and went back into the dining room to look for Arta. He felt a strong twinge of memory when he found her in a corner pretending to listen to a young captain reliving the fight for Majuba Hill. He extricated her. In the carriage on the way back to Kensington, she commented on his unusual quiet.

He patted her satin-covered knee. "Your papa was just reflecting on how pretty you looked tonight, and how much like your mother. You're the age she was when we met."

She laid a hand on his, and they rode in silence through the English night, as dark as patient death.

The Widow of Whitehall stepped down from her carriage-and-four and climbed to her box with the aid of a cane and "God Save the Queen" at her back, looking to the performers gathered with their hats in their hands on the exhibition grounds like a stout crow surrounded by cardinals, the famed black gown and bonnet cutting a somber patch of mourning out of the scarlet livery of the outriders. The imitative dark hues of the dresses worn by the royal women and the gray coats of their escorts lent counterpoint to the swirl of bunting and costumes in the arena. As Lord Gower accompanied Colonel Sir Henry Ewart up the stairs behind the royal party, someone among the Americans, accustomed by now to the comings and goings of princes and prime ministers, stage-whispered: "Why, she looks just like someone's grandmother."

"She is, to half the crowned heads of Europe," replied Nate Salsbury.

Will mounted Old Charlie and galloped up to the royal box alongside Sergeant Bates in cavalry dress, the scout waving Old Glory. The old woman in the center of the box hesitated, then rose with obvious difficulty and bowed. The spectators roared. Overcome, Will handed the colors to Bates, who dipped them. At that point everyone in the box stood, the women bowing, the military men saluting, while the band played "The Star-Spangled Banner."

Watching from the end of the grandstand, Bob Haslam, friend from Pony Express days and a veteran of Captain Jack Slade's raid on the Cheyenne camp, shook his graying head and spat a brown stream of tobacco. "Everywhere that cuss goes he makes him some more history."

The Queen came intending to stay for an hour and remained throughout the show, watching the Indian pony races and the pageant of American history from colonial days and the "First Scalp for Custer" and Annie Oakley and Johnny Baker shooting the blue glass balls and the attack on the Deadwood coach.

Will relieved John Nelson in the driver's seat next to jolly Edward, Prince of Wales, a frequent visitor to the show's rehearsals and, like Will, a poker addict. Inside, the kings of Greece, Denmark, Saxony, and Belgium, representing their countries at the Jubilee, held on to their silk hats and the wooden sides while the coach rocked and bounced and its driver uncurled his whip over the horses' heads to stay ahead of the pursuing Indians.

After the rescue Will helped down the chubby heir to the realm and opened the door for the flushed and chattering monarchs. "Colonel," said Edward, flicking a cinder from a flaming arrow off his sleeve, "I'll wager you've never held four kings like these before."

The scout winked. "I've held four kings many times, but the Prince of Wales makes this a royal flush."

Protocol dictated that female royalty extend a hand, palm down, to be kissed. Sixteen-year-old markswoman Lillian Smith, schooled in custom but overcome with excitement, shook the hand of the Princess of Wales, whose face, lined beyond its years from waiting for her husband's ascension, brightened. She matched the sharpshooter's warm grip. Unaccustomed color came to the Queen's pouched cheeks when the great scout in his white doeskins and the grand duke's diamond stickpin kissed her hand and answered questions at length about his life on the plains.

"Tell us, Colonel, how many red Indians have you slain in combat?"

"Well, Your Majesty, let's just say that I never killed any that didn't deserve it."

Chief Red Shirt lowered his feathered head before "the white grandmother" with the reserved and graceful dignity of a European ambassador, explaining through a half-breed interpreter that he had come across the Great Water especially to see her. "My heart is glad within me." The monarch returned his bow, eyes shining. She complimented the squaws on the papooses they presented for her approval, examined a handsome silver-inlaid Winchester displayed by Miss Smith, demonstrating a keen interest in the weapon, and admired Will's gold-hilted saber, presented to him by officers of the United States Army in recognition of his services. Looking levelly at Annie Oakley, she intoned: "You are a very, very clever little girl."

That evening she filled many pages of her journal with her impressions of the dashing American scout, gushing like a love-struck schoolgirl.

Journalists wandered through the Indian village, sidestepping snarling yellow mongrels and sketching squaws preparing meals over open fires in front of the colorful tipis. Offered a buffalo-horn spoonful of dark stew, the *Evening News* representative tasted it reluctantly.

"Why, this is quite good."

"Fat young dog best," said the squaw, pleased.

"The red man is changing every season," a seated Chief Red Shirt told the correspondent from the Sheffield *Leader* with the interpreter's aid. "The Indian of the next generation will not be the Indian of the last. Our buffaloes are nearly all gone, the deer have entirely vanished, and the white man takes more and more of our land." He was silent for a moment, then spoke in a rush, spitting his consonants. Haltingly, the embarrassed interpreter added: "But the United States Government is good. True, it has taken away our land, but the government now gives us food that we may not starve. They are educating our children and teaching them to farm and to use farming implements. Our children will learn the white man's civilization and to live like him."

"Chief seems cranky," the journalist recorded.

Will and Arta took rooms in Regent Street, where the scout lived in a white tie and received American dignitaries, matching James G. Blaine's politician's grin and shaking hands with stiff, professorial Joseph Pulitzer, ill now and too blind to edit his own New York *World.* (*"Leise, Herr* Colonel, *leise, bitte,"* begged the raw-nerved publisher in German, shrinking from his host's bellowing speech: "Softer, softer, please.") Russia's Grand Duke Michael brought regards from his brother Alexis and confided that although he had come to London to find a bride, he was most honored to have warmed a passenger's seat in the Deadwood coach. Will mimicked Oscar Wilde's terrified expression when the Indians swept near him in that seat, compared combat experiences with Crimean and Franco-Prussian war veterans, and listened attentively to European retellings of Greek myths. "That fellow Hercules must have been a pretty good cuss," he said, pouring. "Now let me tell you about Wild Bill."

The show wintered in Manchester, where the Prince of Wales visited almost daily, finally presenting its star with an engraved gold watch crusted with rubies. Touched, Will embraced the future king and gave him the saber with the gold hilt. At the close of the English season the following May, Will's hearty "Hail and farewell!" was answered by a ragged but thunderous chorus of "For He's a Jolly Good Fellow" from twenty thousand throats raw from cheering. The crowd that gathered on the quay to see the

Persian Monarch off for America bearing its cargo of guns and buffaloes and weary but smiling entertainers was larger than the one that had shouted encouragement to the British troops leaving for Africa.

"Old fellow, your journeys are over."

Will drew a deep, shuddering breath and let it out slowly, nodding to the deckhands gathered at the gunnels, who lifted the canvas and tilted the covered, already stiffening carcass out from under the United States flag and over the side. Twenty-one-year-old Charlie, equine survivor of the war for the plains, slid into the calm water with scarcely a splash, bobbed for a moment, and glimmered away under the gunmetal surface to a rest far removed from the lands he had known.

The Wild West came home to brass bands, gifts, and speeches and got ready for a reunion performance at Staten Island while its star entertained the famous and wealthy who came to bask in the warmth of his energy at the Waldorf-Astoria. When the run finished, he rested with Louisa and Arta and Irma—growing up now—at Welcome Wigwam and visited his sister Julia and her husband Bill Goodman at Scout's Rest, cutting chickens' throats for dinner with bullets from the matched silver- and gold-plated revolvers presented to him in New York by the Colt Patent Arms Company. He toured the ranch with Bill Goodman, planned new irrigation canals and more trees for the southwest section, and shot quail and clay pigeons with Johnny Baker. Correcting galleys for a new edition of his autobiography, he told Louisa, "I played Windsor Castle, but I'd heaps rather be home." She went on sewing without response.

In the fall of 1888, Nate Salsbury started talking about the Paris Exposition.

CHAPTER THIRTEEN

"*Vive* Bouff'lo Beel! *Vive* Annee Oaklee! *Vive les* bock'roos *et les sauvages!*"

Members of the company were recognized in costume and mufti, eating in cafés and drinking in bistros, riding in carriages and trolleys, walking along the Left Bank and the Champs Élysées (where Parisians thronged shops advertising buffalo robes and buckskin shirts and stood in line to buy hasty translations of Prentiss Ingraham's *Border Romances of Buffalo Bill*), and celebrated as no one had been in that city since Austerlitz. Will's graying mane and goatee were as well known as Napoleon's forelock, and those who had seen Little Missy extinguish candles on rotating wagon wheels and snatch six-guns off the ground from horseback at full gallop and then obliterate glass balls flung into the air by Frank Butler needed no prompting to gather around the quiet Quaker girl on street corners, demanding her autograph. During public appearances they pelted the company with questions in fractured English about the American West, the boldest among them running fingers down the Indians' bare arms to determine whether the red came off. The braves, many of whom had accompanied the show on its first trip abroad and recalled the reserved and polite British with affection, cared little for the earthy French.

Will thanked Thomas Edison, visiting the exhibition with his wife, for the incandescent bulb. "If not for you we'd be doing one show per day and shutting down at dusk," he shouted into the inventor's good ear. While Prince Roland Bonaparte tried out his English on the Indians, the star uncorked many agonizing hours spent conjugating French verbs on the trip over to converse with the Vicomtesse Chardon de Briailes and showed off his swift grasp of Spanish with ex-Queen Isabella, who rode in the Deadwood coach. The Shah of Persia wedged his imperial buttocks into the same seat on another occasion, holding the experience the highlight of his European tour.

Rosa Bonheur's Victorian black bonnet and smock were seen in the tents and stables and on the exhibition grounds, where she sat with paints and easel, quietly and discreetly peeling years off the scout posing for her on his white horse Billy in a plain fringed shirt and water-stained Stetson from the old days. When the painting was finished and presented to Will, he had it packed carefully and shipped home to Welcome Wigwam. Within days the Bois de Boulogne was crawling with artists, sketching the Indians and the magnificent sheathed musculature of the Percheron horses that hauled the wagons and helped pull up tent stakes. From old habit the braves begged yellow and vermilion off the artists for war paint.

Annie Oakley, who made her own costumes, commissioned several Paris gowns for fancy dress and contributed ideas to designers fascinated by the frontier attire she kept in a custom trunk that doubled as a dressing table.

At the end of summer the company toured the South of France and then boarded a train for Barcelona. There it rained.

"Some folks like the rain," growled Will, pouring from his steel flask into his coffee cup. Swift drops pattered the canvas overhead, and the military tent smelled like wet hides from his boots and oilskin drying next to the stove. "I never did. Seemed like there was always a message to be carried way the hell out on the prairie just when it was coming down like whores' drawers and I was the only rider handy." He held up the flask, raising his eyebrows inquisitively at Nate Salsbury, who sat on the other side of the camp table warming his hands around a steaming china mug. The manager shook his head. "Plus it reminds me of the weather that season in New Orleans," Will added, sipping noisily.

"Frank Richmond's got the grippe." Salsbury, coming down with a cold himself, sniffed morosely. "If he doesn't get better by tomorrow we'll have to get someone else to announce the acts."

"It's not as if he'd have anyone to announce to."

"Things aren't as bad as all that. We've been drawing."

"We'll be lucky to make expenses. If these Spaniards don't see a bullfight on the card they stay home."

"Arizona John's out taking pictures of the Indians in front of a statue of Columbus he found in town. The newspapers ought to eat that one up. They can print pictures here now." His enthusiasm rang hollow in the mildewed air.

Will sweetened his coffee some more. "I'm thinking we should cut our losses and go on to Italy. The weather's better there anyhow."

"We'll stick it out here until the end of the week. If there isn't any—" Salsbury broke off. Arizona John Burke had ducked through the flap without announcing himself, water streaming from his hat and poncho. His broad face was blood-red and he was puffing like a broken steampipe. "We got trouble."

"What happened, you get your flash powder wet?" The scout's speech was beginning to slur.

"There's a government health inspector down by the Indian village fixing to place the show under quarantine."

"For what?" Salsbury was on his feet.

Burke hesitated. "Smallpox."

Will grabbed his outerwear.

The three found fifteen men in comic-opera uniforms and rain capes rounding up Indians and herding them roughly toward their tipis with side arms drawn. Off to one side stood a sallow little man with a flat-crowned black hat screwed down to his eyes and a tan slicker that hung like a tent to the tops of his shoes and dragged in the mud. He sniffed the air distastefully between himself and Will and introduced himself in heavily accented English as Dr. Miguel Razaforte of the Ministry of Public Health.

"What's this about smallpox?" Will demanded. The rain lancing in under his hat brim steamed on his flushed face.

"The smallpox, the influenza, what else God knows. Your people they are very sick. It is my duty to protect my countrymen from the sickness you bring."

The scout placed a hand on the arm of a Sioux brave being prodded past. "Bad Heart, is anyone sick in your lodge?"

"Squaw of my brother Dog no get up. He beat her, still no get up. Bad spirit climb in through her mouth when she sleep." He hurried off, wrapped in a soaked stinking buffalo robe.

"Six of your Indians have the influenza," rapped Razaforte. "Much vomiting, purging, fever. Your man Richmond has it also; he will die before the week is out." He went on, ignoring the stricken look on his listeners' faces. "One of your laborers, your *trabajadores*, your—" He struggled for the word, his fierce black moustaches twitching.

"Roustabouts," Burke provided.

"*Sí*, roustabouts. He has the pox. There are many sick in Barcelona, señores." He waved a small nervous hand in the direction of a group of ragged vagrants, Spaniards not connected with the show, huddled in the warmth near the mess tent entrance. "It is a bad thing that you allow this filth in here. Someone should have warned you they breed disease."

Salsbury made an involuntary shift away from the wretches. "Are you shutting us down?"

"It is my duty. No one goes in or out for six weeks. Longer if there are deaths."

"Six weeks! Just sitting here is costing us four thousand a day."

"That is not my concern. These men have orders to shoot anyone who tries to leave." His black eyes were impassive. "I shall arrange for medical help and disposal. You will of course be billed for everything, including cost of cremation. Welcome to Barcelona, señores." He bowed smartly and left.

Enraged, Will swung to face Arizona John and almost lost his balance, which made him madder. "It's your job to ride herd on the Indians. How come I didn't hear about this before?"

"It's news to me, Will." The publicist shrank back slightly. "They're always complaining about something, it's in their nature. How was I to know there was anything behind it this time?"

"You're paid to know."

"Have you dealt with influenza and smallpox?" Salsbury asked the scout, seeking to draw his wrath. He was genuinely afraid his partner would strike Burke.

"Some." It was working; Will's brow knitted in thought. "Find out which Indians are sick and separate them from the rest. Post guards at their tipis and see they don't leave, but for Christ's sake don't let the guards touch anything. Get some sulphur fires going. Burn gunpowder. I want everyone in the show to stand in the smoke five minutes each day. It helps to kill the miasma. No exceptions, Nate; that means you and me and John too."

Salsbury and Burke saw to the arrangements, rounding up cowboys to serve as reluctant guards at the contaminated lodges while the healthy Indians pitched their tipis several hundred yards upwind, the squaws and children with relatives in the quarantine camp wailing. The stricken roustabout was moved to a cot in the tent where the light equipment was stored. Soon he was joined by another, and then two more came down with rashes and fever. Frank Richmond, the ringmaster, seemed to rally the second night, and died the following morning. By that time the first roustabout was dead and two others were delirious. Meanwhile, from the Indian village rose the rhythmless death chant that had never failed to lift the hairs on the back of Will's neck after bloody skirmishes on the plains.

"How many dead now?" He raised his voice over the roar of water lashing his tent. The rain had turned into a gale. Through the open flap he could see performers and roustabouts struggling to secure canvas torn loose by the mounting wind. Lightning shattered the lampblack sky.

"Two from smallpox," Salsbury shouted back, "and eight Indians from influenza. I don't hold any hope for the others." Panic haunted the whites of the manager's eyes above the gauze wrap he had taken to wearing around the lower half of his face. He was a lifelong hypochondriac, and terrified of death. Will had never thought higher of his partner than in the past few days, during which he had come into daily contact with his chief fear and yet still continued to function. Now the scout recognized the first cracks in the façade.

"We got to get out of here, Nate. Smallpox wiped out the Mandans and damn near did for the Pawnees. If we stay here we'll all die."

"How? The government's doubled the guard. They'll shoot to kill."

"Either way we're dead. This way we got a fighting chance." Seeing the fear sharpen in the manager's eyes, he chuckled reassuringly. "It won't come to that. I listen to you in matters of business, Nate, but now we're in my jurisdiction. I've not been just sitting here drinking while you and the others were lighting fires and separating sick from well. I got passage for the whole company aboard a tramp steamer for Italy."

Salsbury tore aside the gauze. "But how are we going to get on board? No one gets past those guards."

"Don't insult me. I once snuck a band of gunmen into a Cheyenne camp without so much as waking up a dog. I can ride clear through these thick-eared Spaniards a hundred times out of a hundred and they won't hear anything louder than my shadow."

"When are we leaving?" After six years of listening to tall tales, Will's partner was still dubious. But he wanted to believe.

"Tonight."

"Tonight? In *this?*"

"Maybe you'd rather go at high noon on a nice bright day with the whole Spanish fleet sunning itself in the harbor."

"It's too risky. Even if we don't sink, how do you plan to smuggle two hundred and fifty-odd people past all those soldiers?"

"Not just people. We're taking along the livestock and equipment. We'll need it when we play Naples."

"Damn it, Will, this is a poor time to uncork that famous backwoods sense of humor." Salsbury's fury bordered on hysteria.

The scout was tugging on his boots. He stamped the carpeted tent floor with a sharp report that startled the manager into silence. Will stood. The two were the same height, but the scout's two-inch heels gave him an edge. "I wasn't always a showman, Nate. You forget that sometimes. Listen. Go to the treasury tent and draw two thousand in tens and twenties. Tell Jule Keene I sent you and sign for it. Bring it here. Then go find Arizona John and Buck Taylor and Johnny Baker and any ten roustabouts you can get hold of and tell them to break camp. Leave up the tents and tipis with the sick in them, and leave the sick for doctoring here. Everything else is to be loaded in the wagons and ready to roll in two hours. There's no telling how much longer this thing will blow. Got all that?"

Salsbury nodded. "What's the money for?"

"Phil Sheridan once told me you can't mount an attack without the proper weapons."

Responding dopily to their handlers' cursing, hoofs skidding in ropy mud and water to their hocks, the great Percherons snorted and whinnied and pulled down the tents, which were swiftly folded around the poles and fed into the beds of creaking wagons in total darkness. White flickering flashes bleached out roustabouts bucket-brigading trunks and crates into the waiting vehicles while thunder splattered and rain slashed their faces. Members of the troupe, allowed one piece of luggage each, climbed into ambulances and buckboards, their oilskins rustling like sheets of tin. Thunder-shy buffaloes and longhorns mooed and milled restlessly in their respective corrals.

"John, can't you get those Indians to move any faster?" Salsbury prodded the publicist, who was supervising the dismantling of the tipis.

"Not when they're working and looking back over their shoulders at the same time. They think their slain enemies come looking for revenge at night. The ghosts' powers are strongest when the sky is angry, Red Shirt says."

"They haven't seen Will."

In the downpour they waited, a train of wagons and animals half a mile long across a plain of bare mud that had been a city of tents two hours before. The horses stamped and shivered. Then Will, mounted on a black mare near the head of the column, shouted to the lead driver, who flipped his reins and started his team forward. The others fell in behind. Lightning illuminated the remaining tents and tipis as they rolled past, washing out the grim watching faces of the families who had chosen to stay behind with their sick. Then darkness poured back in and they were gone.

Johnny Baker, privileged to ride the colonel's white horse Billy, rode with the cowboys, flicking his quirt from time to time at the ears and rumps of straying buffaloes. A white bolt blasted a tree two hundred yards off, and in that instant of blinding clarity the youth found himself staring into the wooden face of a uniformed Spaniard standing close enough to touch his mount with the end of his rifle. In the blackness that immediately descended he waited, frozen, for the guard's reaction. Would he cry out, or shoot without warning? Johnny jumped at a deafening report, then realized that it was just thunder. There was no reaction, and he decided that the man had been too dazzled to see. The boy hadn't been told about the two thousand dollars Will had instructed Salsbury to draw from the treasury.

The livestock were driven and the cargo was carried up a reinforced gangplank onto the slanting deck of a rotting freighter, rolling and creaking on a wild sea while Will shouted in English and Spanish and exchanged gestures with the black-bearded captain on the bridge, eventually settling the dispute by shoving a fistful of cash into the other's sooty grasp. Deckhands and cowboys rigged a network of ropes between decks to prevent the tense animals from falling, and the ship cast off without running lights into the roiling blackness of the Mediterranean.

"Look!" exclaimed Johnny, pointing over the railing.

Nate Salsbury watched the uniformed Spaniards spilling onto the dock, Razaforte in his soaked hat and shining slicker shaking his fist in the light of a raised lantern and shouting soundlessly into the gale.

"Gentlemanly of him to see us off." The manager went below.

Will shared the first mate's cabin with Arizona John, who dragged in and dropped with a squish and a howl of strained bolts onto the edge of his bunk. The cramped quarters stank sourly of coal oil and stale sweat.

"Everything square?" The scout lay in the top bunk composing a letter to Arta in the light of a swaying lantern.

"The Indians are chucking buffalo jerky all over the hold, and the long-horns are doing their level damnedest to gore each other to death from fright. Aside from that I'd swear we were safe on Staten Island. I believe I'll stay home next trip. I'm getting too old and fat for all this European luxury."

Throughout the night the Wild West climbed oily waves and slid down the other side.

Naples glittered under a fat sun, blue Vesuvius standing in for the super-fluous Wyoming mural while the Indian pony races and the "Drama of Civilization" played themselves out against its smoking backdrop. When a brawl broke out in the stands over reserved seats, Salsbury ordered a check of all tickets and learned that one of the city's notorious confidence men had counterfeited and sold some two thousand over capacity. He averted a riot by sending Johnny Baker and Will's nephew Ed Goodman among the angry ticketholders with free passes for later performances. The Neapolitan police came and wrote down his complaint in their little leather-bound notebooks and tipped their absurd caps and went home. But the jammed shows quickly made up all losses. From there the exhibition went on to attract huge crowds in Milan and Verona and Venice, where Will had his picture taken aboard a gondola with four worried-looking braves and smoked cigars with Red Shirt in St. Mark's Square while Venetians and pigeons flocked around them. In Rome the American cowboys, challenged by the Duke of Sermoneta to tame his fierce stallions, made short work of the mankillers, to the intense disappointment of the watching Romans, who had come anticipating a bloodbath. Some of them booed. To placate them Will challenged the Italian horse handlers to try the broncos. The Americans laughed good-naturedly when the would-be riders were thrown, but Will put a stop to the contest when the terrified horses started bleeding from the irons and chains of local custom. He inspected the Colosseum, sighed, and chose a sturdier arena for the show's performances. The Indi-ans, unnerved by the vaulted echoing splendor of the Vatican and Arizona John's strict lectures on protocol, hooted at the Swiss Guards in their striped pantaloons but looked on in awe as Pope Leo XIII was borne be-tween their colorful ranks in his high tiara and yards of white satin and cloth of gold. Christian braves knelt with some of the cowboys and Burke to receive the pontiff's blessing. A pregnant squaw fainted. Non-Christian Indians murmured superstitiously as a Sioux holy man stepped forward to attend her. That night another woman died in the village. The holy man painted himself and danced and threw phosphor in a fire.

"White holy man bad medicine," a tall Oglala with gray hairs in his roach told Arizona John. "Kill squaw."

"Nonsense. The woman was frail before we left Spain. It's a miracle she survived the voyage across the Mediterranean."

"We go home now. Nine Oglala, four Miniconjou, some Cut Fingers." He made the sign indicating Cheyenne. "Some squaws and papooses. No more Europe."

"You can't just come and go when and where you please. You're wards of the United States Government under the Wild West's guardianship. Colonel Cody will be heap angry when he hears what you're planning. His heart will be bad."

"You tell Cody. We go home now." The Sioux turned away.

Arizona John found Will conversing animatedly with a uniformed customs official in his tent, augmenting his crash course in Italian with broad gestures. He heard the publicist out, then said, "Once an Indian's mind is made up, no white man can change it."

"You're not going to just let them up and go!"

"They're our charges, not our captives. But they'll go nowhere unless someone arranges their passage. Tell them to stick it out till Germany and if they still want to go I'll send someone back with them."

"If they leave, all the rest will go with them."

Will sighed. "John, you've spent more time with Indians in the past fifteen years than I did in all my years on the plains. Haven't you learned anything about them by now? They don't just all take off like birds leaving a telegraph wire because some of them are homesick. It took them twenty thousand years to get together for a few hours at the Little Big Horn. Do you really think they'll do it again for the sake of one dead squaw?" Burke didn't answer. The scout nodded as if he had. "Now go tell them what I told you and let me get back to some serious bribery. This poor excuse for local authority wants me to pay an entrance duty by weight on every animal in the show before he'll let us perform in Florence." He returned to the discussion. The dark little man had sat through the Americans' conversation with olive eyes darting back and forth between the speakers, uncomprehending.

The towering Oglala received the publicist's message without expression.

"I have heard you," he said when it was finished. Then he turned and went back into his tipi, leaving Arizona John standing outside, wondering. But the Indians stayed through the German tour.

In Germany the painted red men and their mock foes seized and held Berlin's Kurfürstendamm for a month while a generation reared on Karl May's tales of the frontier followed the action as informed as any of the audiences in New York and Chicago, counting each falling brave with guttural exhalations like a team of Prussian master sergeants calling cadence. Fat burghers in feathered headdresses strutted down the Wilhelmstrasse, their distended vests strung with their orders of office and tomahawks in their hands.

Between performances, Will inclined his head politely to a Junker in a tight black uniform and monocle, who shot to stiff attention, snapping his heels and dipping his bearded chin in salute. He had a drawing board in one hand and a charcoal pencil in the other.

"He doesn't look much like the artists I saw in Paris," Will remarked to Arizona John, watching as the officer sketched with quick deft strokes the trainers feeding the horses.

"He's Colonel von Something-or-Other of von Hindenburg's personal staff. You can't spit around here lately without hitting a uniform. They seem damn interested in how we feed and move the personnel and livestock."

"Maybe they're fixing to put on a show of their own."

"That's what worries me."

Rheumatic Joseph William Louis Luitpold, uncle of mad King Otto and Prince Regent of Bavaria, visited the show with his grown daughters at Munich, and returned to inspect Annie Oakley's guns and watch her plug a tossed coin in the arena. While he was wandering around, a bronco the cowboys called Dynamite broke loose and charged him. Annie shouldered the Prince Regent out of the way. Throughout her stay with the Wild West, the markswoman wore a gold bracelet engraved with the crown and monogram of Luitpold, a gift from the grateful future monarch. Prentiss Ingraham wrote up the incident for the pamphlets.

The company train loaded in Munich and wound through the Alps, its teakettle whistle echoing among the snowy peaks. Will weaved his way back from the club car and thudded into the seat beside Nate Salsbury, who was sitting with his eyes closed and a ledger open on his lap. "You all right, Nate?"

"Just tired." He spoke without stirring.

"Comes as no surprise. I don't know when you sleep."

"I don't."

"It ain't healthy, pard."

"It's been a busy couple of years. Your cut alone from this run figures out to a million. You can write Louisa and tell her you finally made good on your promise." Salsbury had heard about his partner's town-building venture in Kansas in 1869.

"I'll need it. Arta's getting set to marry that Boal fellow. I cabled them a

THIS OLD BILL 159

bank draft from Munich." He paused, watching the sunlight glittering silver in the dapper manager's beard. His cheeks had a sunken look and there were dark leeches under his eyes. "You sure you're fit?"

He nodded and closed the ledger. "Getting old."

"You're my age."

"Not if you count time spent adding up columns of figures while everyone else is sleeping or out having a good time." He paused. "There's a fellow I want you to meet when we get back home. His name's Jim Bailey."

"The circus man?"

"That's him. I'm thinking of taking him in as a third partner."

Will glared. "What for? We're doing all right."

"We'll never do better. The trick is to stay where we are, and that won't be easy with competition like Pawnee Bill and Adam Forepaugh and half a hundred others planning their own European tours. It'll take fresh ideas, new blood. Bailey's got both. I'm running low."

"You're just tired. You said so yourself."

"I lied. I've a dozen things wrong with me, any one of which I'm assured will kill me if I don't draw rein. The short of it is this tour has knocked a number of years off my life I can scarcely spare."

"You don't drink enough," joshed Will.

"I've dealt with Bailey before. He has some ideas I think you'll like."

"No sideshows or freaks, Nate. That's one of the things Arizona John and I agreed on before you came in."

"Just meet Bailey, that's all I ask. If you don't like him, he stays out. That's fair." He slid back into his former slouch and resettled his hat over his eyes.

The scout frowned. "Every time I hear the word 'fair' I feel around to make sure I still have my wallet."

Salsbury's only response was a mild snore. The train chugged on in counterpoint.

CHAPTER FOURTEEN

The study was a museum.

The walls bristled with mounted buffalo heads and bows and lances and Melton Prior's framed sketches of Queen Victoria greeting the Wild West. Yellow Hand's warbonnet and cured scalp flanked an enormous stone fireplace over which hung Rosa Bonheur's impressive painting of Buffalo Bill astride Billy, while Lucretia Borgia, her original bluing worn down to bare steel, leaned in the corner. The rest of the decor had a crowded, haphazard look, items dumped in corners and larger souvenirs propped like disused storm doors against the walls. A photograph of William Tecumseh Sherman, signed in the general's crooked hand, stood incongruously in a jungle of family portraits on a rolltop desk mounded over with papers. For all that, the place had a warm untidiness about it, the tobacco-reeking carelessness of a room in which work was done, an occasional drink spilled, and a life lived. An old shoe of a room in which the visitor felt oddly at home. It was part of a suite that included a bedroom and a bath, and every room stamped with the seal of its inhabitant.

The door opened, admitting more warmth and a burst of sunlight in the person of a big man in worn riding clothes topped off with a big hat set at a jaunty angle, a large slab of raw youth with rusty iron in its long hair and beard and wrinkles around the eyes, emitting an outdoor aroma of leather and horse. The visitor's hand was seized in a surprisingly small paw with piano-wire tendons and wrung until the blood retreated protestingly up his wrist. The iron smile parted and a voice like a sustained blast on a steam whistle said: "Welcome to Scout's Rest, hoss. Didn't my sister Julia have a glass filled for you? No one leaves this place empty-bellied or sober."

"She made the offer, Colonel," replied the other, drawing back slightly, as anyone does when the door of a furnace is suddenly flung open in his face. "It's a tad early for me, I'm afraid."

Will laughed, the famous baritone fairly rattling the windows. "We'd've cured you of that quick enough on the hunt. I taught the Grand Duke to open his eyes with rye every morning and I hear tell he's still doing it with vodka."

"That was the Russian Grand Duke Alexis? Or Michael? You've met them both, I believe." The guest produced his pad and hunted for a pencil.

Will pulled at an ornate bell rope. "Alexis. You said in your wire you were with the Omaha *Herald?*"

"Yes, sir. My editor is anxious to publish the first in-depth interview with Buffalo Bill since the Wild West's return from Europe."

The maid came to the open study door. Determining that the journalist craved nothing, Will asked for rye and branch. "Just a twig," he added, winking broadly. When the servant withdrew, he transferred a stack of thick scrapbooks from one of a pair of stuffed leather armchairs to the floor, apologizing for the room's cluttered condition. "My house in town, Welcome Wigwam, burned to the ground while I was in South Dakota. Thank Christ no one was hurt. When I heard about it I wired orders to save Rosa Bonheur's picture and the rest could go to blazes. But our brave little party of brigaders got out almost everything of value, and it looks as if I'll have to rebuild just to make room for it." He removed his hat with a graceful flourish and sailed it at a peg next to the door. It caught and hung there.

Sitting, his guest explained that he'd heard of the family's misfortune. "It must be crowded here with all of you and your sister's family living under one roof."

"Well, Scout's Rest isn't your typical sod hut with a little building out back, and with Julia and Bill's boy still in Europe and my Arta making her home with her new husband, we don't all rub up against each other too much." He grinned down any potential argument. Actually, Julia and Louisa barely tolerated each other at the best of times and living together got along like bitch badgers in season. Whether he sensed the lie or not, the journalist changed the subject.

"How did you find Europe?"

"Easy. I just got off the boat and there she was. Much obliged, missy." He accepted a huge tumbler full of clear liquid from the maid, who curtsied and swept out, drawing the door shut behind her. "But I got to clear up something you said before. The Wild West didn't come back with me. It's waiting for me back in Alsace-Lorraine, where I left it along with some Sioux and Cheyenne to settle all this buffalo shit about me mistreating the Indians in my charge. *Pardon ma français,* hoss." His eyes crinkled over the glass.

"That seems as good a place to start as any. How do you suppose that rumor got started?"

"The herd's full of young studs fixing to pull down the old bull. I reckon they saw their chance when that bunch got homesick in Italy and started making noises about leaving the show. But they were the same bucks I brought back with me and they put a stop to that kind of talk in a blue-tick hurry."

"Some thought they were coached to say good things about their treatment."

For an instant Will's benign features hardened. Then he smiled and leaned forward and patted his guest's knee. "You ever try to get an Indian to do or say a thing he didn't want to?"

The journalist admitted that he was not long from Philadelphia and that he had not yet met an Indian in the flesh. His host chuckled.

"Let's just say it requires a brand of patience and perseverance I never could afford."

"But surely that press conference back East was just a side trip. You were recalled by President Harrison to deal with the Ghost Dance crisis."

"No, that come up after I got back." He was serious now. "I offered my services to General Miles and he accepted them with gratitude. The plan was for me to talk my old friend Sitting Bull into federal custody and let this Indian Messiah thing that's got the Army jumping like scorpions in hot sand peter out on its own."

"What stopped you?"

"Cheap politics, hoss. I was on the very threshold of Sitting Bull's camp at Grand River with a wagonload of his favorite hard candy and a band of armed men to handle the hostile braves around him when a wire came from Washington City countermanding Miles's orders. If not for that, the Hunkpapa would be safe under house arrest right now and the biggest worry at the agency would be whether the drought will kill the corn."

"But instead the Army is preparing for another Indian war."

"War, hell!" This time the windows really did rattle. "It will be the 7th Cavalry all over again, only in reverse. The Indians are counting on their painted shirts to turn away bullets. They'd better, because all they got to fight back with are a few Winchesters and those rusty old single-shot Springfields they took from Custer. Sweet Jesus, there ain't even buffaloes enough to make sinew for them to string their bows!"

The tirade had startled the journalist. When at length he resumed writing in his pad, his host sat back and sipped his drink. Quietly: "You're wasting your time here, son. You ought to be out in the Badlands, watching a proud race dangle to death on the end of a memory and an old man's wild dream."

For a space the young man's scratching pencil crowded out all other sounds. Then he brought up the scout's youth on the frontier. Will brightened somewhat and retold the whole thing, borrowing heavily from Ned Buntline and the play *Buffalo Bill*, forgotten after nearly twenty years. "When I was eight years old my father was stabbed in Salt Creek, Kansas, by a man named Dunne for speaking out against slavery. The mob would of cut him to pieces then and there except I fought them back until a neighbor came forward to help me get him to a wagon."

The reporter, a slim youth with innocent eyes and a hopeful moustache, took it all down with a child's faith. It helped that when Will thought back to that long-gone trading post, what he remembered was the way the incident had been portrayed on the stage. He spun a few lies about his Civil War experiences, then invited his guest to tour the ranch. He selected a roan gelding for himself from the stables and saddled up a sorrel mare for the journalist. "We always rode geldings on the scout," he explained, mounting. "Stallions got your hair lifted whistling at the Indians' fillies when you were trying to keep cover."

He pointed out the twin lakes he had named Arta and Irma for his daughters, and cattle grazing in the largest existing stand of buffalo grass, stretching tall and green to the horizon. Pointing southward: "Not three days' ride that way I had an altercation with Major William B. Royall, who was in temporary command of the 5th in '68. He sent me out for buffaloes to feed the regiment, but when I asked for wagons to bring back the meat he said, 'I am not in the habit of sending out my wagons until I know there is something to be hauled in.' " He mimicked a West Point tone of voice. "Next day I cut seven healthy cows out of a small herd and shagged 'em right into camp before I cut them down. Pony soldiers diving every whichway. Royall was standing there with a big curly at his feet wanting to know what the hell I thought I was doing. I said I thought I'd make the buffaloes furnish their own transportation."

"Colonel, you're arguably the most famous man of the century," said the other, trying to write and ride at the same time. "Any thoughts on that?"

He thought a moment. "Well, it beats hell out of waiting in line at the theater."

They rode to a rise from which they could observe the broad irrigation canals that linked the twisting braided Platte in the north to a swift creek dividing the ranch from east to west. Along the eastern boundary the buildings of North Platte stood like chess pieces on a board. The surrounding countryside was as flat as a wagon bed.

"You don't see anything like this in Europe," said Will. "There you can't turn around without sticking your elbow in someone's eye. I think that's one reason they're always fighting; someone's always sticking his elbow in someone else's eye."

"Do you think there will be war between France and Germany?"

"Son, I'd rather fight an Indian naked than answer a question like that."

They made their leisurely way back to the house while the sky to the west went from blue to bronze. Several times they crossed paths with lean-jawed cowhands heading out toward the big pasture. Invariably, they flipped him the casual two-fingered scouts' salute and said, "Afternoon, Colonel." He called them all "hoss." Asked why, he admitted with a shamefaced grin that while he could remember the troop strength of any of the outfits he had scouted for at any given time, he couldn't hold a name. Before they parted company at the stables, Will clamped a punishing hand on the journalist's shoulder.

"Remember what I said about going to the Badlands, hoss. When that's done you'll not see another Indian making a stand anywhere but on the grounds of an exhibition."

The young man shrank under his grip and assured him he'd think about the advice. Will looked at him closely, then sighed and released him and shook his hand again and watched him climb into his buggy.

"Philadelphia." He shook his head and went inside for a drink.

Coming up dawn at Standing Rock, red fire painting the low tops of the buttelike hills to the east. Will's breath and white-haired James McLaughlin's curled and mingled in the silver-thin air. The Indian agent and Yellow Hand's slayer had little to say to each other.

Presently a trooper wearing the absurd Prussian-inspired spiked helmet and flared tunic of the new cavalry appeared around the corner of the commanding officer's headquarters leading an old stallion whose fresh iron shoes rang on the frozen earth. Although it had grown gaunt and slat-sided from years of grass feeding, the beast had firm muscles on a frame larger than any Indian pony's. Will stroked its dished white face. "Easy, big fellow. You remember me, don't you?"

"Sitting Bull's family asked that the horse be returned to the Wild West," McLaughlin explained. "He never forgot your generosity and spoke of you often."

Will scratched the hollows behind the flicking ears and said nothing.

Suddenly the agent cursed. The horse shied at the abrupt exclamation. "It was a stupid misunderstanding. The Indian police thought Sitting Bull's Sioux warriors were going to shoot and Sitting Bull's Sioux warriors thought the Indian police were going to shoot. So someone shot. We're still sorting out just who."

"Why trouble with it? He'll still be dead when you've finished."

"Your way was no good either. Maybe you'd be dead too, and then we'd have a full-scale war on our hands. The War Department is burning to test its new Hotchkiss guns under actual battlefield conditions."

"I think that's what you were scared of from the start. That's why you tried to get me drunk that night here on the post, figuring I'd be too sick to go out in the morning. When that didn't work you sent a telegram to Harrison to get him to rescind the arrest order."

McLaughlin smiled grimly. "You outdrank some cast iron constitutions that night. Some of those whiskey-tough veterans are still wobbling."

Will tethered the horse behind his buckboard. "For what it's worth, I think you're a good man with Indians. Seems like no matter what stand we take with them it's over their cold carcasses." He offered his hand.

The agent hesitated, then took it.

"Strange thing," he said as the scout mounted the driver's seat and untied the reins. "When the shooting was still going on and Sitting Bull was dead, the horse reared and started dancing on its hind legs. The Indians who saw it swore the old man's soul had entered its body."

"He's trained to dance when he hears gunfire. I reckon he thought he was back in the arena."

"Maybe."

Will returned to Europe with the horse and replacements for the Indians who had gone back to their reservations. Black Heart, Short Bull, Kicking Bear, Long Wolf, Yankton Charlie, Scatter, and Revenge wandered seasick among the gingerbread villages and ice-cream peaks of Alsace-Lorraine and posed for Arizona John's inescapable camera with the Tower of London at their backs. Victoria entertained the company at Windsor Castle, confiding to her journal that Colonel Cody's beard had gone gray. "Sitting Bull's Last Mount" outdrew every other act in the show except Annie Oakley's and the star's own. Subsequently he rode it in place of old Billy, who like old Charlie before him died on board the *Persian Monarch* on the way home. Indians who had made the previous trip identified the sea burial to curious tribesmen as a tribute to the Death Spirit to insure a safe voyage.

"Good-bye, William. Write the girls."

At the door Louisa presented a powdered cheek, which he brushed lightly with his lips. Her skin was coarse, her figure growing matronly, and there were leaden threads in her hair. She had stopped accusing him of deserting her when he left on his frequent excursions. Moreover, she no longer accompanied him to the railroad station.

Bill Goodman helped load his bags into the carriage. "Are you going too, Irma?" he asked.

"Just to the station." Will laid a gentle hand on his daughter's shoulder.

Caped and bonneted against cinders, she was a bright, pretty child who took after her father in looks and energy, as lively and mischievous at thirteen as Arta had been quiet and withdrawn. Goodman helped her into the rear seat and turned to face his brother-in-law. A man measures his age by the people around him, and the scout wondered when Goodman's hair had finished turning white.

"Will, this is a hell of a time to bring it up, but you're a hard man to tie down lately. The ranch accounts are scraping bottom. I'm going to have to squeeze to make this month's payroll."

"What happened to that ten thousand I deposited last summer?"

"You used most of it to finish rebuilding Welcome Wigwam. I didn't want to say anything—"

"I haven't time to see to it just now. When I get to Chicago I'll wire the bank to transfer over another ten from my personal account."

Goodman looked embarrassed. "I was thinking you might give me permission to sell off that southwest five hundred. That way we could make expenses and still show a profit this year."

"No. Matter of fact, I'm considering taking on another thousand up north. It's for sale at a good price."

"This is getting to be a costly pastime."

Will patted his broad back. "Just keep on running her the way you been, Bill. I hear they're talking about Scout's Rest clear down in Mexico."

"I shouldn't wonder." Goodman climbed into the driver's seat.

At the station Will left the baggage to Goodman and a colored porter and lifted Irma down. He grunted. A bullet of pain sniped at his lower back.

"Your old father shook hands with Alexis on this very spot. He was as tall as a telegraph pole, but he could stick a rifle in the air and miss the sky. His brother Alexander is Czar now. Phil Sheridan was there. And Custer. His hair wasn't really yellow, but red like a prairie fire."

"I know, Papa. You told me."

He bent to kiss her, feeling again the sharp tug in his back. At the conductor's warning bawl he shook Goodman's hand, mounted the step, waved, and went inside to wave again from his seat in the coach. The hoarse whistle made the floor buzz under his feet. As the train rocked back and then rolled forward, he reflected that his daughter was almost as tall as his brother-in-law. Time slid like a shadow over his thoughts.

He spent much of the journey to Chicago in the club car with James A. Bailey, a small, wiry, jerky man his own age who wore rimless spectacles and a goatee and affected a pedantic superiority that irritated the scout. Some of the alcoholic conferences began with Nate Salsbury present, but after a few minutes the graying manager would invariably excuse himself to go lie down in his compartment and rest an aching head or settle a sour stomach. Bailey would then produce his own sketches and diagrams for reconstructing the show, chattering away to Will about lights and equipment and order of entry like some mad cross between an excited professor and a sideshow barker. Will looked at the circles and squares and nodded as if he understood everything, thinking that if all this was good enough for Nate he was no one to stand in front of it. But he backed up when his new partner mentioned one-night stands.

"It can't be done. It takes us days just to set up."

"That's what Barnum said, but I showed him how to scale down and take on a specially equipped circus train and doubled the circus's profits the first year."

"The Wild West is an historical event, not a circus. I'll not have it scaled down."

"I'm talking about padding, unnecessary duplication. Trick riders *and* trick shots, when we should be hiring performers who are both. And Will, have you ever in your life fired anyone? The publicity train alone is almost as long as the whole rest of the organization."

"That's Major Burke's department. Talk to Arizona John."

"Arizona John hates my guts. It will have to come from you."

"I'll not have him hate mine."

Bailey's spectacles reflected the scout's drawn features. "That's your trouble, Colonel. You're too decent for the show business."

Will walked in on Salsbury taking pills in his sleeping compartment and told him of the exchange.

"Hear him out, Colonel. He may have a point." The manager had taken to calling Will almost exclusively by his military title.

"You weren't there, Nate. He holds decency a fault."

"There are as many indecent successes as there are decent failures."

The scout left under a darker cloud than he had carried in with him. Bailey entered minutes later and presented his side of the argument.

"He has a skull as thick as a bull buffalo's and the business sense of a sixteen-year-old," Salsbury agreed. "For ten years I've been afraid to let him out of my sight, thinking he'll get in one of his generous moods and give those bloodsuckers he calls his pards shares in the show free gratis. I've spent hundreds of hours when I should have been working listening to his stories about Kit Carson and Wild Bill and all the rest and he's never told any of them the same way twice. I never know when he's giving me the straight of it. Now it's your turn, Jim. Why do you think I brought you in?"

"I assumed it was because you liked my ideas for improving the show."

"That's what I told the Colonel. I don't think he believed it any more than you do."

"You feel that way, why didn't you offer to sell me all of your interest instead of just half?"

"Because in spite of all our differences the Colonel and I are a prosperous match." He tunked the cork back in his pill bottle. "And because I like him. God help me, I like the silly prancing son of a bitch."

In this accelerated year of 1893 the Chicago World's Fair pulled in more people than had ever assembled in one spot in United States history. Their buggies and carriages invented the traffic jam on State Street and Michigan Boulevard, they hung out of trolleys and stood in the aisles of the Illinois Central, their combined weight strained the fresh construction of the elevated railway built just for them and threatened to swamp lake steamers paddling to and from the Loop. Fair organizers reported sadly that there wasn't room for the Wild West on the grounds. Rallying to the occasion, Salsbury leased a large empty lot across Sixty-third Street from the main entrance and had Arizona John announce that the show would be open seven days a week including Sundays, when the fair was closed. Between the end of April and the end of September, six million people came to boo the Indians and watch the glass balls burst.

"Ladies and gentlemen, permit me to introduce to you a congress of the rough riders of the world."

A magician's sweep of the great white Stetson, swelling ground, and then the charge of the feathered braves—Sioux, Arapahos, Pawnees, and Cheyennes aboard ponies painted bright as hobby horses, fresh-looking scalps braided into their manes and tails; behind them the black beards and fluttering pantaloons of the Cossacks on their great Arabs; Victoria's parade-dress lancers; Wilhelm's Potsdamer Reds in their plumed scarlet helmets and matching tunics; the U.S. Cavalry, slouch-hatted and gauntleted; Mexican vaqueros in black velvet and silver lace; American cowboys in chaps and kerchiefs; gauchos from the Argentine, whirling their deadly bolos; the clash and clatter of French cuirassiers in archaic breastplates; the loose order of the Texas Rangers under the Lone Star flag. Spectators punished their palms and unlimbered Kodaks to capture the event. The popular little black boxes bled color from the Pony Express re-creation and petite Annie Oakley shattering her old sharpshooting records, blurred the Sioux raid on the wagon train and the "Cowboy Fun" of the rodeo. In the smaller tents surrounding the big top, the fans bought autographed pictures and Prentiss Ingraham's Buffalo Bill dime novels—now selling for a quarter apiece—in case lots. Reporters fluttered around Arizona John and his six-foot Oglalas, pumping Chief Rain-in-the-Face for the details of how he killed George

Custer's brother Tom at the Last Stand. "The white longhair's pup brother slap and kick me at guardhouse in Fort Lincoln. I wait. I take hair." He posed for pictures leaning on crutches.

Will held open house in his Chicago hotel. Johnny Baker, a man grown now, wearing the Cody uniform of shoulder-length hair and buckskins— "Johnny" only to Will, who when he looked at the other's lean frame and clean square jaw still saw an underfed boy holding a squirrel rifle—came with his new wife and stood by grinning while the old man spent an afternoon charming the young woman, who had come expecting a swaggering Indian killer with whiskey breath and came away in love with him. In the buggy on their way back to their own hotel, she went on about the scout's polished manners and the strikingly beautiful woman who had graced the opposite end of the table. "You didn't tell me he had such a young wife," she chided.

"He doesn't," said Johnny, and changed the subject.

The woman's name was Viola Katherine Clemmons. A British actress of small renown when they had met on the Wild West's second appearance in London, she was taller and trimmer than Louisa and wore her golden hair pressed into flat curls on either side of a careful part in the center. Will liked her soft accent and the way she listened to his stories with wide eyes and many innocent questions, demonstrating an interest that his wife had long since ceased to pretend. They had begun meeting in secret, but with the suitor's likeness plastered on every outside wall between Gravesend and Soho they had soon abandoned the grotesque charade, and photographs of the two attending the opera and theater, the old scout grinning as if at gunpoint as he helped her out of carriages and opened doors for her, appeared in newspapers throughout the empire. In spite of Arizona John's Herculean efforts to prevent it, rumors of the affair made their way across the ocean to Louisa. Will had accepted her shrill harangue upon his return, and in the boldness of his injured pride cabled Viola boat fare to America. When she complained that she had no work waiting for her there, he made contact with a New York theatrical agent and offered to back a play, any play, that would star Viola Katherine Clemmons. By his own reckoning he had spent in excess of fifty thousand dollars on properties for his new love.

In his haste to get back to the hotel and Viola, Will strode rapidly through camp, puffing a cigar and trailing reporters scrambling to match his pace and write in their pads at the same time.

"Is it true that when you met the Pope at the Vatican you offered him a spot with the Wild West?"

He steered them toward Nate Salsbury and the Bedouin horsemen the partners had brought back from the Mediterranean, and slipped away while

Salsbury was showing off his studied Arabic with a tall chieftain in burnoose and beard. Twice visitors stopped the scout to have their pictures taken with Buffalo Bill. Just in time he spotted Arizona John heading his way with more reporters and ducked through the Indian camp, approaching his own tent from the rear. There he shook hands with the shiny-eyed children gathered around the entrance and invited them inside to touch Yellow Hand's scalp and examine his ornate Colts. The tent was always full of children, the boys all looking like Kit, dead these seventeen years.

CHAPTER FIFTEEN

"I'm obliged, Mr. Beck, but I had my fill of founding towns back in '68," Will said.

George T. Beck shook his large pink head. "It won't be like that, Colonel. We anticipate a thriving resort trade from the hot springs nearby, so there would be nothing gained from moving to another site even if we wanted to, which of course we wouldn't without notifying all our people. I have other investors interested in the irrigation project, including Mrs. Phoebe Apperson Hearst, mother of the New York newspaperman, and I am opening negotiations with the Burlington Railroad to build a branch line into town. I lack only fifty thousand dollars and a name like yours to get the show on the road, so to speak, heh-heh." The developer unsheathed prominent teeth in a premature ejaculation of a grin.

"What are you fixing to call the place, Mr. Beck?"

"Shoshone, after the river that will provide the water."

Will leveled off their glasses from the amber bottle on the desk in his study. "I like it," he said, raising his glass. "Damned if I don't."

They started building at the foot of Carter Mountain in northwestern Wyoming in the spring of 1895. They laid out hundred-foot-wide streets for fire control, built a hundred and fifty miles of sluices, threw up a commissary building for the graders and carpenters and a schoolhouse for their children. Will came to inspect the site, erected a cabin on the mountain, and wired Bill Goodman for ranch funds to buy more land in the vicinity. When Goodman explained that every cent was tied up in the operation of

Scout's Rest, his brother-in-law asked Nate Salsbury for five thousand dollars.

"I don't know, Colonel," the manager demurred. "The residents aren't going to like having to pay a quarter a barrel to ship water down from the Shoshone River."

"That's just till we get the sluices working. The loam there is twenty-one feet deep. Farmers will be able to stand out in the field and watch their crops grow. Tell you what, I'll sell everything I own to pay you if we fail to make money next summer."

Salsbury made out a bank draft for the requested amount. "I hope you're not planning to approach Bailey with the same offer," he warned, rocking a blotter over his signature. "He'll believe you."

The investors applied to Washington for a post office, but the Postmaster General, who had an existing office on the Shoshone Indian Reservation, vetoed the name. The partners put their heads together and made a happy decision. They called the town Cody.

Will sent for Louisa and Irma, who toured the sawdust-smelling city and the country beyond in an open carriage while the proud founder pointed out the site of the future Irma Hotel and the sulphur springs where Indians once bathed to rid themselves of evil spirits, and talked about the stagecoach stops he would construct along the road to Yellowstone National Park to house tourists. Louisa wasn't impressed.

"The only difference I see between this place and Rome, Kansas, is there are no savages," she said. "No red ones anyway."

"I was younger and dumber then, Mama. This time it will be me using the railroad instead of the other way around. The spur will go in along that ridge yonder."

"William, you're fifty years old. When will you grow up?" She and Irma left for North Platte the next morning.

The old scout's cabin was always full of guests who came to dip their pale bodies in the hot springs and hunt elk and bighorn sheep. One, an abrasive young Easterner with a barrel chest, beribboned spectacles, and an overwhelming energy to match Will's own, would bare his wealth of teeth in a friendly grimace as he wrung the other guests' hands, then proceed to lead the unfortunates assigned to his hunting party gasping up steep mountainsides and wading across swift-running streams and thrashing through dense undergrowth from first light to last, holding forth all the while on the virtues of the strenuous life. He would then stay up half the night drinking whiskey and discussing the ranch business and the growing trouble in Cuba with Will, retire for two hours, and be up again at dawn for another foray into the wilderness. Few of the survivors remembered his odd name, but their host called him Teedie and introduced him as the Police Commissioner of New York City. Nate Salsbury, now a full partner in the Cody project (albeit a reluctant one), stayed at the cabin only one night. When his partner and the neighboring Earl of Portsmouth tired of shooting playing cards out of each other's hands and started standing tin cans on their heads, the ailing manager of the Wild West chose to spend the remainder of his visit amid the comparative peace of the clattering hammers and creaking wagon springs in town.

Show members trooped in and out of the cabin between seasons. Annie Oakley and Frank Butler shot the heads off running squirrels in the surrounding woods. Johnny Baker showed off his two small daughters, much to the astonishment of Will and the delight of the childless markswoman, who had her picture taken with the girls. Viola Katherine Clemmons declined Will's invitation politely, wiring from Chicago that she was tied up in rehearsals for a play he was financing. He consoled himself with some of the women his hunting guests brought with them, brass-laughtered Denver sirens with hard faces behind the paint and southern belles in ruffles with honey voices and dollar signs in their eyes. Good times and whiskey flowed freely on Carter Mountain.

Not so water. The workers digging the sluices fought mosquitoes and each other and hacked their way through roots and broke their shovels against rock and cut up the construction gang's faces in the Cody saloon over the games and women in back. When gold was discovered in Alaska, many of them collected their pay for a stake and bought passage to San Francisco and points north. The manpower reserve dried up almost overnight. The developers asked the investors for more money with which to advertise for laborers and raise wages. Will was among the first to kick in with funds borrowed from Jim Bailey and from the banks against Welcome Wigwam and Scout's Rest.

Nate Salsbury kept out of it. On the advice of physicians he had cut his schedule in half, heaping most of the managerial responsibilities on Bailey, who was busy streamlining the show for one-night stands. Will took his mind off this blasphemy and his own problems of the heart by pouring more money into Cody. He bought land, advertised back East for customers, shipped in a printing press from Duluth and established the town's first newspaper, the *Shoshone Valley News*. Prospective buyers jammed the buggies and traps he placed at their disposal, thronged the bar six deep to "have one on Buffalo Bill"—and went home with their bank balances intact.

"The freeloaders always precede the serious investors," George T. Beck encouraged his famous partner in a letter that caught up with the Wild West in Brooklyn during the 1897 season. Will didn't answer.

The warship *Maine* blew up and sank in Havana Harbor just as rehearsals were getting under way for spring. When McKinley declared war against Spain and Will's old friend Teedie recruited some cowboys from the Wild West for a cavalry regiment he planned to lead to Santiago de Cuba, borrowing the name "Rough Riders," Arizona John persuaded his employer to issue a statement to the press that if the Army would place him in command of six hundred Sioux braves he would bring the war to a victorious conclusion within weeks. "It would be like getting back at Spain for '89," he pressed.

"All right, write out something and I'll sign her," said the Colonel distractedly, inspecting his loads. He forgot about the conversation by the end of the week.

"John! Arizona John!"

Young Dexter Fellows, an earnest-faced former journalist who had assumed much of the rheumatic Burke's publicity burden, hastened to the tent with the scout's head sticking out through the tent flap. "Get the major," Will snapped.

The publicist appeared moments later, puffing away in a gray flannel undershirt with the dickey and cuffs he wore in place of a shirt under his jackets. Will thrust the telegram under his nose.

WAR DEPARTMENT
WASHINGTON DC

COLONEL CODY:

DELIGHTED TO WELCOME YOU EXPEDITIONARY FORCE CUBA STOP WHEN CAN YOU COME ACCEPT YOUR COMMISSION

GENERAL NELSON A. MILES

"Now what, John? I'm up to my ass in bookings and you got me drafted." He stuffed his paunch into a pair of canvas riding breeches and struggled to button them.

"I don't know." Burke reread the wire. "We did it when Wounded Knee was coming up and again when it looked like we might go back to war with Mexico, and Washington turned us down both times."

"Get me out of it."

"I suppose I can tell the papers you're waiting for your orders or something."

"I don't care what you tell them. Get me out of it or I'll get you real major's clusters and take you with me."

Dewey took Manila and Roosevelt San Juan Hill while the hero of Warbonnet Creek was still sputtering and fuming for the papers about the criminal sluggishness in Washington, a strain he was playing yet when a battered and bloody Spain sued for peace. At the end of the tour, Will fled the reporters and Louisa for the TE Ranch, the new spread he was developing in the Big Horn Basin on the strength of a new Salsbury loan and a second mortage on Scout's Rest obtained from a Cheyenne bank. Four hundred thousand acres of pasture fed several hundred head of Herefords and Black Angus—over the vociferous objections of Bill Goodman, who had advised him to maintain a sturdy core of Texas longhorns against another winter like the disastrous one of 1886–87. On Johnny Baker's first visit without his family, Will took him on an overnight tour.

"Windy as hell up here," the young sharpshooter observed, huddling close to the fire on a bank of the Shoshone River. The flame wriggled and twisted in the icy gusts off the mountain.

Will blew steam off a tin cup of coffee with whiskey in it to cut the bitter taste. "This country is so close to paradise you can feel the breezes from heaven. When the angels flap their wings the wind comes right down this valley." He paused. "I've asked Lulu for a divorce."

Johnny looked at him over his own cup. "Oh?"

"She won't give it to me."

"Did you expect her to?" The younger man drank.

"Truth to tell, yes. I thought she was as miserable as me. I signed every bit of the North Platte property over to her and offered her an annual income if she'd cut the tether. But I reckon she's dead square set on making me more miserable. I'm taking her to court."

"Don't do it, Colonel. She'll make a prize fool of you."

"I just got done paying off the Waldorf-Astoria for a batch of furniture she busted up last month after she called my room at the Hoffman House and Viola answered. If she can make me a greater fool than she did then, it will be worth seeing. She tried to poison me once," he added.

"She did not."

"I was sick for days. But it would of been kinder than what she's been doing to me all these years. She's not given me one minute's peace from her nagging since we got married. A man can take being told he's not a man only so long." He doctored the contents of his cup some more from the steel flask he carried. "Soon's I get shed of her, I'm fixing to marry Viola."

"It will look sore as hell."

"There's a new century coming. Divorces aren't looked down on as they used to be. People are getting more enlightened. I gave her the chance for a quiet legal separation. Now it will be war and publicity."

"Folks are always on the wife's side in a divorce. Her lawyers'll drag out all that baggage about you and Viola and you'll lose your case. Worse than that, you'll lose your public in the bargain."

"I'd welcome it."

Johnny looked at his mentor.

"As a fellow gets old he doesn't feel like tearing about the country forever," Will said. "I don't want to die a showman. I grow very tired of this sort of sham worship sometimes."

Orange firelight crawled over the old scout's haggard features, scoring his cheeks and scooping black hollows under his eyes. As Johnny watched, something came into those eyes briefly, and he felt the cold wind from the mountain on his back. He laid another stick on the fire and lifted the smudged enamel coffee pot from the flat rock where it was keeping warm next to the flames. "Let's finish off this pot, Colonel," he said. "Get an early start in the morning."

"As I said to Barnum, a circus is a living organism. In order to remain successful it must continue to breathe, move, grow. You can't just keep giving the public the same things and expect them to remain loyal."

As he spoke, Jim Bailey towed his partners through the sideshow tent, introducing them to the fire king, the juggler, the mind reader, and the snake charmer in her skimpy attire with a python wrapped around her masculine body, finally having Will pose with a midget on his shoulder for one of Arizona John's photographers. "The sideshow is just that," he was saying. "The main draw will always be the Wild West, but the freaks will take care of the overhead. It's a new century, brimming with new concepts and undiscovered promises. We can't go on using the ones that worked in the last."

"No," said the star doubtfully, "I reckon we can't."

Salsbury said nothing. He had fainted once during a heated altercation with Bailey over the sideshow idea, but had managed to keep Will from learning of the incident for fear of upsetting the precarious balance of his confidence. The former circus man's high-handed irreverence for the ideals upon which the Wild West was founded irritated Salsbury only half as much as the awareness of his own mistake in bringing him in as a partner. It bothered him that he was too ill to fight back with the weapons he knew and that Will was too unschooled in business matters to understand that the problem went beyond approving the addition of a feature they both found repugnant. Moreover, Bailey seemed of the opinion that the show had been in trouble when he came along to "rescue" it; the happy accounts for the year preceding his involvement failed to dissuade him from this view, and the manager's suggestions were haughtily brushed aside with a speech that invariably began: "As I said to Barnum . . ."

But Salsbury, white-bearded now, his custom double-breasted jackets hanging on his skeletal frame, was in no condition to bear grudges, let alone his crushing responsibilities as manager, scaled down though they were. He missed many of the show's inaugural one-night stands, and as the company was preparing for a new European tour at the end of the 1901 season, he thrust a pale, shaking hand into Will's and informed him that he had sold the rest of his interest to Bailey.

The old scout's face worked. "You sure this is how you want it, Nate?"

"It's not a case of wanting. The flesh is weak."

"Wish I was going with you."

"You'll never retire, Colonel. The people won't let you."

Salsbury died the next year. The news staggered Will, unaccustomed to the mortality of show people. He was doubly stricken when Salsbury's family answered his condolences with a note that made it clear whom they held responsible for his early demise. He remembered having his picture taken once with Nate and his wife and new baby and couldn't reconcile that memory with this turn. By this time the show was making money in London and Marseilles, but was drawing smaller crowds and less publicity for all Arizona John's aging efforts.

"It's that J. T. McCaddon and his International Shows," Will grumbled. "He stuck that Wild West exhibition onto his circus just to spite us."

Bailey agreed. "He's got you in a pincers with George Sanger's circus on the other side. As I said to Barnum, this is a jungle, not a business. Plaster your posters over your competitors', and if they complain, make what publicity you can out of it."

"Wish to hell we had Butler and Oakley with us this trip."

At 3:20 A.M., October 29, 1901, the second section of the white train had slammed head-on into a slow freight near Lexington, Virginia. The show was traveling in three sections that year, but no one had informed the engineer of the freight, which had pulled back onto the main line after letting the first section pass. Both crews leaped clear just before the two locomotives swallowed each other in a hell of shrieking metal and spraying splinters, but Annie Oakley was flung out of her bed against the corner of her special trunk, tearing something loose inside her. Steam poured from the torn boilers and firearms popped and crackled as uninjured cowboys saw to the screaming horses. Frank Butler carried his moaning wife to a siding where the third section had become a makeshift infirmary.

"We lost about a hundred mounts, Colonel," Buck Taylor reported later. "Pap and Eagle among 'em. I reckon God was looking out for the people."

"What about Little Missy?"

"She's on her way to some hospital in New Jersey for an operation of some kind."

"Will she be able to shoot when she gets better?"

"I asked the doc about that." The cowboy paused.

Will looked at him from the entrance to his tent. He had been in the first section, and hadn't learned about the accident until reaching Danville. "Well?"

"He said he'd have to know if she's going to get better first."

At St. Michael's in Newark the doctors performed surgery to stop the internal bleeding, set her fractured wrist, and treated her for a sprained back. Will sent flowers and had the medical bills forwarded to the show. By that time the entire staff was referring to her as Little Missy, and Butler and Oakley had announced that they would no longer be performing with the Wild West.

"Nor with anyone else," Will confided to Jim Bailey sadly.

Old friends to see in London and on the Continent—Edward, on the throne now, white of beard and ailing, but with a sparkle in his eye for the days of the Deadwood coach and Buffalo Bill's "royal flush," and Grand Duke Michael of Russia, meeting the scout in Vienna with a bear hug and a special saddle standard, a gift from his brother the Czar.

"How old are you, Will?" Michael asked.

"Sixty."

"Is that all? Why, you are quite a boy yet!" They roared and Will refilled their glasses.

Before they left England, Johnny Baker read a social note in *The Times* of London about Viola Katherine Clemmons and her new husband, Howard Gould of Wall Street. Shown the item, Will moved his shoulders and accepted a child's program for autographing. "I would rather manage a million Indians than one soubrette."

Johnny quietly celebrated the end of the Colonel's divorce plans.

In Italy, visiting American humorist George Ade presented the snake charmer with a candy box from which sprang a mechanical snake when she opened the lid. Her shrieks alerted the entire troupe.

In France, glanders swept through the horse herd. Health inspectors representing the French Republic examined the stricken mounts and signaled the soldiers they had brought along, who unbuttoned the flaps over their side arms. Will stopped them and selected a firing squad from among the cowboys traveling with the show. They shot forty-two of the best horses the first day, and two hundred by the end of the week.

"We leave here with only a hundred mounts," Arizona John told reporters grimly, wincing at each report from the corrals. "The less said the better."

No bands or dignitaries, and only the New Yorkers and tourists who happened to be there, were waiting on the docks when the Wild West returned from its four-year European excursion. The show played a special engagement at Madison Square Garden. During the charge up San Juan Hill—a popular feature in England and France, where distrust for Spain had run almost as high as in America—Will gravely pointed out the banks of empty seats to Jim Bailey.

"Yes," said his partner. *"The Great Train Robbery* is showing on Broadway."

"Actors making believe in front of cameras." Will smoothed his hat brim with a disgusted gesture. "Why truck with that when they got the real thing here in person?"

"I don't know, Colonel. Maybe they're tired of the real thing."

In Cheyenne the bailiff borrowed city officers to hold back the crowds, and still the temperature in the courtroom rose from the body heat of too many people jammed onto the hard narrow benches and standing along the back wall, smelling of wool and sweat and fried chicken from the gaily covered baskets on the laps of some of the women. The standees made a path for the striking old man in his gray Stetson and three-piece black suit and the seated spectators leaned forward to hear the stout woman in mourning black occupying the witness chair.

"William is one of the kindest and most generous men I ever knew. When he was sober he was gentle and considerate. If I had him to myself now there would be no trouble. His environments have caused him to put this upon me."

A woman in the gallery wept loudly. Will, sitting at a table inside the railing with his attorney, didn't react to the speech or to the glares he knew he was attracting from the watchers. He wore a black armband on his sleeve for Arta—quiet, darkly beautiful Arta, dead in Spokane. "Her father's decision shattered her frail heart," Louisa had tearfully told the court. He remembered how well she rode.

Louisa's lawyer, hitherto the family retainer, pudgy and balding, with the face of a professional mourner and flecks of gray ash on his vest, questioned her obsequiously in a hushed, reverent tone that made everyone in the room strain to hear his words, including the judge. "Mrs. Cody, your husband has accused you of repeated failure to submit to your, er, conjugal destiny. Would you care to answer that charge?"

She flushed slightly and met Will's gaze. "I will make no answer, other than to remind him of the four children I bore him."

"Four times in thirty-eight years," muttered the plaintiff.

"You spoke, Colonel?" barked the judge.

"Nothing, your honor."

"Mrs. Cody," the attorney continued, "your husband further alleges that on a certain Christmas Day you attempted to poison him by introducing a gypsy love potion called"—referring to a paper in his hand—"Dragon's Blood into his coffee. Is this true?"

A nervous titter rippled through the gallery, quickly silenced by the judge's gavel.

"I admit to the act," she replied, "but not the intention he has assigned to it. It was both a vain and desperate attempt to reclaim William's love and to release him from the wicked bonds of alcohol, temperance being an advertised property of the elixir. Only a wife who is truly devoted to her husband would enter into such an endeavor."

"We're with you, dear!" called a woman seated two rows behind Will.

"Remove that woman," the judge told the bailiff.

Louisa's testimony and those of her witnesses ground on for days, inexorably eroding Will's case. He sat head high and stone-faced while his affair with Viola Katherine Clemmons was examined ("I suppose he wants a young wife") and his frequent desertions of home and family were clucked over, laughing out loud only once, when a Mrs. H. S. Parker declared that Will had been "romantically involved" with Queen Victoria during his London engagements. The judge gaveled down the general mirth and instructed the court recorder to strike the statement from the transcript. The press was there to relate the events to readers across the country.

Will's petition was denied and he was directed to pay his wife's court costs in the amount of $318. He did so glumly, and disappeared from the courtroom while Louisa's friends were congratulating the victor, knocking down a photographer who tried to take his picture on the courthouse steps. Two days later a hand on his TE Ranch outside Cody found the owner sprawled on the floor of his cabin in a litter of empty bottles and managed to force half a gallon of piping-hot coffee down his throat before the scout broke his jaw.

CHAPTER SIXTEEN

Wyoming hibernated under a pewter sky, last year's slain grass lying flat under silvery leprous semicircles of crusty snow. Distant haze furred the mountains to the west, with their dead white caps. The horses' shoes clanged on iron earth as they stamped and blew clouds of milky vapor. The tight-faced cowmen in their crimped hats and reversed-hide coats with standing collars exhaled gray smoke and spat glistening brown juice that crackled when it hit the ground. Their weapons bulged obviously under their coats.

"I don't give a standing fuck whose protection they're under, least of all the goddamn U.S. Government," said the spokesman for the group, a wolf-faced rancher with a circle of black moustache and beard like a coal smudge around his mouth and tiny eyes glittering in knife slits in his brown skin. "My daddy fit the Cheyennes for this here land and I ain't fixing to let any more hair grow whilst a bunch of digger Utes is living tall off the herd he started." The others in the band murmured agreement.

Will wrapped his piebald's reins around the horn of his saddle and cut a quarter-size chew off a frozen plug of tobacco with the knife he had used to lift Yellow Hand's scalp. He hadn't chewed in twenty years, and the bare thought of it set his remaining teeth to aching, but it was important to draw the confidence of these hard men with the taste of blood on their tongues. "This is an unofficial expedition, not connected with the government," he explained, parking the slice in his right cheek to thaw. "General Miles has asked me as a personal favor to talk the renegades into returning to their reservation in Colorado. These here are George T. Beck and Hank Fulton, pards of mine from Cody." He indicated the cherry-faced developer and blond-bearded Fulton, a fellow investor. The spokesman didn't return their silent greetings.

"You're going to have to do a heap of talking with just one gun 'twixt three old men."

Chuckling, Will patted Lucretia Borgia's scarred buttstock protruding above his saddle scabbard. "Indians are sensitive creatures. I am eager to avoid the impression we're looking for a fight."

"We ain't so particular," announced one of the other cowmen. His companions grunted.

"They're just a bunch of hungry orphans who have forgot how to live off the land the way their fathers did," Will said. "Many of them are women and children. You would do yourself no credit killing their like."

"That ain't what we heard." Black Beard looked doubtful for the first time. "We was told they was blooded braves armed with new Winchesters."

"They are not. Do you think General Miles would risk sending three old men with one rifle to talk to them if that were the case?"

The cowmen withdrew a few yards to confer in whispers.

"What do you think?" Beck asked.

Will shook his head.

Presently the spokesman kneed his horse back toward them. "You can talk to the bastards. If it don't work we'll let Mr. Colt and Mr. Winchester do our talking for us."

"Hard bunch," Fulton remarked, as the trio rode away, feeling the cowmen's eyes hot on their backs.

"They talk a good fight. Wave a wet papoose in their faces and they'd light a shuck in every direction but up." The scout leaned over sideways and got rid of the tobacco.

At night they slept on the hard ground and awoke the next morning stiff and sore and hacking up quarts of phlegm. The cold settled in their joints, and as they rode, the saddles rubbed the insides of their thighs raw and needles pierced their backs between the shoulder blades. They found the fugitive band the fourth day out, camped on the bank of a sluggish creek with slabs of dirty ice drifting in the brown current. Their tipis were made of patched blankets stretched over squat green poles. The party of whites had been watching them from a rise for some minutes before a group of young men slipped the hobbles off a string of hollow-flanked ponies and mounted to ride out and confront the intruders.

"Your man Major Burke should be here to see this," Beck told Will.

"I invited him, but he said he was too rheumatic to sit a horse. Anyhow, there's little enough here for his pamphlets."

The Utes wore Army blankets and balding buffalo robes over homespun. Many of them had on white man's hats with the crowns cut out so that their heads could breathe. Their squaws watched anxiously from camp as they drew rein ten yards from the newcomers. Babies cried.

Will picked out the leader, a brave in his early twenties with Negroid features and hair hanging in twin plaits down his dirty white cotton shirt-front, and spoke slowly, punctuating his words with signs. "The Sioux call me Pahaska, Longhair. The white war chief your people call Bearcoat Miles has sent me to ask you to return to your home in Colorado or there will be much trouble."

"This is our home," said the Ute without signs.

"No more. You build your lodges on land that is not yours and feed off the cattle of them that own it. They are angry. They would destroy your people. The white chief does not want this to happen. Here the cold wind blows freely through your blankets that are not as good as buffalo robes. Your children cry for food that you cannot give them and your ponies are weak and skinny. Go home to the reservation, where you will grow fat and strong and live in warm cabins."

"No one grows fat on the reservation. The white chiefs eat meat while our children fill their bellies with water. We will stay here."

"If you stay here, bad white men will shoot your squaws and children while you are out rustling their cattle and burn your tipis."

"If the white men come we will meet them with guns." The Ute spread his blanket to expose a battered Henry resting across his mount's withers.

"If you shoot one white man, two more will take his place like always. They will shoot your squaws and children and burn your tipis."

"Maybe," said the Ute, "we will shoot you."

Now the other braves shifted positions and displayed weapons. Fulton and Beck choked up on their reins. Their mounts snorted protestingly.

Will remained unmoving. "It would not be a great victory. We are old men and our time draws short. When you have shot us, others will come and shoot your squaws and children and burn your tipis."

"What crime have our people done that we must live like slaves?" The brave's voice broke. "Your people are without honor. What is their medicine?"

"They will shoot your squaws and children," Will said, "and burn your tipis."

The Indians looked at one another, and Will could see that he had won. The leader spoke quietly, without looking the scout in the eye.

"We will go back, Longhair. Alone."

Will said that it was a decision worthy of a great chief, adding: "It would be just as well if you didn't kill any more cattle than is absolutely necessary on your way back."

The young Ute replied gravely that he would try to follow that mandate, and wheeled his pony, leading the others back into camp. For a time the white men watched as the tipis were struck and converted to travois to carry the children and cookstuffs.

"Kind of hard on them, weren't you?" Hank Fulton asked Will.

"It was pure truth I was telling them. They'd of seen through anything else."

Beck rubbed a coarse sleeve over his face, wet and shining in spite of the cold. "Is this how it was during the Indian wars?"

"Not hardly, seeing as how we're still alive."

"When they showed off those repeaters, I think I knew how Custer must have felt. Telephones and motorcars and Indian powwows just don't go together. Like dancing the minuet to ragtime."

"Poor bastards." Will gathered his reins. "Poor dumb beautiful fornicating bastards."

He no longer lived in North Platte, receiving friends and business acquaintances in the cramped cabin at Cody instead and donning an armor of inebriation in the club car on the way to Nebraska to visit grown-up Irma while Louisa, more resentful and sharp-tongued than ever since the divorce attempt, dusted off the old weapons. Each time he returned to Wyoming it took more drinking to get over his visit. Hunting expeditions into the Shoshone River country left trails of empty bottles and women's underthings while the hunters sang bawdy frontier ballads at the tops of their lungs and potted at trees, stampeding game for miles. Will sold off land and cattle to keep up with the taxes and mortgage payments on Scout's Rest, but somehow the money always went for other things: a copper and gold mine in Arizona, a printing plant for sister Helen and her new lithographer husband, grading and building on the real property in Cody, irrigation canals for both ranches. The federal government had stepped in to supervise the town's water system, relieving him of that headache, and now that the Burlington spur was in he was making money from the Irma Hotel and, at last, from settlers buying lots, but most of that went into staying ahead of the interest on his many loans. Bailey had ceased to be a reliable source; like Salsbury before him, he was showing signs of weakening under the burden of managing the show, and doctors and patent medicines devoured most of his share of the dwindling profits. When the circus man arrived at the TE Ranch to begin arrangements for the 1907 season, his partner was shocked at the change in him. Bailey's graying whiskers seemed to be pulling his professorial face into a gaunt mask, and his self-assured barker's bawl had become the hesitant quaver of age. One day, while his specially designed circus train was setting up the tents for another link in the endless chain of one-night stands, Bailey went to bed to sleep off a splitting headache and never got up. Within days of the funeral, Will received notice from a New York firm of lawyers that the family of James Anthony Bailey was foreclosing upon his share of the Wild West in lieu of monies owed his late business associate.

"What'll I do, John?" he asked Burke.

The publicist, up to his cottony whiskers in steaming bath water, shrugged one larded shoulder. "Retire."

Will sold Scout's Rest to a syndicate of eastern developers for a fraction of what he had pumped into it and used the money to settle a bank lien against the ranch in Wyoming. He winked and shook hands with those show members who were leaving to find work elsewhere, embraced Johnny Baker, watched the wagons and the tents and the venerable Deadwood coach roll out of the great barn for the last time, and went home. Home to Welcome Wigwam and Louisa. The cabin at Cody was too full of echoes.

"The old reprobate," said Louisa, as he was coming up the front walk.

Major Gordon W. Lillie, "Pawnee Bill," friend from the old days, an aging giant growing thick through the middle, with long chestnut locks, a modest handlebar, ornately embroidered buckskins, and thigh-length boots, himself often mistaken for Buffalo Bill, posed for photographers seated across from the original at a camp table, his pen poised over the contract merging Pawnee Bill's Far East with Buffalo Bill's Wild West. As the last flash faded and the pen began scratching in earnest, the white-haired scout's fierce scowl softened and he let his chest drop back into his belly.

"Is the show going to be as big as before?" asked a reporter.

"Bigger than ever," Lillie replied in his rumbling bass. "Big as all outdoors."

"What about the Deadwood coach?" asked another.

"I acquired that along with everything else when I bought out the late Mr. Bailey's interest in the Wild West."

Questions tumbled over one another, among them: "Is Buffalo Bill a partner or just an employee?"

Major Lillie winked at Will, who chuckled low and said, "Boys, I've not worked for a soul save my own since '76 and I am too old to go back. I have a half interest." In fact he had been handed a partnership free and clear by Lillie, an experienced promoter well aware of Buffalo Bill's crowd-drawing potential.

"What about Annie Oakley?"

"She is touring the country independently," said Lillie. "We hope to have her with us in 1912."

"I thought this was Buffalo Bill's last tour."

"It is," said Will, mildly irritated at his being referred to in the third person.

"Tired, Bill?"

"If I thought I was to die a showman, I would go out of business to-morrow. I don't want to die and have people say, 'Oh, there goes another old showman.' When I die, I want the people of Wyoming who are living on the land that has been made fertile by my work and expenditure to remember me as the man who opened up Wyoming to the best of civilization."

"Wants to ranch," wrote the journalists.

There were many more questions, but Major Lillie, with the all-encompassing eye of an entrepreneur, noted the growing strain in his partner's features and herded the reporters out with much back-patting and promises of free press passes to the opening. "You all right, Will?" he said, resuming his seat.

"I'm dandy."

"Come on, old hoss. This here is Pawnee Bill you're talking to."

"Body'd think you really came from out West to hear you talk like that." He let his face fall. "It's my bladder, Bill. It's filled to bursting all the time, but when I try to pee I can't get rid of but a few drops. I feel like a cow that needs milking all the time."

"Seen a doctor?"

"Seen several. It's something called my prostate. I didn't even know I had one till it started in giving me hell. It has to be operated on, they say."

"So have it done."

"After this season, maybe. When I got time."

"If it's a question of money, I'll advance you whatever you require."

"It ain't money. My name's on this contract, promising a full tour for half the profits. I don't sign anything or shake a man's hand without delivering."

Lillie sat back. "Well, it's your bladder."

"Wish to hell it was someone else's."

"Buffalo Bill's Last Tour," said the advance publicity. Adults who had never seen the great scout in action, and those who had sat in the gallery as children, came with *their* children to see him shatter the glass balls and wrestle Yellow Hand, applauding explosively as the paunchy old man rose waving the great headdress, having agreed to refrain from exhibiting the scalp any more at the special request of a women's organization. They sat in silence, tears starting the long crawl down their faces, as the old man came out under the calcium spot alone, sometimes on horseback, but more often in a phaeton as the pressure in his crotch increased, to take off the great hat one last time and say good-bye.

"This farewell visit will be my last hail and farewell to you all . . ."

They wept openly in Detroit and Chicago, in Wichita and above the border in Toronto, and rose to cheer the standing figure with bowed white head, the slayer of Tall Bull and Yellow Hand, the man who had saved Wild Bill Hickok's life when the Cheyennes lanced him and left him for dead, Custer's avenger, the man who shook hands with Kit Carson and Queen Victoria and crated up the old West and sent it around the world to perform on a tabletop.

"This farewell visit will be my last . . ."

In Austin and Atlanta they gave him a rebel yell, closing the bloody wound opened at the Salt Creek Trading Post in 1854. A Confederate veteran of the skirmish at Westport got up from his wheelchair with the help of his grandsons to salute his old enemy.

"This farewell visit . . ."

Big Bill Taft dined with him at the White House in Washington and had his picture taken with his great suety arm lying across the scout's shoulders, Will grinning to keep from screaming at the pain of it.

"This farewell . . ."

Attendance fell off the second year. The familiar speech met dry eyes and an occasional raspberry. Major Lillie added a string of nickelodeon machines to the sideshow and sent out telegrams. Old friends joined the show in Denver, Johnny Baker with gray in his locks and Little Missy, sinewy and white-haired at fifty-two, recovered from her injuries, still breaking her old sharpshooting records with revolver and rifle before smaller crowds. A newsreel camera recorded the reunion, copper-colored figures jerking like flies on a trout line.

"Miss Oakley, is it true you once shot the end off a cigarette in Kaiser Wilhelm's mouth?"

"The wrong end."

Resting between performances at sister May's home in Denver, Will accepted an invitation to lunch in a private railroad car belonging to a large, soft man who introduced himself as Harry H. Tammen, owner with Fred Bonfils of the Denver *Post* and the Sells-Floto Circus.

"Yes, Annie Oakley once toured with that organization," the scout recalled, smoking one of his host's seventy-five-cent cigars amid the red plush and polished yellow brass.

"No, that was the Sells *Brothers* Circus." Tammen, pink and shiny with a small white smile like a fat chipmunk's, chortled and fiddled with a gold elk's tooth on his watch chain. The pair were lodge brothers. "I orginally called mine the Floto Dog and Pony Show, after the sports editor on the *Post*, then signed a relative of the Sellses for his name. You would have blushed to hear Ringling Brothers take on, after they had gone and bought the entire Sells works to the same end. But, of course, everything was perfectly legal and above board. That's the way I do business."

A colored porter served highballs, and then the two sat down to a dinner of roast beef and stuffed crabs from Alaska and caviar and red wine. Finding an appreciative audience in his companion, Will spun yarns about the frontier and acted out his first interview with the late Queen, taking the parts of Colonel Sir Henry Ewart and the Duchess of Athole and Victoria herself while his listener chortled and poured more wine into the scout's glass. At length, Tammen dismissed the porter and they retired to a pair of deep overstuffed chairs with fresh highballs in their hands.

"What can I do for you, Mr. Tammen?" Will asked, loosening his belt a notch.

The other wiped away his tears of laughter and blew his large nose into a silk handkerchief. "Rather, that might be my question to you, Colonel. I am a speculator by trade and by avocation. Communications, real property, entertainment—whichever way the winds of progress are blowing. Word has reached me that you seek an investor."

"It's news to me. The Wild West is doing better than ever," Will lied.

"Come, come, sir. I have sources."

"What are you offering?"

"What are you asking?"

The frontiersman swirled his drink. "I require twenty thousand dollars to square a number of personal obligations."

"Twenty thousand dollars you shall have, sir." Tammen drew open a drawer in the oak table at his left elbow and set a pen, a bottle of ink, and a leather-bound checkbook on top. Will watched, fascinated.

"Just like that?"

"Oh, no, no, no. Certainly not. I am not St. Nicholas, for all I am told I resemble the reverend gentleman." His speech and girth reminded the scout favorably of Ned Buntline. "I will accept a six months' note on your share of the Cody-Lillie exhibition as a gesture of good faith that payment will be received at the end of the period."

"It will be, and on time."

"I am confident that it will. But my partner, Mr. Bonfils, would insist upon collateral." He leaned forward, cradling the quivering mass under his vest between fat thighs. "I would also, separately and apart from this agreement, admire to offer you a most lucrative assignment as headline act for the Sells-Floto Circus at the close of the current season."

His guest hesitated. "Pawnee Bill is a good friend and an agreeable partner."

"He lacks my facility to properly promote your contribution. Buffalo Bill, my dear Colonel Cody, is an institution, not a sideshow freak. He should be thus presented."

"You say 'Buffalo Bill' as if he's not right here talking to you."

"He is more than one mere man, and bigger than the both of us." Tammen extended a very clean, very pink and pudgy right hand. "What say you, sir; have we a pact?"

For a fraction of a second Will teetered. Then he clasped the hand. It felt moist and very warm.

When Major Lillie learned of his partner's decision, his showman's face sagged and the light from the electric drop-cord in his tent made the dye in his moustache and hair obvious. "You've not signed anything yet?" he asked hopefully. "If you haven't I can get you clear of it, tell Tammen you're committed to this show."

"We shook hands on it, Bill."

"A thing like that doesn't mean anything to a man like H. H. Tammen."

"It does to me."

"You shook my hand, and signed a contract to boot. You sat at that very table and gave a pretty little speech about how good your word and signature are."

"A lot of other people whose hands I shook are after me for money I don't have and Tammen does."

"The Buffalo Bill I knew stood by his obligations."

"It's not that I'm ungrateful," the other said softly. "It's a question of surviving."

The fire died from Lillie's eyes, leaving an ash of concern. "Why didn't you come to me first? We could have worked something out."

"You're as broke as I am. I wouldn't put you to the chore of thinking up a polite way to say no."

"You have more friends than anyone I know."

"They're not my friends, though I thought they were. If I had a buffalo nickel for every time I heard 'If you ever need anything, Colonel, just call on me,' I would not be in this fix. They are always busy when I call."

"What I've heard about Tammen isn't good. The Indians would say that he is a man without honor."

"Right now that doesn't concern me. What does is that he is a man with twenty thousand dollars."

"I hope it solves all your problems." The major's tone was glacial. "He bought you for it."

The show pulled out of Sacramento and Reno owing several thousand dollars in feed bills, ducked an advertising commitment in Portland, and limped back to Denver in July 1913 leaving a trail of angry hotel owners and indifferent crowds.

"It's the damned moving pictures," Lillie complained. "They reel in paying customers like bass, travel in cans, and you don't have to feed or clean up after buffaloes on film."

Will said, "I went to see one last time I was in New York. They're too hard on the eyes. Folks will tire of them before long."

"I hope we're still here when they do."

Tammen received Will in his private car, wearing what looked to be the same immaculate black three-piece suit and elk's tooth. The scout made three trips to the bathroom in the course of their conversation. Over highballs the speculator brought up the note. "I wouldn't mention it at all, except it's long past due and you've not paid a cent of the interest," he added with a show of embarrassment.

"I will make good on it."

"I was never in doubt that you would." Smiling his chipmunk's smile, Tammen topped off his guest's glass and lifted his own. "To prosperity."

Will awoke in his tent the next morning in mid-snore to find a hand shaking his shoulder and a strange young face hovering above his own. So many cowboys had moved in and out of his and Lillie's employ in such a short time that he had given up trying to keep track of them. "Big trouble, Colonel," this one was saying.

Groggily, the scout, still wearing the suit of clothes he had worn to see Tammen the night before, relieved his swollen bladder into an enameled pot and stumbled outside, squinting in the harsh sunlight. Among the performers in costume and roustabouts in work clothes milling about the grounds, the four men in gray suits stood out like blisters. Three were carrying shotguns. The fourth, a stringy brown man under a gray slouch hat, spotted Will and jerked his head in that direction. The group started moving his way.

Will swung about and grasped the young cowboy's arm. "Get the cash box from the treasury tent and off the grounds, quick."

"It's no use, Colonel," the man told him sadly. "They have it already."

He looked again at the four. One had his shotgun under one arm and was carrying the black strongbox in both hands. Will's fingers slackened and the cowboy withdrew his arm, rubbing circulation back into it.

"William F. Cody?" inquired the man in the slouch hat.

When Will nodded, the man pulled aside his coat flap to show a star on his vest. "We're from the Adams County Sheriff's Office. We have a court order directing you to surrender all property belonging to Buffalo Bill's Wild West and Pawnee Bill's Far East in lieu of sixty thousand dollars owed the United States Lithographing Company." He produced a long fold of paper from an inside pocket.

"I wired them last Monday we'd make good on those posters soon."

"I wouldn't know about that. I have orders to impound everything on the lot."

"After you've done that, what?"

"These officers will remain on the premises. Any attempt to remove property will be regarded as theft and the offender will be arrested and prosecuted." Turning away, the sheriff's man directed two of his companions to their stations and relieved the third of the cash box. That man walked beside him carrying the shotgun while the other carried the box by its handles through the Indian camp toward a new beetle-black Model T touring car parked inside the main gate with its top folded. Will walked along with them.

"I mean, what happens to everything here? You just going to let it rot and the livestock starve?"

"That's up to the judge. Likely he'll authorize an auction if some kind of payment isn't made within a specified length of time."

He hoisted the box over the low door on the passenger's side and placed it on the floor. Then he got in and started the ticking engine, but before releasing the brake he looked across at Will with an expression that puzzled the scout.

"I'm just doing my job, Colonel Cody. A job I wouldn't have except I decided to become a lawman after I read a book about Buffalo Bill when I was twelve."

He shifted gears with a groan, backed around, shifted again, and clattered out through the gate, laying down a brown cloud of dust and sweet exhaust. The man with the shotgun moved off between tents.

"Tammen," said Major Lillie.

Will turned and saw his partner standing in front of his tent, watching the retreating vehicle. "It's not his doing," he replied.

Pawnee Bill went inside after treating the scout to a long look that put him in mind of Louisa.

The auction attracted a larger crowd than the show had seen in two years. They came from all over to watch and bid on cattle from India and camels from the Sahara and broncos and workhorses and oxen and cages and mirrored wagons ablaze in the sun. The white train was broken up, its rolling stock sold to eastern railroad interests to have its gold letters painted over and its aisles narrowed to make room for more seats. The crowd ignored Major Lillie's "buyer beware" leaflets, laughed when a bony nag was led into the arena on the heels of a breathtaking Percheron, and gasped when a tall, weathered Westerner with a short cigar clamped in his teeth bid a hundred and fifty dollars for the animal.

"Sold to the gentleman from Lincoln." The auctioneer cracked his gavel.

The man was Colonel C. J. Bills, a fellow rancher and old pard who had spent many lazy Sunday afternoons with Will picking buds off Scout's Rest trees at forty paces. "If I can't buy that bag of bones," he had vowed on his way to Denver, "I'll steal him." The horse was Isham, the show mount Will had ridden for years, and when the transaction was complete, Colonel Bills handed the paper to Will and arranged to have the old horse shipped to the TE Ranch.

"In the old days we called a man without a saddle horse a farmer," he muttered, before his friend could thank him. "And, by God, I'll die before I lay eyes on Buffalo Bill behind a plow."

CHAPTER SEVENTEEN

The late-summer sun burned color out of the tough ugly bunch grass, throwing into high relief the blood hues of the painted and bonneted Indians in the village of bright tipis and many-colored horses milling on the ridge overlooking the river. Will, in scuffed brown buckskins and a Stetson stained dark with dirt and sweat such as he hadn't worn since he'd posed for Rosa Bonheur's painting almost thirty years earlier, shifted his seat carefully in the saddle and waited desperately for the order to move. He felt faint.

"Charge!"

He put spurs to the white stallion and plunged forward down the slope and into the village, firing his Colt right and left the way he had seen Wild Bill Hickok do in the Cheyenne camp the year he turned fifteen. His feathered targets yelped and fell. Finally, he drew rein before the chief's tipi just as the Indian was raising his tomahawk over the head of his white woman captive and used up his last shot, sighting down his outstretched arm. The chief arched his back, dropped the weapon, and slumped over sideways.

"Cut!"

Will waited for an agonizing two seconds, then slid out of the saddle. His knees buckled when his feet touched ground, but he maintained a shaky grip on the horn until the dizzy spell passed.

"Great job, Colonel," said the director, slapping a cloud of dust off the scout's back. "We're going to call you 'One-Take' Cody from here on in."

He grinned weakly. "That does it for me, then?"

"One more shot, Colonel. I like to get at least two angles of everything."

He tried not to groan. The director was a thickly built man in his middle years whose broad jaw and boyishly upturned nose made him resemble Bronco Bill Irving, he of the Smith & Wesson religious denomination and the steer-riding exhibition that had nearly made casualties of the visiting press at the Wild West's first opening in Chicago. This one called himself Bronco Billy, in fact, although his sole connection with the history of the plains was a flickering few moments on screen during *The Great Train Robbery,* filmed in New Jersey, and a series of popular western shorts starring him and produced by his company, Essanay Productions. Abruptly he turned his back on his featured player and instructed the man standing behind the hand-crank camera on the open side of the three-walled tipi where and how to set up for the new angle. The Indian chief got up, dusted off his leggings, and looked around for his tomahawk. Meanwhile the blue-clad cavalrymen with whom Will had ridden into the village led their horses back to their marks on the hill. The crew members were also dressed in cavalry uniforms to avoid spoiling a take should one of them wander into a shot.

"Places, everyone," Bronco Billy said, turning back. "That means you too, Colonel."

The shot required three takes. Something went wrong with the camera the first time, and on the second try Will developed a sudden excruciating cramp in his right hand and dropped the revolver just as he was getting set to fire. The blank cartridge discharged on the ground. Finally they had a print and he handed the reins over to a grip and walked back to the tent that served as his dressing room. Once inside he took down his trousers and emptied the India rubber bag he wore strapped to his thigh into a chamber pot. He could no longer control that basic function. While the prescription bag spared him embarrassment in public, it made riding an even more uncomfortable experience than the condition itself. He was refastening the trousers when Johnny Baker entered.

"When you going to have that operation?" chided the sharpshooter.

"When you going to learn to announce yourself before coming into a man's tent?" Will pulled the cork out of a fresh bottle of rye and filled an oversize beer stein on the camp table. His contract with Tammen allowed him only three drinks per day. It didn't say anything about how big.

Johnny dropped the subject and then his lanky frame onto a folding canvas stool. "Well, how do you take to the moving picture business so far?"

"It's harder to organize and run than three circuses. Other than that I don't see a great deal of difference between it and the arena."

"You're just saying that because it was your idea. All Tammen did was put up the money."

Will lowered himself carefully onto his stool and drank. Waiting for the warmth to crawl up his spine, he said, "Miles giving you a hard time again?"

"He never stopped. For a seventy-four-year-old retired warhorse, he behaves a powerful lot like a temperamental actor. Now he's insisting that all eleven thousand troops he commanded during the Wounded Knee campaign be represented when we restage the battle."

"How many we got?"

"Just three hundred. The Army won't loan us any more. I asked."

"March them past the camera forty times. Nelson never could distinguish one pony soldier from another."

"I reckon it's worth a shot." Johnny yawned bitterly and then became grave. "The Indians won't be so easy."

"What's their complaint this time?"

"Same as before, they don't want us filming the Battle of Wounded Knee on top of the graves of them that died there. Talk is they're planning to use real cartridges when we film the fight instead of blanks."

"Iron Tail told me. I'm meeting the tribal elders here this afternoon."

"To hear them carry on you'd think we were still at war."

"For them it never ended."

Wild West veterans Iron Tail, Short Bull, and No Neck came to the council, along with two younger Sioux whom Will didn't know. Their faces were dark, mouths set in brutal lines. In the dim light of the tent it was hard to distinguish the old friends from the strangers. Most volatile was No Neck, who when the dust had settled at the bloodbath at Wounded Knee was found squalling outside the smoldering tipi of his slain parents. Whenever a brown fist struck the folding table it was likely to be his.

"You are calling this a battle," he said sharply. "It was a massacre. My people were outnumbered fifty to one. For every warrior in the village there were ten women and children and old ones too sick to fight. They came to surrender and were met with the white man's peace—fire and lead." His eyes burned in their sockets.

"The War Department will not let us use their soldiers if we intend to place them in a bad light," Will explained.

Iron Tail said, "This is the thing that makes No Neck's heart bad, but not ours. My people will not trample the resting place of their ancestors."

"General Miles insists we film the event where it occurred. It was the only way he would agree to appear."

"Bearcoat Miles is a great warrior but a stupid man," Iron Tail pointed out. "There will be trouble."

One of the younger Sioux grunted. "He will not speak so loud when our guns talk and his pony soldiers fall down and do not get up like those who fell today. Maybe he will be with the ones that stay down."

"That would be very unwise," Will said calmly. "If your people fire real cartridges in the sham battle, the Army will pursue them. There will be no place to hide. They will be captured and stand trial for murder. The hangman will tie ropes around their necks and hoist them into the air and they will die with their necks broken or strangle to death. The tribesmen who told their brothers to do this thing would be among the first to hang."

A number of the Indians stroked their throats uneasily. No Neck pounded the table.

"The white man's peace is ever the same. We will not help him to tell this lie."

Will smacked the table openhanded. The sharp report made the Indians jump. Johnny Baker, seated off to one side, looked quickly at the Colonel. The skin of his face was drawn tight. As the silence grew his expression softened. At length he drew a deep breath and let it out slowly.

"In the white man's world," he said quietly, "you do as you're told."

After a long moment Iron Tail rose, closing his blanket around the spotted old flesh of his torso. "We go now."

The Indians filed out, No Neck last, raking hot eyes over the two white men.

Johnny was still staring at Will. Alone with him, he said, "I never heard anyone talk to an Indian like that before, Colonel."

"I told him true."

"That's what I mean."

Will blew dust out of his beer stein. "Reckon we'll find out tomorrow if it took."

Wounded Knee shook again under the beating of many hoofs, firearms crackling like a brushfire, smoke scudding across the blue and red bodies on the field. There was a pause after Bronco Billy yelled "Cut!" and then the dead rose, fumbling ready-made cigarettes out of their tunics and scowling at new rips in their moccasins and leggings. The picture, released under the hefty title *The Last Indian Battles, or From the Warpath to the Peace Pipe*, swept through the nation's theaters in the spring of 1914, drawing as many viewers as the Wild West's first three seasons combined to watch the great scout leaping and jerking across bedsheet screens in pancake and rouge. Will's portion of the proceeds stopped at H. H. Tammen, who loaned some of it to his star in advances against his salary as a performer for the Sells-Floto Circus. Unlike Nate Salsbury and Jim Bailey, the Denver tycoon parted with the sums cheerfully, extending as he did so more promissory notes for Will's signature. "A hundred dollars per day plus forty per cent of the gross over three thousand dollars per day," he told the scout the day of the fall opening. "That makes you the highest-paid entertainer of this century. You will be in the black in no time."

"No time" was it. Will borrowed from his employer to quiet his creditors, wired more to Hank Fulton in Cody to see about organizing the dude ranch Hank and George T. Beck had been after him to start, and sent the rest of the cash on hand to his sister Helen and her husband Hugh Wetmore, whose printing business had failed. Each entreaty to Tammen was met with the familiar rodent's grin and another note to sign. The scout's participation in the show consisted of leading the parade around the arena, picking off glass balls launched by a young sharpshooter whom in his absentmindedness he sometimes called "Johnny," and the farewell speech, always the farewell speech, made more often from the driver's seat of a phaeton because his crotch was too tender for the saddle. St. Louis, Topeka, Omaha, and most of the smaller cities in between. Another night, another city, and he seldom knew the name of the one he was in. Between appearances he rested in his tent, drinking his three steins per day and snarling at whoever poked his head inside, unless he was a fan or a child. Tammen saw that Will's picture was taken often surrounded by children.

The clown of Denver swaggered down crowded streets in linen as white as the caps of the Rockies and trousers with a crease as sharp as a scalping knife, hailing old pards across the street with a bellowed "Hey, old hoss!" that turned heads for blocks. He gave quarters to the children following him and when he ran out of quarters he handed out silver dollars until his pockets were empty. By this time his rounds would deposit him in front of the *Post;* he would go in and tap Tammen or his partner, Fred Bonfils, for more. On slow news days reporters called him over to their desks and asked him questions about Wild Bill and Sitting Bull, smirking when the stentorian voice brought editors' heads popping out of their offices.

Once on the street he met Johnny Baker, just back from his own London tour. The two pumped hands and slapped each other's shoulders and stepped into a saloon where everyone knew the old scout.

"How are things, Colonel?"

"Just larruping. Hearst wants me to write a series of articles for his monthly magazine and I am negotiating to buy the 101 Ranch show from the Miller brothers. With the war in Europe I look to put on a military spectacle that will outdraw Jess Willard."

"You're no longer with Tammen, then?" Johnny sipped his beer.

"Once the papers are signed for the Scout's Rest sale I will buy out my contract."

The sharpshooter smiled thinly and nodded, but the smile died short of his eyes. The bright Colorado sunlight streaming in through the front window found strands of silver in his long hair.

The money from Scout's Rest went to collection firms and lawyers. Major Lillie was suing Will for breach of contract. Will signed another note for Tammen.

When Sells-Floto played Lawrence, Kansas, near the end of the 1914 tour, Will sent a roustabout to tell Tammen he wanted to see him in his tent. The speculator, imbibing wine in his private car with an attractive redhead in green satin, replied irritably that he was busy and that the scout should come see him if it couldn't wait until morning.

"Sorry, sir. He said to tell you he's too ill with rheumatism to make the walk."

An impatient Tammen found his star seated at the folding table. The gold- and silver-plated revolvers presented to him by the Colt Patent Arms Company lay in front of him. "Have a seat and we'll discuss my contract," Will invited.

"I don't see what we have to discuss." But the visitor sat down opposite him.

"I am quitting the circus when we reach Denver."

"You are not. We have a contract."

"After two years with you I consider my debts repaid in full."

Tammen chortled, his chins quivering. "You have barely kept ahead of the interest. You have not so much as touched the principal. If you think otherwise, you may see my lawyers." He started to push himself to his feet.

"When I could, I avoided killing in the bad days," Will said. "I don't want to kill you. But if there is not justice left I will."

The speculator tried his small, toothy smile. But it was dead in his doughy face. He had frozen in mid-rise. "You can't threaten me."

A quaking old hand slid toward one of the revolvers. Tammen spoke swiftly.

"Where do you think you are, you old fart, still on the frontier? I'll haul you into court for attempted extortion. I'll break you!"

"You've done that." Will's fingers closed around the butt of the nearest Colt.

Tammen rose the rest of the way and took a step backward. His pale eyes rattled in their sockets.

"All right!" he said, releasing his breath with a shudder. "All right, you've got what you wanted. I am releasing you from your contract. But that means your money fountain has dried up. Think about that a minute. What will you do when your creditors eat you alive?"

"Wait for them to cough me back up, I reckon, like you just done." He was pulling back the hammer now with both thumbs. His visitor left.

After a full minute, Will poured what was left in his bottle into the stein. The neck jingled wildly against the edge of the glass.

When the time came to buy the 101 Ranch he hadn't the money, and so Will joined the show as a salaried performer. This time Johnny Baker was along to hoist him into the saddle and help him off at the close of his act. The urine bag sloshed.

"You going to have that operation soon, Colonel?" Johnny raised his voice. Years of exposure to loud reports had callused the old man's eardrums.

"The doctors tell me it's too late to fix it."

When winter came he accompanied *The Last Indian Battles* in a jouncing automobile across the continent, painfully mounting the stages of converted opera houses and lecture halls to talk about Little Phil Sheridan and Cump Sherman and Curly Custer and the duel at Warbonnet Creek while the projectionist threaded the film into the machine. Then spring, and another tour with 101 and Johnny. As the summer wore on, fear crept in to join the pain he saw when he shaved. "I'm afraid of dying out there in front of all those people, Johnny. I dream about it." The sharpshooter tried to josh him out of these moods, and changed the subject when it didn't work. He scarcely went to the bathroom anymore, and when he looked in the mirror, he saw the yellow jaundice in his eyes, as if his urine had backed up to his skull. He made his last farewell speech in Portsmouth, Virginia, with the November cold gray in his joints and shook Johnny's hand when he was back in his tent. The old grip was still there.

"You stay in touch, hear? I'm stopping in Chicago on my way back home to see some men about backing a new show and I'm going to need all the crack shots I can scrape together. Annie Oakley too."

"It'll be just like old times, Colonel."

They stood shaking hands until Johnny realized that it was an effort for the old man to remain standing. When they released grips, a skirl of air too cold for Virginia came in under the wall of the tent and touched the younger man's bare palm, chilling him. He said good-bye again and left.

In Chicago, where General Sheridan had introduced him to society the winter he turned twenty-six and where the Wild West began its first successful season in 1885, Will postponed the meeting with his potential backers, pleading a touch of the grippe. His groin was on fire, his lungs full of fluid, and he hadn't the strength to climb a low flight of stairs. He slept on board the express to Denver over rails once ridden by the white train. Noting the alarm in his sister May's face when she saw him, he gently turned down her invitation to stay with her. "I'll feel better among my mountains." He did improve for a dinner held in his honor at the Irma Hotel in Cody, where he compared accounts of Captain Jack's one-night Cheyenne campaign with Bob Haslam and raised a glass with an aging fellow victim of the Mormon wagon train raid in memory of Alexander Majors, apologizing with a broad wink heavenward for the hard liquor in the glass. The guests grasped his pale hand and laid hands on his bony back and looked in his eyes and went home saddened. When Ned Frost, the foreman at the TE Ranch, hesitated to drive his employer around the grounds in his new Dodge, Will fetched him an astonishingly healthy blow on the shoulder and joshed, "You needn't worry, Ned. I have said too many times I'll not be caught dead riding in an automobile on my own ranch." The foreman complied, at the colonel's request stopping and turning off the engine from time to time while the old man rubbed frost off the windshield with the heel of his hand and looked out over the endless acreage slumbering under blue-shadowed drifts.

"Getting dark, Colonel," said Frost, when they had been parked at the top of a hill long enough for hard ice to form on both sides of the glass. The snow had rusted over and was going gray.

"It is that," Will agreed, and told him to drive back to the cabin.

By morning those hours in the cold had thickened his congestion, and as he took his seat on the morning train, coughing with a deep rattle and sniffling, the passengers sitting near him moved to the opposite side of the aisle. In Denver he took to a bed in May's house, missing another appointment with possible investors. Young Dr. East examined the whites of his eyes and took a blood sample and diagnosed uremic poisoning.

"What can you give me for it?" Will asked.

"I? Nothing." The doctor closed his bag with a final snap. "There are mineral baths in Glenwood Springs that may make your time easier. I'll make an appointment for you with Dr. W. W. Crook there. He has a reputation for miracles."

"That's what it's going to take, is it?"

Dr. East adjusted his black-ribboned spectacles. "Colonel Cody, from what I've been told of your habits, I would say you've been running on miracles alone for ten years."

He toppled over in Dr. Crook's office at the springs. When he came around smelling ammonia on the examination table, the miracle worker, a very tall thin man with fine black hair and puffs of white like mortar smoke over his ears, told him to go home. "I will accompany you."

Will asked no questions.

In the sleeper on the way to Denver he dreamed. Wild Bill in buckskins with a pistol in one hand and his reins in the other, plucking the eyes out of standing prairie dogs along the road from Horseshoe Bend to St. Louis, where Old Mountain had lost by a hair to a flat-running Illinois mare. Carson and Bridger arguing at Fort Laramie over the way a Northern Cheyenne mimicked a screech owl. Ned Buntline swilling pure trade whiskey out of an Army canteen on the back of Powder Face without missing a beat in his oral history of rum's degradations. The light in Sitting Bull's odd gray eyes when Will handed him the dancing horse's reins. Custer galloping up to empty his revolver into a young buffalo bull, his hair flying behind him, glowing like coals in a copper pot under a bright steel sky. Grand Duke Alexis, teeth liquid white behind his sleek moustache, blue eyes childlike, watching Spotted Tail's braves dance while the firelight crawled over their glistening bodies. Yellow Hand crossing Warbonnet Creek on his lean paint, feathers fluttering, lips peeled back in a leer of challenge against the black and vermilion on his face. Johnny Baker's features splitting into a broad grin when his bullet shattered a clay pigeon. Little Missy flushing to her bangs when Queen Victoria told her she was "a very, very clever little girl." Dust and black-powder smoke in Wyoming and a big shaggy dropping within spitting distance of the excursionists from St. Louis to beat Billy Comstock's score by twenty-three.

The horses, almost as famous as he was. Old Mountain, swift as thought in the Wyoming crags. Powder Face, the warrior, responding to bugle calls like a thirty-year man. Brigham and Buckskin Joe, buffalo hunters born and bred, ungorable, living just for the mad dash into the herd and Lucretia Borgia's deep bellow and the quick red blood, sharp and musty in their nostrils. Old Charlie and Billy, graying veterans submitting moodily to circus life and voyages in the stinking tween-decks of ships. Isham and McKinley, the born performers, hamming it up from New York to San Francisco, growing fat on oats and applause. All bones but the last, wintering with the rest of the 101 stock and awaiting his next rider.

Winter on the Great Plains. A sheet of blinding white stretched taut between horizons, wind peeling off the top layer and hurling the hard grains like hot sparks against exposed flesh, needles in the nose, the spent breath of horses and mules and men mingling in thick clouds. Wild Bill turning raw red hands over a tiny blue fire.

"Down's the easiest direction there is. Run down, slide down or fall down —just get down."

"You're dreaming, Colonel. Calm yourself."

He opened his eyes, focusing on Dr. Crook's goatlike face. The physician was seated next to his bunk in the sleeping compartment. Pale sunlight fluttered on the wall opposite the window. Will asked his companion if he was any relation to General George Crook, who ran into a buzz saw with his troops on the Rosebud a month before the Little Big Horn. But he fell asleep again before hearing the answer.

Louisa and Irma were waiting at the station with a carriage to take him to May's house, his daughter approaching middle age gracefully, with laugh lines like her father's at her eyes and pewter dust in her dark hair, Lulu's face grown broad and scored from years spent squinting at close needle-work. Will grinned at her weakly.

"I told you I'd quit, Mama, when I got too old for the other."

Her lips parted in puzzlement. She didn't remember.

There were reporters and photographers on the station platform, slinging questions like Sioux arrows and popping bulbs in his face as he leaned on the doctor's and Irma's arms and tried to look like he was not leaning. Whatever happened to flash powder? The first time he ever saw the stuff go up, his heart bounded against his teeth. Now any idiot with one eye and a finger could make pictures. Old Fire-in-His-Hand would turn over in his box.

"How you feeling, Bill?"

"Ask yourself that one when you're seventy."

"You fixing to retire?"

"Hell, no. Come spring I'm starting up with a bigger and better show than Mr. Griffith could rig for all his cameras and fancy tricks."

"Buffalo Bill Arrives in Denver Too Ill for Removal to Wyoming," intoned the *Post*. Tammen had instructed his editors to play up the story to its finish. Reporters camped on the front lawn of May's house, eating fried chicken from greasy sacks and washing it down with whiskey from hip flasks, their coat collars turned up against the bitter January wind. They glanced up toward the second-floor windows and bought numbers in the pool at a dollar a throw.

The old man lay in fat sunlight, dimly aware of Dr. East's birdlike movements at his bedside, awake but dreaming. Editor Stringfellow's mad eyes and open mouth scooping angry holes in his hairy face, damning abolitionists. Big Isaac Cody, Will's father, a rock in the torrent until the knife's white arc released a scarlet fountain and the rock crumbled. The Mississippi Jaeger pushing Will's shoulder, and a lone Indian tumbling down and down, rolling like a loose bale of rags into the muddy Platte. The charter citizens of Rome, Kansas, lifting rifles and six-guns to rattle a salute to the founder and his young wife. Red-hot picket pins hissing in cups of beer rerouted from Evans' cavalry. The giddy stench of pure alcohol in a close room, Wild Bill wounded and howling, his shoulders heaving under Will's hands. Ned Buntline in the alcoholic throes of creation, pantomiming scenes from *Scouts of the Plains* in a flyblown hotel room. The curtain going up and Will with it, his lines as gone as George Washington's horse. Kit's girlish face and blond locks in the balcony. *Good house, Papa!* Will dancing with Little Missy to Sergeant Bates's banjo in the aisles of the white train while scenery streaked past in a blur of green and yellow. Audiences mangling his name in French and German, Italian and Swiss dialect. Arizona John Burke, wide as a buffalo's behind in fringed and beaded buckskins, teaching the Indians how to genuflect for the Pope and struggling back to his feet like a cow caught in river mud. Breaking ground for the Irma Hotel in Cody and knocking the necks off champagne bottles to celebrate. Nelson Miles pulling his seventy-four-year-old frame into a saddle for Bronco Billy's cameras. A baby's warm breath on his weathered cheek; Arta's? No, Orra's. Both with Kit now. A man shouldn't outlive his children. Scorched canvas tickling his nostrils, the secret satisfaction of burning "William Frederick Cody" into a clean wagon sheet. *Who slew Abel? It wasn't me, sir.* McCarthy looking from the dead Indian to the boy with the smoking rifle and scratching his beard.

"He hasn't long now. I can scarcely feel a pulse."

I never believed any of it, Pa. Even when the show was netting a million a year and there was talk of running me against Cleveland I never took a word of it for gospel. "God never made a worse fool than a man who's a liar to himself," you said. But you never said it would be so much fun, Pa. I reckon maybe you didn't stay around long enough to learn that part.

The oblong of butter-colored sunlight shortened, sliding off the counterpane. Dr. East, timing the patient's pulse by his pocket watch, felt an abnormally strong throb in the thick vein on the underside of the pale wrist at 12:05 P.M. and waited for the next. After ten seconds he pocketed the timepiece. The patient's eyes, half open, grew soft and moist, like wet brown velvet. The family, Irma and May holding the other hand, May's husband Lew Decker and Louisa standing next to the doctor looking at everything but the man on the bed, weren't aware of the change yet; the moment was one of those in a doctor's life that are filled with secret knowledge. As he chose his words, Dr. East reflected with mild surprise that the tiny hall bedroom seemed much bigger than it had a moment before.

When Johnny Baker read the telegram in his North Platte home his reaction was exactly the opposite. Without telling his wife what the wire was about or where he was going, he stamped his heels into a pair of fur-lined boots and put on his padded canvas jacket and selected an old Winchester from among the many newer and more reliable rifles in his arsenal and saddled up his favorite horse and went riding. The air was sharp under a dull metal sky. Brown grass stuck up through retreating patches of snow, painting the flat countryside the color of freshly cured buckskin. When he had ridden out far enough he dismounted and pulled a spring trap and a stack of yellow disks out of a saddlebag. He spent some minutes loading the trap on a low rise and paying out string while the horse nuzzled for new grass in the snowless spots. Then he loaded the carbine, levered in a round, and pulled the string. The first disk described a lazy yellow arc against the overcast. His bullet shattered it forty yards out.

For the next hour he shot clay pigeons while the man-made forests to the west caught fire in the sinking sun and night hammocked down purple from above.

POSTSCRIPT

This Old Bill is a fable, distilled from fact and legend, based on the life of William Frederick "Buffalo Bill" Cody—buffalo hunter, scout, Pony Express rider, stagecoach driver, rancher, developer, showman, and liar. Because of his love for tall tales and his shrewd sense of self-aggrandizement, and because many who knew him were only too glad to promote their own interests by going along with the joke and at times bettering it, the researcher's task as regards this remarkable American is doubly difficult. Implausibility, normally a useful tool in separating truth from fiction, is of scant assistance when what is known about the subject is every bit as outrageous as what has been proved spurious. Such is the case with Buffalo Bill, and such is the reason for this book.

Hence the fable. Some of the distortion in these pages is deliberate, and made in the interests of pace and entertainment, the telescoping of Cody's first two wagon train trips and of the Wild West's two separate performances before Queen Victoria in 1887 being the most notable examples. In other cases, faced with two or more conflicting accounts of the same incident with no clear historical indication as to which is correct, the author has chosen the most believable. In still others, upon encountering a flat plausibility and a romantic unlikelihood, he has opted for romance at the expense of accuracy. It is his book, after all, and the reader who has come this far may be expected to agree at least partially with this decision.

One final note seems appropriate. While preparing this book, the author had the pleasure of meeting a most vibrant elderly gentleman who as a small boy met Buffalo Bill during one of his late tours, and of shaking the hand that shook the hand that shook the hands of Kit Carson, Wild Bill Hickok, George Armstrong Custer, Sitting Bull, and Queen Victoria. In this manner is the living wheel of American history ever turning.

Loren D. Estleman is a prolific and versatile author who, since the publication of his first novel in 1976, has established himself as a leading writer of both mystery and Western fiction. His novels include *Mister St. John*, *Murdock's Law*, *The Glass Highway*, *The Midnight Man*, *Stamping Ground*, and the winner of the Western Writers of America's 1981 Golden Spur Award for Best Historical Western, *Aces & Eights*.